QUINTANA MCCONNELL

The Last Great Almost

Gilded Horizon Books

https://gildedhorizonbooks.com

Copyright © 2025 Gilded Horizon Books LLC.

All rights reserved.

No part of this book may be reproduced in any form or by electronic or mechanical means, including information storage and retrieval systems, without written permission from the author, except for the use of brief quotations for the purpose of a book review.

Cover Art by Anastasia Poli

This narrative is fictional, though it may blur the line between imagined and remembered. Any parallels to real people or events are coincidental and not intended as representation.

This one's for the girls who watched Rory Gilmore spiral, cried during Little Women, and downloaded The Archer in the middle of a breakup.

And for the guys who listen more than they speak. Who love out loud and in silence. Who see tenderness as strength, even when the world insists it's not.

I see you. I raise a glass to you. I support you.

Content Warning:

This book contains references to sexual trauma, mental health—including anxiety, depression, and suicidal ideation—grief, and emotionally complex family dynamics.
I've written with care, but if any of these topics are tender for you, please proceed only as it feels safe. Reader discretion is advised.

Prologue

(Nora's Version)

[DEMO]

Wednesday, November 12, 2008

Dear Journal,

No one really knows me. Not the way you do.

The trouble is, you're just a simple mixture of ink and paper. Strokes of a pen on a dead tree.

You don't have a brain. Reasoning ability.

You hold the facts about me and keep them like a vow. Like a confidential case, you aren't at liberty to discuss.

When, in truth, writing all this down is really just talking to myself.

Flopping down on my bed, headphones on, and ruminating over the events of the week. Month. Year.

I've gotten pretty good at embodying someone who is living, while, inside, I'm slowly wasting away.

Maybe it's this town or the people in it. Save for Elliott, of course.

Everyone here is so… small-minded.

My parents included.

It's like we're stuck in a nativity scene—but instead of divine grace, I'm slowly unraveling under the weight of Mary and Joseph's expectations.

Only, in this version, my parents weren't chosen by God—they just act like they were.

I can't seem to escape the constant spotlight they keep turning in our direction.

But when it's my turn to speak, I forget all my lines.

It's not stage fright though. No. It's something much worse.

It's imposter syndrome. It's post-performance shame.

The emotional hangover from having to play the part that's been chosen for me.

And every time my act falls short, I risk exposing us—exposing who we really are.

I wish I could tell Elliott how often I think of escaping it all.

I've considered it since I was ten or eleven.

Since the evenings I used to spend, locked in my bathroom, floating in a tub of water, ears just below the surface.

Listening to my boombox play a carefully chosen emo song at a volume loud enough to rattle the mirror on the wall.

Sometimes I'd practice holding my breath.

I knew if I ran out of breath, I could drown. I knew it wouldn't take much.

Aspiration. Unconsciousness. Then, nothing.

The thought was oddly peaceful.

They probably should've taken me to a shrink, but I'm not sure they even noticed it was happening. That I was slipping.

That I still am.

Though now, I want to feel the pain of it.

I know it's selfish, but I want to know people will miss me.

Track 1

Touch & Go, But Mostly Go

(Nora's Version)

My earliest memory is of being three years old. 1995 was the year of Elmo, Teddy Grahams, and a plastic kiddie pool in the front yard filled with rubber duckies. The kind that squeal and squirt water when you squeeze them. Oddly enough, it was also the year of Elliott Ashby. And so was every year after that.

I distinctly remember standing on the lawn in my Huggies pull-up, clutching a Ewey the Lamb Beanie Baby, and sucking my thumb. It was a hot summer morning, and the humidity was just creeping in. My mom sat on a plastic patio chair, thighs sticking to the seat and fanning herself with the TV guide she swiped off the coffee table. Looking back now, she was most likely counting down the hours until my nap so that she could curl up on the couch in the air conditioning and binge the episodes of *General Hospital* she'd taped.

When I woke up and crept out of my toddler bed, sometimes I'd walk in on a scene of someone crying or kissing. I guessed it was a hospital for very pretty people.

I didn't know it then, but now I recognize the rumble across the street as a moving truck. Even at that young age, though, I knew that something new was happening. *Someone* new. A little boy, who looked about my age, with a mop of light brown hair, bounced around on the porch of the house that faced ours and husky men carried boxes back and forth from the truck to the front door. One of them occasionally stopped to muss the boy's bangs and tickle him under the chin before returning to unload more items from the overfull U-Haul.

His giggle echoed over the scorching asphalt. I shuffled a few steps forward, planting my feet right at the edge of the sidewalk.

My eyes were glued to the way he swung his little legs over the banister and sat, wriggling with excitement; wild-eyed and barely contained. The neighbors were probably peeking out from their cool living rooms, behind their lace panel curtains, wondering what a family with a Calvin Klein-model-looking father figure and a mom who looked like the offspring of Cindy Crawford and John F. Kennedy Jr. would want in a small town like Moonridge Creek, Ohio.

"Cridlers lived in that house in '86, didn't they?" came a voice from behind me. Right on cue.

Mrs. Snyder, the very elderly and extremely nosy neighborhood gossip who lived next door, strode over, cane in hand, to speak to my mother on occasion. She always chided me for having my "disgusting, germ-ridden fingers" in my mouth and chastised my mom for letting me have, what she called, a filthy habit like thumb-sucking.

"I once babysat for them," she continued. "Weren't right from the start, that bunch." Mrs. Snyder shook her head with disappointment.

My mom smiled politely, but her jaw tightened. She was probably anticipating the moments until the good manners would give way to unsolicited advice or the latest rumor about Joann's husband spending too much time at the church rec room, where the Bible study ends at seven, but his car stays parked until nine—usually beside that white Caprice with the tinted windows and questionable bumper stickers.

My mother has recited all of this to me many times over the years.

Murmuring something I couldn't hear, my mom stood while the sun-bleached plastic chair creaked underneath her. She excused herself, took me by the hand and tugged me toward the house. But just as I was about to turn and follow her inside, I caught the gaze of the boy on the banister. He had his feet hooked behind the spindles and tilted his head to one side, like he was trying to decide if I was a feral little girl, easy to ignore, or an invitation to trouble.

If I was the latter, I guess he didn't mind because he raised his hand and waved.

I swallow hard and push the surfaced memory back to the dark recesses of my mind where it came from. Funny what a midnight run to the convenience store on the corner and catching sight of a Flintstone push-pop in the freezer can do to your mind. I hadn't thought about Elliott Ashby in at least fifteen years.

Okay, that's not true. I think about him a lot. But I removed him from my Facebook friends fifteen years ago. Blocked his number from my cell phone. Boxed up every picture of the two of us, and the journal that I kept in high school. I'm making progress. I call it progress. My therapist calls it avoidance.

Avoidance. Sounds like progress if you say it fast enough.

Strategic forgetting maybe.

Repression? Probably.

I'm finished with him. That's the lie I tell myself most often.

I'm different now. Lie number two.

But it doesn't matter what label I slap on it, does it? Life is going okay. And, after all these years, there is no way he is still thinking about me. Little miss American Midwest and my big dreams. I had moved to Portland and had really put myself out there. Grayson and I are on the same page for the first time in what feels like forever. I have a stable job, even if I want to claw my eyes out most days. Things are good. Things are good—great, even—and I'm determined to appreciate it.

What business do I have being discontent? I'm successful, my boyfriend is driven and charismatic, if not a little overly analytical, and sooner than later we will probably be planning our wedding and looking at vacation homes in Bend or on Cannon Beach. Everything is moving forward.

But here, under the fluorescent lights of the Plaid Pantry, I am human enough to admit that I am having a weak moment. I grab the box of Tampax I'd crawled out of bed for, and a king-size Snickers bar, slap a ten-dollar bill on the counter with a nod at Barry—the manchild manager who I am on a first-name basis with—and walk out.

The hum of the coolers and the dubstep playlist Barry is headbanging to follows me out the door. I stare down at my teal sweatpants and worn-in Superstars. Middle-of-the-night me doesn't even remotely resemble the put-together professional I am when I'm in the office Monday through Friday.

I shake myself to get rid of the residual chill that clings to my skin from the icy interior of the store, and I remember a similar shiver that ran down my spine the year Elliott and I had decided to do the polar plunge in Lake Erie. We made my dad drive us all the way to Presque Isle in near-blizzard conditions to prove our bravery. Fifteen and stubborn and huddled close to the tiny vents pumping out subpar heat in my dad's Camry, we had more determination in our veins than common sense.

I used to think jumping into freezing water with him was proof of our unfailing bond. Now I call my therapist after I cry watching Parenthood reruns. Back then, I thought surviving hypothermia together meant we'd weather anything. Turns out, emotional frostbite lingers longer than lake water.

In my youth, I chased pain that made me feel alive. Now I crave quiet—warm socks, slow mornings, my usual coffee order waiting for me on the counter at Sterling. The walkability of my neighborhood in the Pearl District is a curated blend of urban sophistication and Pacific Northwest charm. Artsy, cool, and a little overpriced. A long way from small-town Ohio and I want to keep it that way.

I don't miss Ohio. I miss the way I used to feel there, before everything got tangled. But feelings aren't places you can revisit, and I remind myself of that at least a hundred times a day. Especially during the times when I imagine showing up there, on my parents' doorstep wearing wet sneakers and a homesick grin. But I know better than to think it'd be a soft landing. Doorsteps aren't time machines.

I shove my hands into my pockets and linger under the dim streetlights, wedging the box of tampons between my elbow and ribs. Shifting on my feet, I debate whether Flamin' Hot Cheetos would've paired well with this week's train wreck of diet choices, then shrug at myself. I hope Grayson never has to see this side of me.

Maybe by the time I become a wife, a mother, I'll be a more polished version of myself. Like the ones I used to see in the *Good Housekeeping* magazines my mom read. Someone who memorized all the latest cleaning tips and beauty advice. A woman who seemingly did it all, with grace.

I like to believe grace will come with practice. But sometimes, I feel like I am learning a lost art. Something my mother and grandmother had that just didn't get passed on to me. Still, I try. I hang eucalyptus in the shower and whisper affirmations I don't quite believe. I show up anyway—exhausted, underpaid, and well-dressed. The mantra of all millennial transplants in this city.

All but one. Grayson is the exception to every rule. Like a pair of well-worn leather loafers that doesn't beg for attention but always makes the whole outfit feel right. He doesn't need curated playlists or gratitude journals. Everything about him is effortless.

I am costume jewelry posing as a Tiffany tennis bracelet. But, around Grayson, I feel like the diamond I try so hard to be. The one I am sure is hiding beneath the surface.

Glancing up at the crescent moon, I wonder if I will ever be able to shed the self-deprecation. One day, perhaps I'll be able to look in the mirror and say, *you're exactly who you were meant to be.* But, for now, with half a Snickers stuffed in my mouth and scuffs on my shoes, I walk back down the empty sidewalk to my apartment building.

All that awaits me at home is white subway tiles, polished concrete, and a wrinkled duvet I can't wait to snuggle under. Maybe that is enough. But what if it isn't?

Track 2

Scout's Honor

(Elliott's Version)

Early sunlight streaks through the tall, rectangular windows facing the west side of Moonridge High as I sit at my desk, thumping the cap of my red pen against a thick pile of homework papers. They'd been turned in at the end of last week and now it's Tuesday. I hadn't wanted to spend my weekend alone with my thoughts, marking them and assigning grade percentages.

Today is May 26th anyway. Memorial Day weekend had given me respite before the last few days of the school year ensued. What does it matter if the extra credit I'd given out on analyzing TikTok book reviews waits an hour more?

I really try to make learning fun but I'm beginning to think after the last twelve years of teaching at my alma mater, the concept of enjoyable learning is pretty foreign to the eleventh graders that rotate in and out of my classroom nine months out of the year. If I'm honest with myself, I'm looking forward to summer, to living life without an alarm clock, as much as they are.

It's only 6:30 AM but I've already been at work for twenty minutes and students don't usually start rolling in until at least 7:15. I drag a hand across my face and feel the stubble from the last few days of not shaving. That's the thing about me—I notice everything. I always have. It's both a blessing and a curse.

Some might call it OCD. Others might say I just hate being uninformed.

But what they don't know is that the things I notice are mostly things I wish I didn't. I've always been too in my head to care what most other people think though. So, I collect the things I see like pennies in a piggy bank. Each moment I've saved rattles in my mind—like coins I'll spend when the time's right. Only that time was more than a decade ago.

I hear the click of heels coming down the hall and groan quietly, recognizing that it's the unmistakable footsteps of Jessica Sorrell. She's the principal at Moonridge High and I do everything I can to avoid running into her, at school or anywhere else. It's a small town and people talk, specifically about Miss Sorrell and me.

Jessica seeks out my truck every morning, like it's some kind of beacon. Maybe I should be driving something less flashy than a souped-up King Ranch, but that's beside the point. My usual parking spot is near the only shade tree in the lot because I've got to protect the investment I made in that truck on a teacher's salary.

I gave Jessica a ride home in it one day after classes when her Prius was on the fritz. But nosy neighbors and small towns go together like peanut butter and banana sandwiches. Once one of them saw me helping her out of the passenger side on the corner of Walnut and Maple, I was doomed to be dubbed the playboy of Moonridge.

After that, the F-150 wasn't just a mode of transportation. It was a symbol of a moment I couldn't control. A narrative being told without permission. But Jessica ate it up. In fact, if I didn't know better, I'd have thought she started it herself.

She waltzes into my office with an easy smile. The kind that would knock most guys off their feet.

"Good morning, Elliott," she says. Her voice is smoother than the leather in my cab. "You missed the faculty breakfast on Friday."

"Did I?" I chuckle wryly. "Guess I'm not much of a breakfast person." I glance over at the protein bar sticking out of my bag as if I'm considering entering it as evidence.

She doesn't laugh. Just studies me like she's waiting for an explanation I don't intend to give. Jessica Sorrell is stubborn, but so am I.

She shifts her weight onto one foot. "They asked about you," she states, impatience lacing the words.

"Did you tell them I'm too busy stressing over next year's football roster? Or that I'm married to my truck?"

"Very funny," she replies. We both knew it wasn't. It was a deflection, and I'm great at those. I've been practicing for a long time. She exhales briskly and I steal another glance out the window. Golden sunbeams dance through the glass and onto the floor at her feet. They reflect onto her face and illuminate the dark circles under her eyes.

"Is there something I can help you with?" I ask. More out of concern that I care to admit, but the words come out slightly harsher than I mean them to. Her eyebrow twitches and I do my best to plaster on a genuine grin to soften the moment.

"I just wanted to tell you, have a great summer," she sighs, as if there was more to it but she decided to give me the abridged version. "I won't be here for the rest of the week and didn't want to disappear without saying goodbye. Leaving Moonridge for the summer is the best thing for me right now."

"Where will you go?" I stutter. What I really mean, though, is, *do you feel trapped here too?*

She dodges the vulnerable undertone of my question and sweeps her hair back behind her shoulder, attempting to look less weighed down than I can see she is. "I'm going to visit my sister in Boise. She packed up her regrets and I think it's time I did the same. For a while anyway."

I nod like I don't understand, even though I do. The trouble is that I understand all too well. The only difference is, she has options. My only move is not to move at all.

"Take care of yourself," she finally says. It sounds like she's trying to convince herself instead of me. Still, I vow that I will, which is a lie, and tuck her into a quick, platonic hug. Somehow, I hope that I've transferred some kind of comfort. Then again, I'm not great at that anymore.

Jessica walks out of the room, but behind her lingers a familiar scent. Something sugary sweet. Cherry blossom, jasmine, and stone fruit. It's nostalgic, syrupy, and reminds me of the sticky lip gloss and butterfly hair clips every girl adorned themselves with in school. Then it hits me, it's the smell of the hallways after gym class, and the sleepover bags girls stuffed in their locker on Friday so they could stay over at their best friend's house after school.

Love Spell. I'm pretty sure it's the only perfume I know the name of; thanks to Denise Newbury and the surprise kiss she tried to give me in fifth grade detention. Really, though, there was only one girl I knew back then who *wasn't* wearing it. Nora Lowe.

Back then, Nora always smelled like summer storms and oakmoss. She wasn't like the other girls and I think I knew it the moment we moved in across the street. Nora was different. But not in the way that made you point and wrinkle your nose. It was more of a reason to listen when she talked, to lean into the same enthusiasm she had and try to adopt it yourself.

Nora always knew how to press pause on the world. She was someone I looked up to, whether she knew it or not. In the middle of all my football games, she was the one I looked for in the crowd, to cheer me on. When I was at a breaking point trying to prep for the SATs and worrying I wouldn't get into UNC-

Chapel Hill, she was the one who drilled me on Saturday nights. I didn't have to be perfect around her, but she was always perfect to me.

Then, she was gone.

I clear my throat in the silence and wait for the sting behind my eyes to fade. I get misty when I remember how I failed her—selfish when she needed selfless. Now, I do penance by paying a visit to her parents a couple times a week and trying to be the good guy they always believed I was.

Nora had obviously never told them what happened between us and it wouldn't be fair of me to let them down. To let *her* down. Or the memory of who we were all those years ago. All the things we wanted to be.

We were never officially a couple, but there was always something unspoken between us—feelings folded into friendship, waiting for the right time.

Her mom, Cindy, always asks me if I'm eating enough and will sometimes leave a batch of her otherworldly cinnamon muffins on my porch. Living across the street from them still has its perks. I eat the muffins and think of how Nora once said they reminded her of crisp Octobers and homecoming games.

Her dad, Tommy, still sits out on the porch with the news drifting out from behind him, through the open window. He nods from his chair, and I wave back. I sit. I listen. I watch. I wait. I pretend I don't notice the way Nora's picture still leans a little too far to the left above the mantel, like it's waiting for someone to fix it. I never do.

I think if I ever did straighten it, she'd be gone for real.

Track 3

Fake Dice, Real Stakes

(Nora's Version)

After a week of writhing with a heating pad after work and watching *13 Going on 30* three times during my rom-com binge—repeatedly crying over Mark Ruffalo's undying devotion—I decide it's time I called Grayson to see if he wants to grab dinner. *The Observatory* is one of his favorite restaurants in Portland and I have an affinity for their quinoa-mushroom veggie burger. Plus, we still split the bill when we go out, and I know I can at least afford to indulge in a side of aioli and fries.

Grayson usually steers clear of me when Aunt Flo visits and waits around for me to get my groove back before we pick back up on the whodunit shows he likes to marathon and the latest investor he has lined up for his start-up. I put up with paying for my own food on dates and listening to him drone on about Mallorca detectives because it's easier to play house if I let him take the lead.

I shoot him a quick text. Something that says, *I'm desperate for attention*, without drama or the use of emojis. I need his steadiness to pull me out of my spiral. He answers faster than I anticipate, and the air is involuntarily forced from my lungs when I read the five words he sent.

Sure. We need to talk.

Under any normal set of circumstances, Grayson didn't do the hard conversations or anything remotely inviting the answer that everything was other than fine when he asked how your day was. He didn't do messy. Or maybe he didn't do honest. It was something I'd never really considered before. But now, looking down at the tone I was so unfamiliar with coming from him, it seemed plausible.

If I was going to have some sort of confrontation when what I'd hoped for was romance, I'd need to deep dive into my closet, glass of wine in hand, and take control of the one thing I could—how I presented myself to this man who I had imagined getting down on one knee in a matter of months, asking me to spend the rest of our lives together.

Or maybe that was it? Was tonight going to be the night that our talking and my dreams of a steady life without stress turned into something more? What if Grayson was going to propose at the restaurant? Would there be a ring hidden in my dessert?

I decide I want to walk the line between effortless and outstanding. Pouring myself a glass of Merlot—cherry, cocoa, and a hint of surrender—and sliding by the record player, I press play and the soothing sound of Ed Sheeran and Andrea Bocelli's symphony follow me into my room as I try to choose between dressing for a feast or a funeral.

Running my fingers over a silk slip dress, I feel the vulnerability from the last time I wore it creep over my skin. A first date a few years ago with some guy I met on Tinder. It lasted approximately seventeen minutes before he made one too many innuendo jokes and he crossed a line I didn't want to explain. Nothing good would've come from staying at the bar that night. Nothing good came from me going either.

A structured black, tulip-style dress hangs next to it. One that Grayson had complimented when we'd gone to one of his fundraisers. It hugged my ribs a little too tight and I always felt out of breath when I wore it. Many times, it had nearly gone into the donation pile, but Grayson's voice always stopped me.

I've never seen you look more beautiful.

In the end, I go with a flowing midi that accentuates my square shoulders and has a neckline low enough that it catches attention without being gauche. I drag the only matte red lipstick I own over my dry lips and wish I had less freckles peeking through my foundation. Turning to the side, I catch my reflection. I look oddly composed for someone standing on a fault-line.

Meeting at *The Observatory* is Grayson's idea. He was coming straight from downtown and picking me up would've required a detour. So, I take my time getting there because, knowing him and Portland traffic, I'd be sitting in the dining room listening to the tinkling of glasses and the server asking if my guest was still coming for longer than I liked.

As I entered the restaurant, though, and realized that the dim lighting was much less flattering than I'd hoped, I saw Grayson already seated at our usual table. The smell of smoked cocktails wafted over from the bar, and the blue-gray of the walls felt like a storm rolling in. He sipped his dry Riesling and checked his watch. If anything, Grayson was predictable. Being here early and looking anxious didn't suit him.

I walk over to him as he smooths his napkin. Grayson doesn't look up—he seems nervous. But I guess I would be too, if I was about to ask a very loaded question to someone I hoped would say yes. That was the way I was telling the story to myself about how this night would go anyway. Grayson would be softer, more jittery, less himself. I would weep and nod my head as he slid the ring onto my hand, and in twelve months we'd be having a wedding at The Evergreen.

He clears his throat into the silence between us as I sit and adjust the skirt of my dress around my legs. "Still sparkling water for the lady?" a server asked.

"Actually, I'd love some champagne. Wouldn't you?" I nod at Grayson.

"Champagne?" He furrows his brow. "Rather indulgent, I think. I'll stick with my Riesling."

I offer a tight smile. "Champagne for me anyway, please."

The server looks between us, partially expecting Grayson to change his mind. When he doesn't, she raises an eyebrow and disappears towards the kitchen.

Grayson keeps his gaze on the menu and purses his lips as he peruses the entrees. We both know he'll order the same thing he always does. But that's beside the point.

Tonight, I think, *there's a fine line between ordinary and extraordinary.*

The press-on nails I'd glued with precision atop my own nail beds catch the light, and suddenly I'm ten again, surrounded by glitter and possibility. They are plastic, shiny, and reminiscent of the DIY kits from my childhood. Back then, the tiny gems and faux jewels were meant for maximum sparkle. Tonight, I was hoping the sparkle would come from a size six ring on my left ring finger.

My mind flickers briefly to Elliott and the time I spent bent over the kitchen table at his house with my glittery gel pens and Lisa Frank Trapper Keeper splayed out. The glint in his blue lightning eyes as he peered over his Jello Pudding Pop and quirked his chocolate covered lips up.

"Whatcha writing?" he'd ask.

"Mind your beeswax," I'd shoot back.

"Oooh, so probably something juicy about Sawyer Collins. You'll marry him one day."

"Will not! He's got cooties anyway," was my reasoning.

"One day, you won't think that. That's what my mom says."

"Well, she's wrong. Boys are gross. Especially you," I'd laugh.

But she wasn't wrong. And sitting here at the table with Grayson, I realize that the shimmer on my nails isn't half as bright as the one in Elliott's eyes when we were just kids. Only that doesn't matter because I'm here with someone else.

Grayson's voice cuts gently through the memory, but it takes me a second to place the words. Something about the new chef. Something about whether I want an appetizer. I nod without answering, fingers curling around the stem of my glass.

"You said you wanted to talk," I sputter. The words come out like I've been holding them in a bullpen. Too fast, too eager.

Grayson blinks, not startled. He shifts in his seat, and the air between us thickens. Turning the fork over in his hands, he stares at the empty plate in front of him.

"I did," he says finally, and I hear something brittle in it.

I reach for the menu, just to have somewhere to look. The font blurs and bleeds like it's been dipped in water, and suddenly the restaurant feels too curated. Too clean. Like someone plucked ambiance from a Pinterest board—and forgot real life would show up, too.

"I've been thinking," he continues. Then, he pauses, as if the moment was suddenly upon him to perform and he'd gotten stage fright.

"Say it," I whisper, though I don't know what I want him to say. Only that I've come all this way to hear it.

He sighs. It sounds resigned, and complicated. I decide I don't want to hear him say anything other than that I look nice tonight, or something to that effect. He hasn't commented on much since I got here, other than the wine list, and I'm beginning to unravel.

A laugh from a nearby table reminds me how out of sync I feel right now. The weight of the unsaid words he's holding onto is crushing. I feel too hot and too cold all at once and the room is beginning to spin. Grayson fidgets with his napkin, still avoiding my eyes.

"I think some space would be good for us, Nor," he says. The anvil drops. My heart is shattered.

I don't answer. Not with words.

Instead, I stare at a menu I couldn't read even if I wanted to. My vision swims. The laugh from the next table sounds like it's coming from underwater, and

Grayson's face blurs like a portrait painted in haste. The expression he's wearing is all wrong.

Space.

It's what I yearned for when I first got to Portland. Anything that would give me time and miles to distance myself from Elliott and everything Ohio no longer held for me. The kind of space where I could make up fantasies and live in them undisturbed. Or, even worse, the real world.
But this? The kind of space Grayson was asking for wasn't freedom. Not for me. It was cutting the last rope of a suspension bridge that I hadn't completed crossing. And now, I was dangling for dear life as he dared to walk away.

I blink, slow and stupid, like it might rearrange the reality I've just been handed.

Grayson's gaze flickers toward the candle, like maybe it'll offer something to read from the flames. His expression is unknowable.

"I don't want space," I choke. It feels childish, small. But true.

"Nor, I'm not sure you know *what* you want," he replies. It scorches. "We've been together for long enough that I thought we'd be headed in the same direction by now," he continues. "But it seems like the Nora I know and the Nora you really are, are two different people."

"What are you talking about?" I whisper-scream. "I've done everything I could to be the type of woman you'd be proud to be with. And now you want space? To take a break or breakup?"

He's exasperated. I can see it. He doesn't want to fight. But it's less because he's angry and more because I'm not worth fighting for.

"I don't want to make this dramatic. Breaking up seems so… high school. Let's just call it, going our separate ways. No hard feelings. Yeah?"

I nod, slowly. Not because I agree. Because I know the argument's already over. I'm not losing a relationship tonight—I'm losing the version of myself I built to survive it. And I was delusional enough to think I'd be walking out of here a fiancée.

"Yeah," I hear myself say. It sounds like someone else's voice.

I scoot my chair out, slow enough that maybe he'll stop me. He doesn't. Of course he doesn't. He's already rehearsing life without me.

Track 4

Trip Of My Life

(Elliott's Version)

I'm still trying to find it. The part of me that feels comfortable without the blanket of ambiguity I carry around. In my head, I look something like Linus, Charlie Brown's friend. He's probably a little more thoughtful than I am, truth be told. Linus is the deep thinker of the Peanuts group and I always thought he carried around the blue blanket because of his anxiety. Needless to say, I carry around mine for the same reason.

If my metaphorical blanket were real, it'd probably have a hole worn through it by now from running my fingers over the same spot so many times. Maybe I'd be able to put it over my head when I was feeling particularly grumpy.

I remember one newspaper cutout from the comic section that hung on our fridge for the longest time. Linus had lost his blanket for two weeks and when he got it back it was dirty, ragged, torn, and even moldy, but the joy of having it again overshadowed it all. By comparison, I'd feel pretty lucky if mine quietly slipped away. If I didn't have something to hide behind all the time, I'd probably be forced to do something other than spend my free time with a craft beer and my couch.

The truth is, I don't know who I am without it. And maybe that's the problem.

Tilting my head back and draining the brown glass bottle I have clutched in my hand, I add it to the others on the cluttered coffee table. Surveying my surroundings, you'd think that I was in the middle of moving in, or decidedly on my way out. After my parents died, I looked for ways to do what I called simplifying. Really though, it was a way to disguise the pain I couldn't tolerate by going through their things box by box. Instead, I loaded most of it up and dropped it off at the nearest Goodwill. To me, stuff didn't hold memories, people did. And I was so full of them that I was nearly overflowing.

Simplifying sounded noble. Felt more like cowardice in flannel.

The only box I hadn't had the heart to send away was a bunch of memorabilia from my childhood. It wasn't so much about the great times I'd had with my parents, though there were plenty. It was that I was sure it held a lifetime worth of cards, pictures, and souvenirs of my life lived side-by-side with Nora.

I glance over at the brown cardboard, sitting in the corner of the sparsely furnished living room. A small white piece of paper sticks out from one of the folds and tonight I find myself brave enough to go over and pluck it from the box. I don't know if it's the three beers in, or the freedom of not having to work tomorrow, but I'm holding a Polaroid in my hand. One I haven't seen since junior high.

The edges are slightly curled; the ink faded to the kind of sepia that only time—or a kitchen drawer—can create. In the photo, Nora's hair is tucked behind one ear, her smile half-formed. I am sitting beside her, face turned in her direction, eyes glued to her dimples. Suddenly, I wonder how many moments were captured where I was looking at her like this. With complete adoration.

I hadn't known the photo was being taken. But now I wonder if this was the first time someone else saw it before I did—how utterly gone I was for her. That Nora Lowe was the love of my life.

She was. And maybe still is. But only in photos, because that's the only place I see her. The only time I get to have a conversation with her is inside my own head. And, even then, I usually act like an idiot. The same one that gave up calling when I realized she blocked my number. The same one who never got on a plane. Never showed up on her doorstep begging for forgiveness.

Somehow, even in the make-believe conversations, I still manage to blow it.

I can still recall my mom's voice when she'd come in with the groceries and see us doing homework together or playing Oregon Trail, huddled around the giant desktop in our den. The hum of the tower, the cracked mousepad with peeling corners—it all felt eternal back then.

"You two are gonna get married someday," she'd sing out. Like it was set in stone. Like she could see the future.

"Not if she keeps bossing me around," I'd snort, even though I was smiling harder than I wanted her to see. I didn't realize it then, but the smile wasn't because I thought my mom's idea was crazy. It was because even I didn't picture myself living any differently than with Nora by my side, forever.

I trace the photo's outline with my thumb and feel it

snag slightly on a crease. It's fragile. But so is memory. So is love. And so, apparently, am I.

Sliding the photo into the pocket of my *Levi's*, I head out to the front porch, the creaky screen door swaying shut behind me with a groan.

This is it. The spot where I first saw her. The spot where I'll probably die still seeing her. Barefoot in the grass, thumb in her mouth, the hum of sprinklers in the distance.

I was there; I remember it. And even though I know she's not there now, it doesn't stop me from looking. It never has.

Yellow light shines through the windows of her old house. Filtering through the curtains, I can see the glow of the television screen. *Jeopardy*. But it must be an old episode because Alex Trebek is still the host on this one.

The familiarity of it makes me smile to myself. Just another night in Moonridge, where nothing ever changes. At least, not fast enough for anyone to notice. Except it does—and it's slowly breaking me.

A porch light flickers across the street. A dog lets out one sharp bark. Somewhere inside my house, the sound of Tom Llamas hosting the nightly news.

None of it is profound. Just familiar. Just… enough.

It's like I live in a time capsule. By the time someone finds me it'll be the year 3000 and only bones will be left. A note taped to my ribcage: *Died of boredom. Or too much nostalgia. Hard to say.*

I know that thinking that way isn't doing me any favors. It's the way people joke about loneliness without ever admitting it. That subtlety makes it even more heartbreaking.

My phone buzzes in my pocket. I pull it out, halfway through a sigh, already poised to decline another scam call. But then I see the name—Marquis. It's not like him to call me midweek. He works third shift as a warehouse selector at Buckeye Bend Logistics, one town over. The same company Tommy, Nora's dad, used to work for. At this hour, he'd be eating dinner with his wife and kids, probably wiping ketchup off the baby's face and trying to convince the oldest to finish her carrots. So, with his name lighting up my screen, I know it probably isn't a casual call to catch up. I almost don't answer.

Marquis barely lets me say hello before his bellowing voice fills the line.

"You'll never guess who I was in traffic next to this morning," he says.

"Hello to you, too," I laugh. "You call me to gossip now?"

Marquis sighs on the other end of the phone call. "Are you ever going to start taking me seriously?"

"I haven't since high school. Why ruin a good streak?" I reply dryly.

"Well, you might want to wipe the smirk I know you've got off of your face before what I have to say does it for you."

"Noted," I say, more seriously, and sit still. I try to compose myself so that I can get a better grasp on exactly what's happening right now. Marquis is a jokester, but not tonight. "What's up?"

"Nora Lowe, that's what's up. She was sitting in a car next to me at a red light, this morning on the way back from work."

"You obviously aren't getting enough sleep." I brush off the news as if it's impossible, but my eyes are wide with possibility. My heart pounds against the inside of my chest and I feel slightly wheezy. She wouldn't come back, would she? Not after everything.

I stay frozen, phone still pressed to my ear, listening for the sound of Marquis breathing—half hoping he saw her again, half terrified he did.

Track 5

Off With Her Head

(Nora's Version)

I tug my *Taylor Swift is my therapist* trucker hat down farther on my forehead and slump down in my economy airplane seat. It feels like every person I've passed since I left *The Observatory* the other night can see the sign on my back: *Just got dumped. Please, no pity.*

Grayson tried to call me yesterday. I thought maybe he had reconsidered his lapse in judgment and wanted to beg me to be his again. Instead, he left me a twenty-two second voicemail stating that he needed the pickleball set I borrowed back before the office's weekend match.

Feeling trapped, uncomfortable, and suspended between destinations isn't doing much for my rapidly declining mental state. Low comfort, high vulnerability, and all alone with my thoughts? Please.

Not only am I squished into the middle seat, but my left butt cheek is numb, and my legs have to remain crossed or I am going to knee one of the guys next to me in the crotch. This, however, leaves me plenty of time to come up with a thousand different comebacks to Grayson's less than stellar reason for breaking up with me.

He'd called it "so high school", and he had a point. The way I had waited for him to accept me, want me, and made it a point to change for him—to fit his mold better—was as pathetic as it would've been if we were teenagers. Maybe even more.

The silhouette of the black dress I'd almost worn to dinner haunted me. As soon as I got home, I threw it in the trash. The same place his opinions and superiority belonged. I had spent so long trying to make myself more palatable for him that I'd forgotten what it felt like to love myself. To see my raw edges and not try to stitch them up for the sake of his vanity.

That dress was always too tight, too itchy, too stuffy and, so was our façade of a relationship.

Hearing Grayson say he wanted space—whatever that was supposed to mean—cut. But I wasn't going to bleed for someone who wanted me smaller. As far as

I was concerned, he was the smallest man that ever lived.

I open my messages app and start drafting a text to Grayson.

Try to stretch before the match… Your hamstrings, not your ego.

But I delete it as quickly as it was typed.

A voice comes over the speaker saying that we've hit our cruising altitude and that we should all settle in for a relaxing flight. No weather ahead, the pilot confirms, so there shouldn't be much turbulence. The only problem is the turbulence inside me.

Before long the flight attendants start to make their rounds with the little carts of assorted drinks and snacks. When it's my turn to either order or refuse, I almost ask if they've got anything for heartbreak. But instead, I ask for a ginger ale and throw my headphones on to avoid more questions.

The first song to play when I hit shuffle on my library is *Good 4 U* by Olivia Rodrigo. I know the words by heart. Under normal circumstances I would have been belting out the lyrics about the loser who was so unaffected by her losing her mind over him. Now, my thumb hovers above the skip button as I contemplate my own failed love story.

Grayson and I had never agreed on any music choices. He only listened to indie records and John Mayer, while I dialed up the pop princesses and mainstream dance hits. I cheered for the girls who took life in their own hands, and he tuned into the idea that women were the weaker sex. Sometimes, what I wouldn't give to be a man.

Olivia is nearly at the end of her raging breakup anthem when I decide to scan my playlists for something a little less upbeat and a lot more painful.

The pad of my finger hits a familiar song, and the beginning notes feel like peroxide on a debris-filled wound. It stings and I want to scream, but instead, I bite my bottom lip and scrunch my eyes closed.

A grainy vision of Elliott floods the blackness behind my eyelids until I can see him in full, high-definition color, eleven years old, belting the words to *Here Without You* on a makeshift stage in his backyard. The 3 Doors Down, post-grunge vibe had never really been my style, but his animated performance had made me laugh until my stomach hurt.

He'd only done that karaoke version, which I honestly preferred to the original, to cheer me up. The first boy I'd ever had a crush on—after claiming they all had cooties—had dissed me on the playground in front of all his stupid friends. Elliott, though, was there to patch my broken wings and pride.

I think, looking back, that was the moment I realized that there was a type of love that came without conditions. That some demanded proof, while others provided healing. At the time, it was a reminder of who *actually* showed up for me. Now, it was a reminder of everything I'd lost.

Real love had felt rarer since I left Moonridge. In Elliott's absence, it felt nearly extinct. And I wished, with all my might, that the boy in the backyard with a microphone was still out there somewhere. Even if it wasn't with me.

The sting of the ginger ale fizz burns my nose—and so do my tears. I sniffle, losing a little of the control I was trying to hold onto. At least in the presence of strangers. But the man next to me makes eye contact and, the next thing I know, he's offering me a Kleenex. If I didn't know better, I'd say chivalry wasn't dead. The issue is, I *do* know better.

The exchange with my airplane neighbor in seat 14C is awkward, to say the least. I take the tissue without looking up and murmur my embarrassed thanks, despite my heightening claustrophobia. It isn't just the cabin pressure—it is the pressure of staying silent when all I want to do is riot.

Still, sometimes strangers offer more comfort than people we think we love.

Now that things with Grayson are through, it's clear to me, for the first time since prom night, that you can bet on someone who says they'll never fold. But sometimes it turns out—they are the game.

I'll admit, it's a cynical outlook. One my mom would probably be ashamed of. Then again, she doesn't know anything about what had happened all those years ago between Elliott and me. All the truths that came rushing out when the dam broke.

It seems like every time I dare to love someone, it ends up being an illusion. And I have seen one sleight of hand too many.

Falling into a fitful sleep, I see nothing but tumbling card towers and a cackling Queen of Hearts screaming *Off with her head!* My dreams are haunted by images of Elliott as a magician. Grayson as a mime. My, they make a marvelous pair of pretenders.

Even as I wake up, gather my luggage, and step off the red-eye, I can't get rid of the nightmares. Both the ones I dream and the ones I live. I'm not just a rejected Betty. I'm a rejected Betty headed back to my hometown, waiting for the visceral nausea I feel from bad choices to subside.

Track 6

Rehearsal For A Ghost

(Elliott's Version)

Five times. I've checked five times to see if she's come out of the house yet. To make sure I didn't just conjure up the fact that she's back in Moonridge from thin air. Maybe Marquis imagined that he saw her on the bypass on the way into town. Anything's possible, right?

I didn't want to believe him when he insisted that he would know her anywhere. In fact, his saying that made me a little defensive. *I'm* the one who would know her anywhere. *I'm* the one who knows her everywhere. I can't escape her, no matter how many years pass. No matter how hard I try.

Sure, I'm clinging to the one thing I feel like no one can steal from me—the way her constant presence in my life, for sixteen years, wrote my entire internal map. I've been rehearsing what I would say to her if I ever saw her again since the last time I watched her car back out of the driveway. I'm not possessive, not in the way most guys are. I'm still grieving—the loss of my best friend. That torment masquerades as pride, and I'm not about to let the mask slip.

I haven't seen any movement inside, or outside, the house yet this morning. A sleepless night stretched the morning longer than it should've been. Midnight rolled around with quiet motivation to stay awake. If I didn't go to sleep, I couldn't miss anything. If I kept my eyes open, the possibility of her being here was real.

All night, I bargained with time. Now, every shadow outside is a false alarm.

Hyper-awareness isn't a cozy companion. It's high-functioning angst, at its best. On top of it, my brain doesn't do well with idleness. Sitting at my kitchen table, forcing myself to stare into a cup of coffee, waiting for fate to find me? That isn't my typical approach to life. In fact, I don't really believe in fate anyway.

I'm breaking every rule in my own playbook. But I can't stop.

Robins begin chirping from the large oak tree in my front yard. I can hear the crescendo through the closed windows. Mourning doves join in and then the sharp chatter of a blue jay cuts through the calm. It's the soundtrack to the cataclysm inside me. One that causes my wildest daydreams to collide with reality. Only there's a haze around the edges, a vignette that makes me question what's real and what's not.

The room feels rearranged by unseen hands—just enough askew that the walls might exhale and cave in.

What if she walks out and doesn't even look over? What if I don't recognize her anymore?

I'm not sure I'll survive seeing her again.

It's late spring, the climax to the season of renewal. Summer will stroll in with confidence before I know it. But, somehow, these seasons of growth and sun-soaked permanence feel misaligned. Everything feels off-kilter and ready to collapse. Even me. Especially me.

My body feels heavy and I'm gripping my coffee mug too tight. Behind me, Mr. Coffee sputters in protest to the day's prolonged beginning and I think that perhaps I'm not the only one who dreads finding out if all the speeches I've thrown at the mirror for the last fifteen years have been wasted breath.

The machine sighs again, like it's tired of its routine. Like it knows the speeches I'm thinking of. It's heard them a thousand times and still can't brew enough courage for the end. It coughs once, then settles into quiet indignation.

The speeches were never meant for Nora. Not the Nora behind those windows. They were for the version I adapted every time I needed to believe that, out there somewhere, she was still thinking of me. That the girl in my memory still matched up, freckle for freckle, to the one she was in Portland.

I often imagine her sitting in her chair by a window, looking out at the city. Probably tired from a long week and looking for a lull in the hustle. And, I hope, that she wonders about me.

Or, maybe she doesn't wonder at all. I could've sworn she loved me once. But love is no guarantee. And a guarantee isn't always born from love.

With that thought, I'm transported to a hot, mid-summer night.

July 2009.

Nora and I piled into the car with our school friends. Seventeen and carefree, grabbing slushies from Speedway, and heading to the nearest Flashback 14 movie theater to see the latest Transformers installment.

While the girls swooned over Shia LeBeouf in the back seat, Marquis and I cued up the tunes in the front. The ride to the cinema was a full-blown mixtape, blasted from my iPod Nano hooked up to the auxiliary outlet. We cycled through Owl City, Kings of Leon, and Linkin Park like we owned the rights to the lyrics and they were out on loan.

I caught Nora singing quietly to *Use Somebody*, her fingers wrapped around the straw of her grape slushie. Her lips were stained purple and she was well on her way to a neon brain freeze. Sitting behind me, her voice threaded through the speakers like it belonged there.

By the time we arrived at the movies, we were jacked up on sugar and the idea of overly buttered popcorn spilling on the floor as we passed it between us sounded as good as a steak dinner. Nora, of course, sat next to me so she could whisper about the movie the entire time. A bad habit of hers I'd come to find endearing.

But, as her fingers grazed my wrist when she reached for a handful from the popcorn bucket, I realized that maybe there was more there than the friendly affection that had floated between us since we were toddlers.

It wasn't something I could put words to. It was a feeling. Fleeting, but raw. Something I couldn't desensitize myself to once I realized.

It wasn't loud or public, but it lingered—leaving me suspended between hope and doubt. I was grateful for the feeling, confused by its meaning. And more than anything, I wondered if she'd felt it too. A part of me wanted her to. The other part didn't want anything to change.

Track 7

Lost Girl Logic

(Nora's Version)

I've had precisely three cups of coffee and an apple this morning. I can't stomach anything else. Not when I know he's out there. Elliott Ashby will be down the front steps of his house at literally any moment. I'm preteen and pubescent all over again. In my bedroom at the top of the steep staircase of my parents' American foursquare, staring at the NSYNC poster on my ceiling, and inhaling the lingering scent of cucumber melon on my bedspread.

This is a trauma loop I've been walking through for years. It never becomes less devastating. It didn't when I was over two thousand miles away, and it doesn't now. Because... because no matter what cocktail of meds I'm taking, or how many times a week I go to Pilates class, Elliott is the tripwire I stumble on.

Healing can never be a straight line for someone like me, while someone like him exists in the world.

Even though showering and scrubbing every memory of Grayson down the drain was my first priority when I got here, I still feel the grime of the past on my skin. It's filmy and personal. Not even my favorite hoodie and jeans combo can keep me from subconsciously checking to see if I have a rash. Surely there is a name for the allergic reaction I'm having to being back in Moonridge.

Being so close to everything I've tried to escape seems contradictory on every level.

Why did I return to the murder scene of who I used to be? I guess I never stopped checking for a pulse.

Some part of me still believes there might be life in the wreckage.

Back in high school, my class read *As You Like It*. It ended up being my favorite Shakespearean play. Elliott was mad about it too. Rosalind and Orlando were more than just a love story for us—they were self-discovery and emotional truth. Maybe the truth we weren't ready to tell each other back then.

We often dramatically quoted lines at random and discussed the meaning of "all the world's a stage", in the seventeenth century and our own lives. Today, that stage feels impossibly tilted and I am playing the role of a fool... again.

A dog-eared copy of *As You Like It* still sits on my bookshelf, its spine faded, its margins haunted with Elliott's scribbled metaphors. "Love is merely a madness," he once underlined three times. I'd mocked him for being dramatic. But now, madness doesn't feel like such a stretch.

My mattress creaks as I slide off the bed and glance from the upstairs of this house—full of memories and melancholy—to the adjacent room at Elliott's. It used to be a lifeline—to see his bedroom light on, him hunched over the desk near the window, always working on some new idea. A new play to show the football coach was most common.

Elliott was never just one thing though. He was an artist and an athlete. Dramatist and locker-room jock. Everyone loved him. I loved him. To the moon and Saturn.

I'm still deep into reminiscing when the floorboard outside my room groans under the weight of a person I can only assume is my mom. She has never been able to sneak up on me—she knows. A soft knock on the door follows and I cross the room to open it.

She envelops me for the first time since I showed up unannounced yesterday morning. Our family isn't big on hugs. I guess not seeing your daughter for over a decade will make you do strange things.

It's like those hugs at Disney World. You know, the ones where the character doesn't let go until you do? Like they know how much you need to feel the magic. And I feel it, in her arms. But it isn't real.

Regardless, her perfume hasn't changed. That same faint Estée Lauder she always wears when she needs to feel put together. I don't mention it—but the combination of her scent and her embrace is enough to pull a brain wave loose.

January 1998 stands out in my childhood memory bank.

That was my first visit to Disney World. The Florida heat still baked us, even though it was winter, and I got sunburn on my cheeks so badly it blistered. The Ashbys had agreed to accompany us, and Elliott spent the entire time in a walking harness because his parents were afraid he would wander off. I giggled about it behind his back and felt more mature because my own mom and dad trusted me enough not to get lost. Only, I did.

It was near dusk at the park, and we were just finishing Dole Whip and Mickey pretzels at a snack stand. That's when I spotted the Peter Pan's Flight attraction.

Peter Pan was my favorite childhood story. My VHS tape of the cartoon movie adaptation was so worn that I had to push the tracking button on our remote repeatedly to ever see through the static. But it didn't matter. At age six, the idea of never growing up had me in a chokehold.

I loved the thought of being a Lost Girl, like Wendy. I even begged my parents to buy me a blue nightgown that resembled the one she wore in the cartoon. It's no wonder I wandered into line for the ride. Alone. Led by invisible forces.

Standing there for what seemed like ages, I was all nerve endings and excitement. It never occurred to me that my mom didn't know where I'd gone. Or that, at the same moment, my dad was seeking out security to help find me. I was only told later what a panic I'd caused.

Just as I was about to get swept onto the ride with the other eager people in line, I was pulled aside by a small, sweaty hand. Elliott. Of course.

He never told me how he got out of the harness or how he knew I'd be there—waiting to be taken to

Neverland. He didn't need to. Six-year-old Elliott knew me the way he knew the Sesame Street theme song.

A Disney employee corralled us gently, confirmed we didn't meet the height requirement, then firmly scolded us for straying from our parents. She radioed someone immediately, her voice clipped and professional, and within minutes, a supervisor arrived to escort us to the nearest security station.

Elliott grabbed my hand and held it—the kind of gesture that said he understood my dream. That he was rooting for me. That he'd follow me anywhere, even into trouble.

"Did you sleep?" My mother's voice sounds fuzzy from far away in Neverland.

"Mmhmm," I murmur.

"You know he's home, right? You two should talk. It's been a long time," she says.

"Maybe," I fib. If I can convince her I'm considering it, maybe she'll drop the subject altogether. Maybe I won't have to explain how running to him is the only thing I want and why it's the one thing that can never happen.

Track 8

Shoes By The Door

(Elliott's Version)

It's been a week. I haven't seen her, and yet, she's all over me.

I can tell she's around. The air is different. Sweeter. The days are brighter. Sunnier. Her shoes are by the front door, her rental parked in the driveway. I know it's a rental because no one around here is from Florida. Plus, I'd know the happy little oranges on the license plate were mocking me from a thousand miles away.

Nora is present, and absent. The whole thing is comical and ghostly. And the almost domestic surveillance I have on her house is definitely bordering on creepy.

Internally, I justify it. I brush it off like it's not *that* bad. Or chalk it up to the fact that it's summer, and I'm a teacher. What else am I going to be doing with my time? I'm *supposed* to be resting and relaxing, and stalking my neighbors. It's *normal*.

And yet, I know that she's visited the local coffee shop, Calista's Café, at least three times this week. Her red Chuck Taylor high tops from middle school are still in rotation. Her bedroom light stays on until 4AM because she doesn't sleep.

Obviously, neither do I. Not anymore.

I'm too busy cataloging all of the things about her that I've convinced myself will make it easier, less gut-wrenching, when she goes home. If I can find some idiosyncrasy that I can live without, or prove that I don't know her as well as I once did, the ache will get better.

So far, it's turning out to be the exact opposite.

When Gina, the barista who was incidentally the valedictorian of our graduating class, mentioned that Nora had stopped in, I almost scalded myself on the latte she pushed my way. I was a klutz where Nora was concerned, and Gina knew it. She let me get a couple sips into the foam art on the top of the cup before she dropped subtle details like the fact that Nora ordered oat milk instead of whole.

I thought: *maybe she's changed. Maybe I don't know her anymore.*

That night, when I finally caught a glimpse of her, she wore the same sweatshirt she stole from my car in 2008, and I knew I was deceiving myself.

Sticking to my own routine—going for my morning jogs, catching up on my summer reading list—those things are easy. It's the fact that I know she saw me, noticed I'm here. I'm right where she left me, and she doesn't even have the decency to come say hello. It irks a part of me that doesn't want to stay quiet.

I want to holler at her from my bedroom window or throw rocks at hers. Maybe holding a boombox outside of it would've been more appropriate. Either way, she's tiptoeing around me in a blindfold.

Knocking on her door is an option. I could maybe disguise it as a random visit to her parents. That part is plausible. She could answer the door and be forced to confront me. Either she would be ready for combat or ready to begin again. But what if I was neither soldier nor lover? What if I showed up with my hands in my pockets and a heart I didn't recognize?

Could I stand there and see the anger and hurt without trying to be the bandage? Was it even fair to think I could heal an injury that was my fault in the first place?

What if she wanted to start over? Call a truce. Was going back to being friends even something to consider?

We used to have a rhythm. I'm not sure I could imagine those moments without wondering which ones were sincere. Any type of ease with Nora would beg suspicion. And I'd probably always be chasing the way things were before.

I feel like Sisyphus, rolling a boulder up a hill. Every time I get close to reaching the top, it tumbles back down. The same thing that's been happening forever. No progress. No relief. Endless, futile, emotionally exhausting. But I'm condemned to it. I'm enslaved by her.

I've chosen this cycle. Even as it devours me. She lives in the creases of every decision I make, whether she's in the room or not.

I used to think that was a delusion. Gradually, it became devotion. Now, I'm pretty sure, it's just a disorder.

Shuffling about in my low-lit living room in my bare feet makes me look like I'm eighty-five years old, stumbling around to feed my thirteen cats. The truth is:

1. I'm too lazy to open the blinds.

2. I'm just as stubborn as Nora.

3. I don't own any cats.

I stub my toe lightly on the edge of the dark gold box in the hallway—the one full of keepsakes I nearly opened the other night. My ripped jeans still have the photograph of us tucked in the back pocket. I guess I wanted to keep it close—because at least on film, I can look her in the eyes without shrinking into the version of myself she saw last.

On instinct, I pick up the box and head into my bedroom. I can't do restraint anymore. I won't. It's time to start drowning in the sea that reaches her shore. It's inevitable at this point.

I set the UPS-style box on my bed. Its tape is long gone—the flaps crumble at my touch, nearly disintegrating in my hands. Inside is a flood of artifacts: symbols of a decade, steeped in sentiment. There's a lime green, translucent VTech cordless phone perched on top. Beneath it, a bright orange Harriet the Spy VHS tape, a rack of burned CDs in every genre, pharmacy-developed photo envelopes, and notes folded like footballs—each one a message meant to be passed but never read aloud.

And then it hits me. I've seen all of these things before—but not at my house. This isn't my box.

It's Nora's.

I feel like I'm trespassing and halfway recoil. She wouldn't want me going through her stuff. There was a time when she held nothing back from me. But this—this physical passage into how she lived our past, and how she packed it away—was never meant for my eyes. There has to be a mistake.

Maybe her mom brought things over for the garage sale I never had and didn't realize this was in the mix?

Maybe it was serendipity.

I start putting everything back the way I found it. I want to stuff the box into the attic, and forget the whole thing ever happened, but my gaze catches on a blue book at the bottom. It's fuzzy and it's got a latch that's meant to have a lock. Instead, the latch is ajar and whispers for me to pick up what I assume is a journal.

I couldn't. Could I?

I do.

I start at the beginning, because I'm a coward. A braver man would've flipped to the middle. To find the juiciest parts. In my mind, though, they were all the juiciest. Every part of Nora was the *best* part.

She labeled the entry with the date, and some little hearts were drawn in the corners and over her 'i's' instead of a simple dot of ink.

Even her handwriting is intoxicating.

I run my fingers over the delicate, rounded letters that decorate the page with her innermost thoughts. Swallowing hard, as if I'm afraid I'll get caught, I begin reading.

Thursday, March 18, 2010

It rained today and it felt like it might actually wash me clean. For the first time in forever, I felt like I might cave in and do what I've been meaning to do for months. Like the storm surging outside was giving me courage to brave the storm inside myself.

Telling Elliott… has been on the to-do list for a while now. I just haven't found the right moment. He's the football captain so, of course, he's always surrounded by girls in short skirts. Cheerleaders, especially Kacey, seem to be drawn to him like a magnet these days. I don't know if they are all trying to get a piece of him before we go to college, or something else.

I can't help but think the easy laugh he has when he's with me, and the way his smile lights up all of rural Ohio—that's who he really is. I hope. But what am I supposed to say? I know him better than any of those other girls do. I feel like we belong together.

I know his favorite songs, his dreams for the future… I've seen him cry. How many of them can say that?

Every time I try to bring it up, the words collapse. "Hey Elliott, have you ever thought maybe..." And then nothing. Just silence. Just me.

I stop reading, close my eyes, and squeeze the bridge of my nose.

If she only knew that *just* her was plenty.

Track 9

Choices Are A Luxury

(Elliott's Version)

Soon I'm insatiable. Each page stirs a ravenous hunger inside me to know more about the side of Nora that she didn't share with anyone. Not even me.

It was as if I'd been given the opportunity to look at her under a microscope instead of with the naked eye.

All of her layers were visible from this angle. The things that she thought and felt, things that made her who she was outside of her friendship with me—they were all splayed before me.

Carefully worded, as if she were afraid someone else might read what was written inside, and decorated with doodles and sketches of arrows and squiggles. Hearts and stars.

Page 12 (excerpt)

I got invited to Susie Gibbon's party this weekend, but I don't think I can go. It's not just the rules in my house I'd have to petition in order to be there that makes me feel anxious. It's the possibility of seeing everyone coupled up and sectioned off.

Elliott says I'm being ridiculous, but sometimes I feel no one will ever want me the way I want them.

Page 30 (excerpt)

Sirens weren't sounding when they pulled up, but nevertheless, there's a police car in front of my house and two officers downstairs talking to my parents. They don't know I'm the one who called 911. I can only imagine what consequences would be headed in my direction if they did.

Thank goodness Elliott and his parents are gone until Monday. I'd be so embarrassed if they had heard my dad screaming from across the street. Though I can't imagine what the other neighbors must think.

A domestic disturbance… That's what I'd called it on the phone. Maybe I should've gone with psychotic break.

Page 56 (excerpt)

Alexander Woodruff stopped by my locker today. Actually, he basically plastered me to it. He said he has been noticing me lately and that I'm becoming irresistible. Whatever that means.

He's always come across to me as the type of guy who doesn't have actual relationships. Instead, he has flings with needy girls who aren't interested in attachment. He's a mess. But maybe the kind I should give a chance? Could we be friends? More?

When he looks at me, I feel like the whole room is burning down. And I can't decide if it's because I'm feeling a surge of all the times I was embarrassed by him in front of others, or if his arrogance is electrifying.

My eyes widen at the thought of Nora feeling anything other than disdain for Alexander before twelfth grade. But, judging by the date on most of the entries I've gotten to at this point, I'm reading about something at least a year earlier than that.

Was he really trying to get inside my head even then? Was he wooing her to be sympathetic to him? When did he start planning to swoop in and destroy what we had?

In all honesty, in just these fifty-six pages, I had learned more about Nora's high school experience than I did walking the halls with her there every day for four years.

Did I ever really know her?

Calling the cops on her dad. Why wouldn't she have wanted me to know that?

Feeling unwanted and convincing herself that she might have to settle for someone like Alexander. And what about the entry where she imagined disappearing?

The Nora I knew threw her head back laughing, and made fun of privileged guys who felt like women were a possession. I thought she was the kind of person who sat at the dining room table with her parents, telling them everything about her day—her life—so they could offer guidance and approval.

Had I been wrong?

She had a zest for life—chasing sunsets and hung sideways off her bed doing Sudoku puzzles in pen.

Nora was the definition of altruistically good. But she also had a feisty side, which was my favorite.

Now, staring down at the wide-ruled notebook in my hands, I feel like I should splash some cold water on my face and try to wake up from the hallucination that my best friend hid her most painful and confusing moments from me.

I don't.

I glance outside and notice the river running alongside the curb and the fat raindrops falling from the sky.

I sigh.

It's obvious Nora isn't eager to see me while she's in town. But she just might not have a choice.

Track 10

I Could Be Meaner

(Nora's Version)

Wednesday.

I've been here for a week. I quit my job. I'm in limbo.

Yes. *I quit my job.* I hated it. But that's not the point.

Content creation and social media marketing isn't my calling. Anyone could tell you that. I'm honestly not sure how I ended up working for a company that expected me to use Canva, Instagram, TikTok, MailChimp, and Substack simultaneously. I was good at it. But it wasn't something I was passionate about.

I like glue sticks and imperfect brush strokes, not filters and engagement metrics. I like words that make me feel something and characters that make me root for them. My skill set can be summed up by the fact that opening the camera on my smartphone and snapping a selfie is the extent of my photographic ability.

I feel stifled in corporate environments. And the fact I got a job in one is astonishing, considering I blew off college when I left for Portland.

Leaving Elliott behind had been so much more than that. It meant throwing all my plans out the window and starting over, in the truest sense of the term. I didn't see any other choice but to reinvent myself and find a way to force that persona forward. It worked better than I expected.

But, for as long as I'd been in Portland, I hadn't made any *real* connections. I didn't have a group of girlfriends that took me out on the weekends. I didn't even have a long list of ex-lovers. No calls to ignore. No drama to dodge.

I had myself and the dying plants on my windowsill. Not even a handful of texts from concerned coworkers.

Grayson had filled the void for everything else. Now, I never wanted to hear his name again. I hadn't been under the illusion that our relationship was perfect. However, I at least thought it would be lasting. Suffice it to say that I won't be ordering a veggie burger any time soon. The reminder of impermanence is nauseating.

I've lost my appetite for much more than revenge.

I'm at the kitchen counter, plotting all the ways I'd like to make his life miserable. My parents are on their weekly outing to Costco. Considering the overwhelming silence in this house and how huge it seems in comparison to my apartment, I feel like it should be filled with the pulsing baseline of *Bad Blood*. But before I can switch on the Bluetooth speaker in the living room, the doorbell rings. Westminster chimes echo through the entry.

Who on earth…?

I look through the peephole, but all I see is a sheet of rain falling in the middle of the street. No one at the front door. That doesn't mean anything, except I don't know who it is.

I've been keeping a rather low profile around town, and I don't really want to encounter a bunch of townspeople who want to engage in meaningless small talk. Telling me how I look too fat or too skinny, too tired, and asking me why I'm not married yet.

Hesitating for a beat, I push my hair behind my ear and grab the handle. A rattled sigh escapes my lips, but I try to look less peaked and punchier as I swing the wooden door open.

Immediately, my mouth falls open and SOS flares go off in every direction.

Help. I need help.

Because Elliott Ashby is standing on my front porch, soaked to the bone, backwards baseball cap, and a three-day beard.

He's older, obviously. But age has made him more handsome, if that's possible. There's a streak of gray in his facial hair that looks less like deterioration and more like sophistication. His eyes are dappled with every shade of denim and his muscles are rippled with veins. The damp t-shirt he wears, clings to his body like it's painted onto his skin. Paired with the same Levi's I remember from when I knew him.

This version of Elliott is rugged, intimate, and familiar. Everything I was afraid it would be if I didn't manage to stay out of his path during my time in Moonridge. And here I stand, wearing an oversized top that says, *I Could Be Meaner*, and the look of someone who's been emotionally destroyed in an instant.

"H-hi," I stutter. It's breathy. Exposed. But it's too late.

I'm expecting that he'll start with politeness, that will transition into something awkward. Sooner than later, the conversation will become stagnant, and he'll walk back to his world, leaving me to unravel in mine.

"Why didn't you tell me?" he demands. His voice shakes. It sounds more like hurt than harrowing.

The problem is, I don't know what he's talking about.

"I'm sorry. What?" I blink hard and wrinkle my forehead trying to make sense of what's happening.

"You didn't tell me, Nor. We told each other everything," he says, out of breath. It's then that I see he's holding something. A fuzzy, now wet, book with my signature heart doodles all over the interior pages. My journal from high school. How in the world did he get it?

I scramble. Panic. Blink, hoping this is all a bad dream.

No such luck.

He's there. I'm here. And the journal—somewhere in between. The past and present float around us in the humidity, while the thunderstorm above cracks and booms. This can't be real. I'm not here.

"Nora…" his voice is soft now. Velvet wrapping around my broken parts.

"Don't," I say. It's my only request. The only thing I have the right left to ask of him. To not bring this up. To not make this about us. "It was a long time ago."

"Time doesn't erase what happened," he replies. His face is full of concern that is way more attractive than it should be right now and I'm losing my resolve. He wants to talk, to listen. I'm fraying like a rope held to a flame.

I try to calculate what page he's holding. If it's the one where I wrote about leaving Moonridge before telling him goodbye… then maybe I deserve this. It's possible that the rain soaked the pages and now it's ruined, right? Maybe things can go back to the way they were, and we'll never need to address what's written in that baby blue book.

Track 11

Fire & Rain

(Elliott's Version)

"Are you kidding me, right now, Nor?"

I know I'm getting under her skin, but I can't help it. The confession of feelings that I just read in my bedroom has utterly wrecked me. I made it almost halfway through the journal before I couldn't read anymore. There were so many things she had endured alone, and I was just finding out.

Once I got to page eighty-seven, my chest felt like it was caving in. The night she'd spent crying in the shower, hoping the water would drown out the noise of her sobbing. Page ninety-three: a fight she had with her Dad; calling him narcissistic and emotionally unavailable. It wasn't just sadness—it was erosion. And I never saw it coming.

Why hadn't I paid more attention? She needed me...

I run my hand over my thick stubble and my mouth goes dry. She needed me then. Does she still need me now?

I'm not sure how long I stand on the splintered wooden porch of her house. She's still in the doorway, so I guess that's a good sign. The rain's still tapping on the roof with a rhythm that shouts, *say something.*

Nora still hasn't answered the question about whether she was joking with me—whether her silence had only been my impression or an accurate representation of our senior year. Even more terrifying, had it been a thread that was woven through our entire lifetime together without me knowing?

I was angry. Not at her though. I was irate with myself for not having seen through the smokescreen. For riding the high of popularity and praise without stopping to make sure she was okay. All I ever wanted was for her to be protected and cherished for being nothing short of amazing. Turns out, what I wanted and what I facilitated were two very different things.

I open my mouth. Close it again. There's no script for this.

"Please, can I come in so we can talk?" I ask. My voice is gravelly, dropped a couple registers. I don't know if it's from fatigue or misery, but it reverberates through both of us.

She doesn't say anything right away. Just studies me with that expression she used to wear when we played Scrabble—a silent dare to see if I would make good on my vow to win. Silently, I was making that same vow now. Could she hear it?

The stakes are higher this time. Stitched through clubhouse sleepovers and graduation day and all the summer afternoons we thought were forever. But I owe her something.

Her eyes are dark and conspiring. I can't tell if she's going to kiss me or kill me, and either choice seems relevant right now. I hold my breath and count… *one… two…* I'm trying to wait her out.

A hitched exhale makes her chest fall and her shoulders curve inward like she wishes she had a rock to crawl underneath. I've felt that too. Most of the time, it's when the reminders of her become overwhelming. When I'm teetering on sending a drunk text at 2 AM asking, *who do you love?* Or speeding off into the distance without looking back. But nothing good ever happens in a getaway car.

I stay. Because without her, I'd never get very far.

My hand involuntarily extends toward her, and I aim to rub her shoulder. But she shifts as I reach out and my palm gently connects with the side of her face. I'm suddenly cupping her cheek, and she stills under my touch.

The moment is completely spontaneous, though I couldn't have planned it better. Her skin is smooth under the pad of my thumb that is tracing absent-minded circles over the patch of freckles under her right eye. And, for just a moment, I'm lost to the recklessness of it.

Her hair is the same mix of wheat and ash it was when we graduated. She's cut it a little shorter and it frames her face more loosely, but it's iconically Nora. The shirt she's wearing is embroidered with *I Could Be Meaner.* And maybe she could. I don't know whether to laugh or cry at the implication.

"I can't do this..." she says. But it's nearly inaudible.

I don't move. Mist from the rain is collecting on my eyelashes. I look sappy and undone; a broken-down version of myself. She, on the other hand, looks radiant. The Ohio gloom suits the mood and the washed-out colors around us make hers even more saturated.

"I know," I whisper. I do, actually.

I never, for a second, thought that when I marched over and rang the doorbell she'd fold for me. But I would for her, and I think she knows.

Nora Lowe, the tragically poetic girl-next-door, doesn't let me in. Instead, she backs away slowly and closes the door. I hear the lock click into place. She's trying to pretend I'm not here. But I am. And I always have been.

I wait another beat, just in case.

Nothing. But it's not as simple as that.

Track 12

Pacific Blue

(Nora's Version)

The journal. I didn't grab the journal. Why didn't I grab it?

It was right there, dripping with rainwater and years of regret. And I left it there. Left all my pride in his hands.

I'm pretty sure that was the worst day of June. It's only the fifth.

The exchange, however brief it was, has been living, rent-free, in my mind for the last two days. It's been a magnanimous feat to elude Elliott, but I've managed it. Barely.

I just can't risk him thinking that his rainy-day stroll over to the house, the sight of his bewitching biceps, and the sound of the grit that has lodged itself into his voice box *means* something. Because it doesn't. It can't.

If it did, I don't know what I'd do with it. If it doesn't, then I've already waited too long.

Silverware tings softly in the background, and someone from the kitchen yells, *Order up!* The Bent Spoon is alive with chaos, while I'm slowly fading in a booth of burgundy vinyl. Tabasco sits beside my plate on the eternally sticky Formica table and the striped awning outside ruffles in the breeze. Another American summer is on the horizon. And by the looks of it, so is my finishing these home fries.

Scanning the newspaper in front of me, leftover from the last patron to inhabit this seat, I can see there's a baseball game this Saturday, a bake sale at the church on Sunday after services, and a sale on Honey Baked Ham at Giant Eagle this week. Good to see that some things never change.

It's ironic that the world around us can recycle content so regularly and we never stop to notice. In fact, the sameness is comforting to most people. In places like Moonridge, there would've been an uprising if the grocery store had a sale on turkey instead of ham. Because you knew Emmy's mama was making that ham for Sunday dinner at the Moose

Lodge and the whole town was going to be there.

I, too, used to find comfort in that kind of predictability. I still might if there was a reason to stick around here. If there was more to look forward to than little league and Red Hat Society luncheons.

My dad asked me yesterday how long I was planning to stay. I took one look at the condescending expression on his face that essentially deemed me a *quitter* and told him I'd be gone by the end of the week. I said it more out of spite than anything else.

My parents had only visited me in Portland a couple of times over the years. They were always busy, or so they said. First it was Dad's job. Then his retirement. Eventually, it was just the inconvenience of remembering I exist. The answer to my pleas for more support, more company, was that they were too tied up. Visiting your only daughter before you kick the bucket is a burden nowadays. Who knew?

And then people turn around and wonder why this generation struggles with mental health, toxic relationships, and a lack of self-esteem.

We were trained. A special effort was put into that trauma, and don't forget it.

As I pushed the last few bites around on my plate, I wondered if Elliott had gotten to the part in my journal where I reflected on why I had tried to be so understanding and mature, when I was still so young. I still had so many mistakes to make, but I couldn't. I wasn't allowed. Perfectionism was ingrained on my soul. I wore it like a merit badge and showed it to anyone who passed by. I'd worked hard for that title, *perfectionist*. But it had come at the cost of my innocence. At least some of it.

Seeing Elliott so at ease with his own parents when we were kids stirred a pang of jealousy inside me. They accepted him, just as he was. Someone young, impressionable, born to grow and change. Not meant to be a miniature adult from birth. He was one of the lucky ones. A golden child. He was golden to me.

My mom always told me to be careful around Elliott. Oh, it wasn't that he wasn't a 'good boy', she said. It was just that he was more 'spirited' than others. Secretly, I knew that meant his charm and unburdened air bothered her. Was it her conscience that was pricked? Or did she feel a sense of fear for me because his lust for life was so foreign?

Her warning only made me want to be more contaminated by him. Infected with his charisma and enthusiasm. Seeing the world the way he did made me happier. And when I was happier, I didn't think about dying.

Elliott didn't know it but he was the life raft I needed in the middle of an ocean full of sharks.

He made surviving seem possible. Not just possible—promising.

People like my dad, and Grayson… I loved them. But I had to perform for them. They considered me a reflection of *their* worth. What I did, said, pursued, promoted—it always came down to how it made them look. What it made *them* feel.

I never told all of that to Elliott. Snippets slipped out unintentionally maybe, but nothing that would've aroused suspicion. It wasn't that I didn't want to articulate it, I just didn't know how. Even now, I'm still learning how to speak up for my own needs.

Maybe that's why when Tania—my waitress, who can't be more than eighteen—picks up the bill, I tell her to keep the change. She'll need a little something to start over with one day. A hunch. A good one.

Next door to The Bent Spoon is a bookstore. It wasn't there when I was growing up and my curiosity gets the better of me as I peer in at the organized shelves and bookcases. The lady manning the counter inside sees me through the glass and, though I can't make her face out through the reflection on the window, I can tell she's waving me inside. Obediently, I round the corner to the entrance and step inside.

A soft bell above the door announces me to the dust and the paper, and I notice how peaceful it is beyond the threshold. It smells like lavender and chamomile. I dare to hope that this is a safe haven for someone who's just passing through. Because I'm definitely not staying.

The woman at the register, the one who invited me inside, wears a warm smile and a frilly top. She's the opposite of me in every way, but she fits the atmosphere. I feel welcome, and I haven't had that in a long time.

"Is there anything I can help you find?" she asks expectantly.

"Oh no," I say, shaking my head. "I'm just browsing." It's my go-to answer anytime I enter a shop. My inherent anxiety won't let me ask for help. It's a fatal flaw and one I'm sure will be buried with me.

The woman nods, unfazed by my refusal. She doesn't press, just turns back to organizing a tray of bookmarks. I move slowly past the counter, hands stuffed in my jacket pockets, letting the quiet soak in.

There's a table near the back with a crooked sign that says *All Stationery 50% Off*. An assortment of notepads, packs of pens, and letterheads litter the surface. But as I round the table, I see that, on the back side of the display are diaries and journals.

I run my fingers over the texture on the covers. Linen, cotton, felt, but I come to a stop when I spot an embossed leatherbound version in Pacific blue on the end. It feels like it's been waiting for me.

It doesn't look brand new, though the pages are all pristine. It has scratches and bumps along the surface; enough to make it look aged, but not useless. Well-worn, not used up. Those distinctions matter.

I hesitate before lifting it off the shelf, half-convinced it's in the wrong spot. The weight of it surprises me— a bit heavier than expected, like it's carrying more than blank pages.

I flip it open, curious, even if I won't buy it. The spine creaks softly, a quiet protest, and the paper is thick, almost creamy. I check for a brand name, a sticker, anything that proves its origin, but there's nothing.

Only… there is something—

> — It's high time I started keeping a journal again.

— The color is the same shade as Elliott Ashby's storm-lit gaze on my porch, two days ago.

Track 13

Oh My My My

(Elliott's Version)

On Wednesday, I stepped off Nora's porch into the tears of a thunderstorm. I ended up finding the lock for the journal at the bottom of the UPS box when I got home. Snapping it back into the latch and preventing myself from reading any more of her private thoughts seemed like the right move. I don't know where the key is to reopen it. Probably as lost as the key to my heart.

"Man, you're an idiot," was all that Marquis offered when I met him for a round at Trudy's and spilled my guts about everything. He wasn't wrong.

Now it's Sunday and I roll over in my bed to stare at the alarm clock for ten minutes before I commit to being awake. My mind has been racing since before Nora got here, but my body doesn't want to cooperate. It seems like whether I'm within her reach or not, she's still touching me.

This morning the sheets feel rougher, the clouds are grayer, and my faucet drips rhythmically in the next room. It doesn't seem like the first week of June is over. Inside me, it might as well be December. And while I live in an eternal winter, Nora is the summer sun that shines down and melts the icicles growing on my gutters.

Unfortunately, after a few glasses of Watershed bourbon, I'd told Marquis I was still drunk on the way her eyelashes danced over her cheekbones. Nonsense probably, but I'd put it out into the universe. I think that was around the time he quietly pulled the tumbler out of my reach and told me to stick with water for the rest of the night.

8:24 AM.

I've been lying here fourteen minutes too long and I'm debating on pulling the pillow over my head and putting myself out of my misery when I hear the sound of doors opening and shutting. The distinct sound of a tinny pop song blaring from a car stereo.

For Pete's sake, it's Sunday.

People in our neighborhood don't start mowing the lawn on the weekend until after nine. Let alone getting turnt up in their driveway. If I have to be the cantankerous, almost middle-aged, man who deals with the situation, so be it. I'm entitled to contemplate my demise in peace.

As I assume the curmudgeonly stance of someone about to scold the youngsters outside for being too noisy and inconsiderate for us old folks, I freeze. The window is still a few feet away and I'm standing next to the bed in my boxer shorts, but I see Nora. I see luggage. I see goodbye.

I'm too far to reach the window. Too close not to watch. It has the hallmarks of every movie I've ever seen where *Wide Open Spaces* plays in the background while a broken character, usually a woman, makes the leap into some new territory. Either she chooses herself or chooses love. Sometimes neither. Maybe both. It sent chills up my spine that Nora is having that same moment, right outside, on Redfern Avenue.

From where I stand, it's too much like watching a memory unfold. The kind you only recognize in hindsight as the turning point. I want to call out, but she won't hear me. I need to be closer. I'm craving it. Even if it ends up being the very last time.

So, I do what any self-respecting, albeit ridiculous, thirty-three-year-old man would do. I shuck on a pair of basketball shorts I find on the floor and take off in a sprint towards Nora's. I'm shirtless and don't have shoes on, my hair is standing on end, and my eyes are probably a little wild but there is no way I'm going to let her leave without her at least knowing that I'm watching her go.

The screen door thwacks against the frame as I exit the house with force and continue, with purpose, across the street and stride right up to the Lowes' uncomfortable reunion on the sidewalk. There's tension in the air, not *because* of me but I can feel it there when I arrive. I understand it more because of the journal entries I *did* read, but the concept of them being anything other than a happy family is still foreign to me.

Tommy stiffens and his gaze at Nora is a little more disconcerting than it should be for a father wishing his daughter well on her journey. Cindy, usually quiet and smug, looks dejected and pained. I'm not sure if it's because of Nora's imminent departure or something else that transpired before I showed up. Either way, the mood needs to be lightened, *stat*.

"Morning family!" I chirp. The cheer in my voice sounds outlandish since I've been a walking wall of stone and sarcasm for the last half of my life. But I try my hardest to break up whatever tension is floating around because I don't want this to be my last record of Nora. It's selfish, I'll admit. I'm not sorry for it though. I hope she'd be as selfish with me, if she was given the chance.

"Where are you off to in such a hurry?" I wink at Nora like we're sixteen again. When I started to see she was more than the little girl I'd grown up with, but I wasn't in deep enough to question what I wanted our relationship status to be.

I think I see her shoulders relax a fraction, though she glares at me like she used to when I interrupted the last half of *One Tree Hill* and talked through all of Chad Michael Murray's scenes.

That dude was annoyingly good at getting girls to fall for him.

I chuckle at the recollection while she searches for her words. I think of all the times she would end up curled into me, in her basement on the sofa, listening to me bash the teenage titans of our era. It was sickening to me now, how I'd taken those moments for granted. How I wish I could have them back.

I wonder, now, if she can still hear me grumbling about perfect hair and curated wardrobes. Was the shape of my shoulder under her chin and the way she fidgeted with the tattered hem of her Moonridge High sweatshirt a sign of something more that I ignored? And, if she doesn't remember those moments the same way I do, I guess I don't blame her. Because life taints people and places and

Polaroids. Like the one I keep transferring to every pair of jeans I wear.

It wasn't perfect, but it was *ours*.

"I'm on my way to the airport," she finally replies. The answer I had known was coming.

"Is that so?" I cross my arms and quirk up a brow. I sound playful. Maybe flirtatious.

It's dangerous. I like it.

"Yep. Time to head home," is all she says.

"Home? Hmm." I rub my chin. I just shaved yesterday, but I can feel the stubble returning already. "I thought that's where you already were. Silly me." It's a risky reply. But I'd risk it all if it meant she'd stay.

Track 14

Goose

(Nora's Version)

Elliott. Sculpted, six-pack flashing, championship quarterback Elliott is challenging me. Asking, essentially, *why* I am leaving Moonridge, again. There's a dare dancing in his eyes, but I'm not in the mood to decipher it. We aren't kids anymore, and this is exhausting.

"Some of us have a life to get back to," I quip. I try to sound resolved, but it comes out like a question.

Do I have anything to return to in Portland?

"A life, huh? Yeah, I wouldn't know anything about that," Elliott shoots back. Though, his hands are up in surrender before I can respond. He already knows what I'm going to say, so I don't say it.

"Jobless and soon-to-be-evicted isn't much of a foundation to build on, young lady," my dad interrupts. It slices into me, the criticism. It's always been there—the undercurrent of my being inadequate. I narrow my eyes at him, then turn my attention to Elliott. Full force, for the first time in fifteen years.

"I hate that he's not wrong," I gesture toward my dad. "Although, moving into a different apartment is my *choice*. I'm *not* getting evicted."

"Well, if it's *that* pressing, we shouldn't delay," Elliott says. He's serious. My confusion heightens.

We shouldn't delay? What does that mean? Is he making fun of me?

"Yeah, I should really get going," I reply.

"Let me just grab a shirt and shoes. I don't think it's legal to streak in Moonridge yet," he jokes.

I look at him blankly, still not understanding. But he avoids my disorientation and grabs my suitcase, placing it in the trunk of my rental car. Dust puffs up from the upholstery and I bristle at how much the act means to me.

"What are you *doing?*" I squeal. A half-laugh escapes my lungs, and it feels like a release of emotions I've held onto for a hazardous amount of time.

"I'm driving you to the airport, Goose," he tells me. But it's not a request, it's a fact.

Goose.

The nickname sounds warm and cozy, like my favorite cardigan. Like a word I can snuggle into and stow away until the world is hushed. Until he tells me it's safe to come out, into the open, again.

Did he know how much it meant to me? That I needed it even before I heard it?

I want to protest. Tell him that there's no way I'm letting him trap me inside a vehicle. That I'm fine on my own, and his presence is a nuisance. Instead, I give my mom a pat on the arm that silently says, *let's not make this worse than it already is.* A terse nod in my dad's direction. Then, I round the back of the car, and slide into the passenger seat.

The seat is toasty against my legs and back; leather heated by the early-morning sunlight. I turn down the volume on Gracie Abrams and lean against the headrest, letting the breeze from the air conditioner blow my hair around me.

Getting into this car was a decision. Now, I have to own up to it. Even if it means riding side-by-side with a resurrected vision of the young man I once cared so much for. The older version is even more dangerous.

A moment later, Elliott plops down in the driver's seat. He hasn't changed his cologne—it's still salty and woody. A hint of sweetness and saffron whisks me away to baggy t-shirts I used to swipe from his bedside table and sleep in. Some of them I never gave back.

I shift in my seat so that my legs are pressed together and my hands are clasped on top of them. Last time we encountered each other, there was a touching mishap. I don't want to take a chance on that happening again. I don't think I'd make it out alive.

Confidence oozes out of Elliott's every pore. It's like the letterman jacket he never outgrew. Somehow always the perfect fit for him, while it sagged on me.

"H-how are you getting back?" I stammer. Maneuvering around his free and easy demeanor is going to be a challenge. I'm feeling lightheaded and self-conscious. My skin feels too tight.

He throws his head back and a laugh huffs out. "Don't worry about me, Goose. I'm more than capable of getting around a town the size of Moonridge Creek."

My fingers twitch in my lap.

Elliott throws the car in reverse, and in a matter of seconds we are backed onto the street. He reaches, I think, for the gear shift, but instead squeezes my upper thigh. It feels like a quiet claim to my soul.

"You okay, Nor? You look a little nauseous."

"Mmhmm, all good." If only that was the truth. If only every atom in my body wasn't about to spontaneously combust.

His hand lingers for a moment too long and my mind searches for anything to grab onto other than the way my skin burns under his touch. Not painful—just warm enough to thaw me.

We are one minute and fifty-eight seconds into the drive. We haven't even left our street. His street. Or do I still belong here, after everything that's happened?

Track 15

Two Seconds On The Gear Shift

(Elliott's Version)

I know better than to push Nora past her comfort zone. I did it anyway. Only, I did it with a seatbelt and the windows down. Not with accusations and judgment.

Nora's faults aren't meant to be displayed for everyone to see. They aren't supposed to be compared or highlighted. Annotated and reviewed.

I had been enlightened, thanks to her journal, to the fact that things weren't going as great behind closed doors as I had assumed. I figured everything was fine. That assumption was my fault. But, based on the limited information I'd gathered this morning, standing on our block, things were pretty messed up for Nora in the present too. That made staying out of her way even harder. It's why I'd thrown myself, care to the wind, into a vehicle with her, headed to the exact place I knew she shouldn't be going.

She stares straight ahead, legs tense, as if she's the first domino in a chain. Like her toppling would cause a reaction she couldn't contain. It's avoidant, but adorable. And I happened to adore her.

My foot presses harder on the gas as we enter the freeway and I'm reminded how few times I ever leave our downtown community. It might not be an urban outpost, but it's what I know. And leaving what I know is a huge problem for me.

What I need is some casual conversation over the sound of the wind, and to pretend like this is just another day. Out with my favorite person for a weekend drive. Nothing complicated. Just two people and a highway.

"So, how long's the flight back?" I ease in. We both know the question is lame, surface-level crap. But I don't have much to work with. Just a suspicion that Nora had tolerated me outside her house to keep confrontation from the prying eyes of her parents, and that she doesn't want to revisit the way we left things on her porch the other day.

She shrugs, still staring straight ahead. "Long enough to wish I didn't have to endure it," she sighs.

"Then why are you?" I press. "Doesn't seem like there is much that needs tending to out there."

"And what would you know about it?" she demands. No—it's softer than that. But I know she means it to be abrasive.

"Not much, I guess. Other than I know how it feels to go home alone every night," I admit. It's a mistake. I've given away too much in one sentence. Should've quit before I started.

Her jaw relaxes though. Like my honesty didn't scare her—it saddened her. Or she was surprised we still had so much in common. Even if it is our loneliness. Or, at least I hope she isn't heading back to a brawny, handsome guy who has a fat 401(k) and hidden ring box.

I stare out the window, hoping the wind will carry what I said far away. To another county, planet, timeline. Especially when she turns up the volume on the stereo. Not much. But enough to make me second-guess speaking at all. I do anyway.

"I never did figure out why you came back, Goose. Anything you wanna tell me?"

"Just something I want to ask. Why do you still call me that? Goose."

It's not anything I've ever really given a lot of thought to. Though I know exactly when it started. We were on the monkey bars, competing to see who could hang upside down the longest without their head exploding. The pressure of gravity made it hard to talk when we were dangling from our legs like that, so we would make funny faces at each other until the other laughed so hard they fell.

We could've broken our necks like that, but we didn't care. It was a game, we were kids, it was the 90s. None of those are good enough explanations. Simultaneously, they're everything.

From that day on, I always referred to Nora as Goose. She was my confidant, my playmate. My silly goose.

My mother had immediately taken note of the nickname, deeming it 'darling'. She used it too, on occasion, and it stuck. For my whole family. For me. Nora was Goose, no debate.

"Old habits and all that," I respond, though the rust from the monkey bars seems to have seeped into my voice. I sound dishonest, and I know it. "I feel like it still suits you," I tack on.

To my surprise she doesn't argue. Just picks at a hangnail and smirks behind the hair hanging in front of her face. She thinks I can't see her. It's cute. Not only because I absolutely *can*, but because even when I'm not turned toward her, I know what it looks like. It looks like my whole life.

"I'm not sure how silly I am anymore," she says quietly.

"No? I'm sure it's in there somewhere," I encourage. She's obviously deep in self-doubt. It's a wrecking ball to the heart, when I know that, somewhere inside, is the inspiring person I grew up with. The one who could tell me they knew how to walk on water, and I'd believe it.

"I remember a girl who danced in puddles singing *If All Of The Raindrops* who would probably agree with me," I smile.

She glances at me, like I've said magic words. But they weren't please or thank you. It wasn't even something I was conscious of until the words had escaped me. It was, *Let's be us, again. Whaddya say?*

The wordless plea must echo inside her brain the way it does mine because she places her hand over mine on the gear shift for *one…two…*seconds. I'm waiting her out. I always do. I'd done it earlier this week. I'd done it when we were eighteen. I'd do it a thousand times again.

"I'm sorry," she finally breathes into the silence. "Sorry, we didn't get the chance to…do what people do now—grab a coffee or whatever."

The whole sentence is steeped in shame, and I hate it. Hate that the apology comes from somewhere inside where she's reprimanding herself. Telling herself she should be more, should be a people pleaser. If there was never anything I wanted Nora to do, it was to be less than she was. She deserved to be larger than life.

"Nora, we aren't grab coffee people," I chuckle, trying to ease the mood. "We're burgers and pizza, beer and bourbon people. Paper plates are our secret language."

Then, the single word I'd been trying to swallow for the entire ride, coming out in one fell swoop as we pull up to the terminal.

"Stay."

"Stay?" she asks. Her brows are quizzical, and she sucks in a sharp breath. The request has landed heavily and out of place. For a minute, though, it looks like she's considering it. Maybe my eyes are playing tricks on me.

The smell of engine exhaust from idling cars, travel coffee, and hot metal streams in through the car windows. The canyon between us, across the console, is widening and I can see she's reaching for the handle. She isn't pulling it open yet, though. Maybe there's still time.

"What would I even do if I stayed?" she asks, turning back toward me. As in shock as I am that the words are coming out of her mouth.

"There's always Thursday night Bingo with Marg down at the senior center," I tease. I don't want to pressure her. I just want to make her feel safe.

"Look," I continue, "I know there's some messed up stuff with your dad and that things aren't glamorous in Portland. Much more than that is beyond me. And maybe you don't have a reason to trust me on this but you're better off here than somewhere out… there." I wave toward the sliding door of the airport that leads to arrivals and departures.

"Yeah well…" she rolls her eyes at me. It's exquisitely Nora. "Even if I *could* spend a few extra days, I don't have a place to stay. My parents aren't an option. My dad is driving me crazy."

Time for another roll of the dice. "So, stay at my place," rushes out of me. "It's not like you don't know your way around the refrigerator there, and I promise to be a saint of a host. You won't even know I'm there."

"Likely story," she laughs. It's pure cadence and reckoning. The first time I feel like I've gotten through to her. To the real her.

Track 16

Elephant In The Pool

(Nora's Version)

My bag is being unloaded as I sip club soda at the bar inside the garage apartment at Elliott's. It's been ages since I was last in here. It's tiny, but I own nothing, so it's a non-issue.

I'll admit, I considered Elliott's offer to stay *inside* the house for a whole thirty-six seconds before I declined. It wasn't that I didn't believe he'd follow through on being a caring and considerate host. In fact, it's *because* I believe he'd dote on me that I said no. I don't deserve his adoration. It's hard enough to swallow the mercy he's cramming down my throat.

Don't get me wrong, I'm grateful. Just out of place. Moonridge Creek feels more like being *on* the moon.

No spacesuit, no oxygen tank. Only me. Floating around gasping for air.

The cushion at my back smells faintly of chlorine and mothballs. Like it hasn't been used since we were still on speaking terms. But the pool outside is immaculate. It is so clear it looks bottomless. Bottomless, like the space I'm holding for Elliott to berate me or interrogate me about prom night 2011. Instead, when he comes in, he leans back on his elbows on the floor and declares his immediate need for a swim.

I busy myself with finding the correct Wi-Fi network to connect to, and completely *not* noticing that he is already unbuttoning his shirt. Clearing my throat, I force my eyes down onto my phone screen, but my mind is preoccupied with creative fantasies of the swim becoming a synchronized dance between the two of us, around the giant elephant in the middle of the pool.

In my visions, the elephant is submerged, distorted, and even sort of beautiful, if you don't look too close.

"Wanna join me?" he asks. His hand is extended toward the French doors that lead out to the sublime blue of the water below that promises relief from the gnats and heatwave.

I blink. His body is already halfway out the door, haloed by late-afternoon light. I have half a mind to say yes. But the other half still speaks in morse code. Tapping out dashes and dots only the fluent could decode.

My thumb hovers over my phone, as if I have something urgent to respond to. But the screen dims, betraying me. And I see Elliott trying to decipher my signals from outside.

"I don't think I *can* join you," I reply. It's not a lie. "I didn't exactly pack for an exotic vacation when I was stuffing my holey yoga pants into my suitcase. I don't have a swimsuit."

Elliott shrugs like what I have on is the furthest thing from his mind.

"So?" He scrunches his face and shields his eyes from the sun. "Go in your shorts and tank top. I won't judge."

My fingers tighten around my phone, like it's the only anchor left. But the water *does* look nice. And I can *almost* believe that what I'm wearing isn't a factor to worry about. That I can go back to being fourteen. Leggy and stick-figured, and wondering when my boobs will finally come in.

2006 was the year all the other girls at my school either got their periods or bought their first real, underwire bras. I'm confident I was the only one still wearing a training bra and searching for the first red streak in my underwear that summer. It was mortifying. But so was stuffing my own chest full of tissues. So, I didn't. But that doesn't mean I didn't think about it.

I saw the way cheerleaders like Kacey and Marissa wore tight t-shirts and skorts that hugged their womanlier bodies. In contrast, I resembled a twelve-year-old boy. Flat-chested and straight as a board from head to toe.

The only thing I really liked about how I looked was my long, blonde hair. It wasn't bleached and bright like the typical blondes around town. The shade of mine was more understated, natural. Luminous beige and goldenrod.

When The Ashbys threw their annual pool party that year, I had arrived with my terrycloth bathing suit cover zipped up to my neck, hoping I could blend into the background. But Elliott wouldn't have it. He swore the event would be a 'total bummer' if I didn't swim.

What are pools for, if you aren't going to enjoy them?

Simple reasoning. Everything with Elliott was simple.

He convinced me to leave the robe behind. Said it was living a little.

As the cover slipped off, I felt like I could probably pull off the hoax of belonging with my peers after all. My mom had bought me a new T-back Speedo. It was a whole piece, but the color was a deep ruby red. I liked to pretend I looked as cool as one of the lifeguards at the public community pool. They were seniors and the epitome of tanned and taut.

I was just about to make a run for it and catapult into the deep end when one of the boys from the football team shouted from the lawn chair positioned opposite. Alexander Woodruff. Alex to his friends. In my opinion, he was the definition of a very inappropriate word I wasn't allowed to say.

"Well, if it isn't the president of the itty-bitty titty committee! Show us what you've got!"

A more filled-out girl my age was sitting on his lap, and he was rubbing my nose in it. Not in the fact that I couldn't have a relationship with him. But in the fact that everyone around me at that party, except Elliott, was comparing me to something better.

I glanced at the girl's face, who was now straddling his lap, but she looked away quickly. I was looking for sympathy from another person of my sex. Obviously, though, I wasn't going to find it.

The other boys surrounding Alexander laughed and it was personal victimization multiplied by six. Their glares, stares, and categorization of my body was something expansive, encompassing. The ridicule ricocheted off the water and into the trees. I felt like I was going to be sick.

Before I could make it to the bushes to either hide or hurl, I felt a hand on my back. Sure, strong, safe.

"Ya know what, Alex," Elliott shouted across the pool. "You really need to get your head out of your butt and recognize a good thing when it's in front of you. Nora's twice the person you'll ever be. You're just jealous she's *mine*."

Mine.

He said it without stumbling. Like it was a brand he'd burned onto my heart. We belonged to each other.

"Are you comin' or not? Fraidy-cat!" present-day Elliott calls from where he treads water in the middle of the sky's reflection.

I run toward his voice like it's the only thing I've ever trusted.

Track 17

Same Wavelength

(Elliott's Version)

After the impromptu swim, I feel lighter. Like the baggage I was carrying when she arrived has been left at the bottom of the staircase. Waiting for someone else to carry it the rest of the way. For now, though, I'm content to let it sit there. I think Nora is too.

The time we spent floating on our backs, staring at the maple leaves flutter against clouds of lily white, was catharsis neither of us expected. It wasn't loud and splashy, like the pool parties when we were young. It was more reserved, more grown up.

Grown-ups. I guess that's what we are now.

It's ludicrous that time has evaded me so quickly. That so much has happened, but my life still feels empty. You'd think, by now, it'd be full of evidence that I wasn't chasing the glory days anymore. That I was grounded. Serious. Ready to settle down. Most people who meet me have one of two ideas when they find out I'm not married and am a former high school jock:

1. I'm a noncommittal, pleasure-seeking womanizer
2. I'm a washed-up has-been waiting for lightning to strike twice

The trouble is that those people don't know me. They only know what their narrow worldview allows. And, trust me, the world gets smaller all the time.

I watch as Nora wrings out her hair first, then twists her tank top into a knot. The water spills down onto her feet and I notice her toenails are painted a rebellious shade of orange. Orange.

It jolts something loose—reminds me of high school. Nora always had a way of making even her silence loud.

I wasn't good at physics in high school. Words on paper came easier than inertia and drag. My parents ended up having to get me a tutor, so I didn't flunk out and miss the rival game Moonridge had near the end of the season in 2009. I spent that year cursing myself for not taking elective chemistry with Nora.

During one of my physics classes, the teacher tried to explain to us that the color orange was for specific electromagnetic radiation wavelengths. I tuned out after the first ten minutes and doodled cartoon characters in my notebook to make Nora laugh on our walk home from school. I'd make up absurd stories to go with each of them and most of the time we were so hungover from giggling about it we couldn't breathe by the time we parted ways.

The only thing I remember about orange electromagnetic radiation is that orange light has longer wavelengths. Longer wavelengths make warmer colors. All I know now is: if Nora's wavelength is orange. So is mine. Because I'm pretty warm, seeing her fidget with her cut-off shorts and the splendor of the evening sun shimmer on her skin.

She radiates in that shade. It's like her frequency's always been tuned to comfort colors—squeaky playground swings, summer sunsets, and fall leaves. Orange was always just a tinge on the spectrum for me. Now, orange is Nora. I can't unsee it.

I don't want to interrupt the solitude, but she's already agreed to swim with me. I wonder… what else she might say yes to.

"Since we've established that we enjoy the fine dining experience of bacon burgers and fries," I begin, doing my best imitation of an Englishman, "would you like to join me for dinner this evening?"

At first, I think she'll cackle and wave me off. As if the idea of us sharing a meal at the diner is comical or stupid. If she says no, it won't be the worst thing we've waded through. But I'm not really up for eating alone.

She lowers her gaze to mine and I see a familiar glint of mischief in the metallic shimmer of her eyes. Tinsel threads of hair hang over her shoulder and she grins like the suggestion was right on time.

"Only if we get milkshakes like we used to," she says.

"One Oreo, one peanut butter. Two straws in each," I nod.

"Don't forget whipped cream and extra cherries," she wags her finger at me.

"Like I would ever," I gasp.

It's a simple thing, two milkshakes. But it's not just a memory. It's a ritual. And the fact that she remembered was the only cherry on top I needed.

This dinner isn't a date, and I'm not her boyfriend. I don't expect it to feel like something it's not. I'm relishing what it already is.

Conversation is still slow to come by the time we walk to the diner. It's a nondescript building with a cheeky name. Standing on the corner, ready to welcome whatever weary soul wanders through the door.

The greasy fries, kitschy décor, and jukebox in the corner haven't changed in years and that's what we always loved best. Nora told me she's already stopped once this week, so she's becoming a regular again at this point. It's a joke for my sake, but she giggles and my heart flutters. I know better than to hope, so I choke it down and allow the quiet yearning to fill my chest.

The jukebox wheezes to life just as we slide into the booth, sneakers squeaking on the checkered floor. We're in the same booth we wedged into every Friday night after football games, before school dances, and for cram sessions before a big test.

The music that fills the space is an Alanis Morissette banger, older than both of us. Irony is a repeated theme in the lyrics and, once the chorus hits, so does recognition, and the two of us are suddenly singing along at the top of our lungs. We sway and bang our heads and put up our hands with the *rock-on* symbol fully displayed.

Our laughter is too loud, too bright, too easy and I start to worry that, once the song ends, this moment will linger in my ribs and turn to stone.

Eventually there is a lull as another patron plugs coins in and makes their song selection. Nora's face is flushed, and she lets out the happiest sigh I've ever heard. One truly free from restraint. One that embraces the milkshakes that are set before us, the melty cheese on her burger, and the ranch dressing she dips her fries into.

The next song is slower—Céline, maybe—and Nora hums along, dancing as she eats. I don't say anything. Just count the seconds before this spell breaks. I'd give anything to make it last, but it can't. Reality is the curtain waiting to fall.

"Wait, wasn't this one of your mom's favorite songs?" Nora asks innocently. But I can't stop it. I'm very quickly filled with teenage petulance and all the grief I never dealt with. The expression I wear must say everything my voice doesn't because Nora's mouth makes a small 'o' shape, and she scoots a little closer.

"I didn't realize," she says. It's kind, but it stings. She wouldn't realize because she wasn't here to deal with it. I did it. Alone.

I steal a fry from her plate, the ultimate gesture of forgiveness, even though I'm not sure how to process it. This. I'm pushing through the pain to keep from falling to pieces in front of her. The same way I've been doing for everyone else. Most of all, for myself.

"You don't have to talk about it," she whispers. "But if you want to…" her voice trails off.

"Eh, knock it off, Goose." I nudge her with my elbow. "My mom loved you. She would've loved to *see* you…" I don't mean it to sound like a guilt trip. Just honesty.

"Yeah… maybe…" she hesitates. "I didn't exactly say goodbye to her either. Your dad… I think he was pretty mad at me, for everything."

"Grudges weren't their style," I shake my head. "They aren't mine either, just so we're clear."

The stained-glass lampshade overhead hangs too low and the lightbulb flickers. The sanitized vinyl beneath my jeans smells like bleach. Nora smells like oakmoss. Years pass, but truths stay.

I breathe deeply, then exhale all the tension tied up in my shoulder blades.

"I should've come. For the funeral," she admits. I've been waiting eight years for that. "They meant so much to me, to everyone in Moonridge. I'll always regret not getting to hug them one more time."

"You? You're not a hugger," I say, deflecting.

"I could be," she pauses. "I guess no one ever taught me how."

"How to hug? C'mon, Nora. That's ridiculous."

"It is, but it's true."

"Well, maybe we'll practice sometime. The more you do it, the better you'll get," I offer.

She must like the idea because, a millisecond later, she kicks me under the table.

"What was that for?" I ask.

"Everything."

Track 18

The Precipice And The Freefall

(Nora's Version)

Sunday, June 7, 2026

Hey Journal! It's me, Nora. For the first time in forever. And surprise! I'm back in Moonridge, for now.

Today was the worst-best day. *cue T Swift vibes*

I realized at exactly 7:06 AM that I hate it here. But we all knew that was going to happen.

At exactly 8:25 AM I realized that I'm still in love with my best friend. Gah.

Right around 9:12 AM it was clear that I'm an idiot and Elliott is a godsend. (But I already knew both of those.)

Why he's being so nice after all these years of silence has my heartstrings in tangles. I haven't done anything to earn back his trust. I didn't even get to explain why I wasn't here for Mark and Lisa's funeral service. I didn't explain, but it's like he's already forgiven me. He's too easy, too gentle with me…

I feel like a coward and a con artist. But what can I do now that I'm living in the apartment above his garage?

Being alone here, without Elliott, feels strange. Like I'm hired help. I know it's not what he wanted when he offered for me to stay in Moonridge but paying him rent is the only way this seemed to make sense. I can't take charity. Not from him.

When I got here, I thought maybe we would have an awkward run-in at the car wash and agree to move on in silence.

Wrong. So, so wrong.
I keep rehearsing lines—how I'll tell him everything when the time is right. But they come out forced and insincere, or not at all.

Sometimes I think he already knows. Sometimes I hope he doesn't.

Crickets chirp outside and the moon is hung high in the obsidian sky. I close the leather notebook I bought in town a couple days ago and let out the breath I've been holding.

Wow.

My raw thoughts spilling onto the page before me feel like salve on a burn. The only issue is that I'm bleeding from fifteen other places. No amount of ointment is going to fix the bullet holes and gashes I've spent the latter part of my life inflicting on myself.

I said goodnight to Elliott an hour or two ago under the guise of mental fatigue, after the full-blown shouting contest we got into with my dad. The object? To be the one to raise your voice the loudest so that everyone else had to submit and listen to you alone. I still don't think there was a clear winner.

I mean, it was sweet, Elliott's suggestion to stop and let them know I'd be in town for a while longer while I figure out my next steps. He'd even helped me draft an email to my landlord and set up a professional moving company to pack up my stuff before it got thrown out on the street for the homeless.

Truthfully, going into it, I thought being here with him was going to be harder. More oppressive. And while conversation doesn't exactly come easy yet, we haven't been sitting, staring, and twiddling our thumbs, which I consider a victory. A small one, but a victory, nonetheless.

With everything that had been piled onto my plate the last couple weeks and the obvious midlife crisis I was having, ten years too early, I am tired. And, since my parents are well-informed on my situation, I figured talking to them about extending my stay in Moonridge would be easy. More of an FYI and less of an IOU.

The way things went, though, it was clear my mom and dad *did* feel like I owed them. In more than one capacity. An explanation, an apology, and a thank you—in that order.

For one, they were horrified that I wouldn't be sleeping under their roof. That I would pay rent to my best friend, or whatever he was now, to live in a garage apartment with one suitcase was the kind of millennial life choice they couldn't wrap their heads around. Not to mention, what would people say? What would the neighbors think? How would they explain to everyone?

To them, if I rented instead of owning—like I'd done for years—I was financially irresponsible. A garage apartment? That was exile. But Elliott was the complication they couldn't classify.

I was literally going to be across the street and down the lane. *Not* down the hall from Elliott, like he originally suggested. Yet, they acted like I'd signed up for scandal with a fountain pen. It was more about how their friends might whisper, than it was about the execution. They didn't want to be seated next to someone at the golf club this summer who might lean over and ask about it.

The apartment. The suitcase. The boy.

It wasn't tidy. It wasn't conservative. It was messy and they didn't like cleaning up after me.

They thought adulthood was a staircase—get the job, buy the house, marry the right person. I must've tripped somewhere on step two.

I am always failing them.

Especially my dad. He's the president of the Moonridge Creek Country Club—not the kind with valet parking or lobster rolls, but the kind with folding chairs, potluck brunches, and a bulletin board full of laminated flyers. He organizes golf tournaments and gives speeches at the summer kickoff cookout. People think he's the kind of man who raised a daughter who sends thank-you notes and keeps her tee time.

I don't even golf. But the country club is stitched into my past all the same.

The honeysuckle just beginning to bloom, damp towels, and sunscreen swaddle me in the scent of those childhood summers and settles me back into the peak seasons of my youth. The nostalgia, the freedom, and frenzy of where I am laying my head tonight make the butterflies in my stomach take flight into the stratosphere.

Who would've thought I'd be here, on a night like this?

My parents didn't see the possibilities. They only saw the flaws. It made them unhappy people, and, by consequence, I was unhappy around them.

They were a generation of mortgage payments, high credit scores, and low debt. I was born into one that was dealing with unprecedented circumstances being announced on the news every night. They said my way wasn't reasonable. I said their way was stifling. We were never going to see eye-to-eye.

After the first and last profanities my dad uttered in front of Elliott left his lips, Elliott grabbed my wrist and quickly escorted me toward the door. It wasn't an exit soaked in finality. But it was a statement.

What I was most struck by, though, was Elliott's instinct—his readiness to protect me. I knew he respected my parents, but he existed outside their worldview. Leaving them in their itchy armchairs was leaving the version of myself who kept trying to be understood by people who never asked questions.

It was pathological. It spoke to control and shame. Ideals that their parents ingrained into them, that they were trying to scream into me. Even my mother, especially my mother. She spoke up only to say, *let's not anger your father, dear.* It was the worst kind of complicity.

I'm deep in thought about the difference between conspiracy and betrayal when I hear a hollow knock on the double doors. Already in my pj's, which consist of the same tank top and shorts I wore today, only in softer materials, I peek through the blinds. Elliott stands there with a mug in his hand and a small parcel. His towering frame looks eerie in the light of the strobe mounted to the outside wall, so I open the door to illuminate his face.

He smiles, but the edges are holding exhaustion, and I know we should both be in bed.

"What's wrong?" I ask. My brows knit together, and I wrap my arms around myself, even though it's not cold.

"Nothing," he reassures me. One word and my body relaxes. "I didn't know if you found the kettle in there or if the place was barren, so I brought you this." He holds out a mug of hot liquid and I immediately smell rooibos and vanilla. My favorite. "I didn't forget the honey." The fact that he answers the question before I ask makes me melt against the doorframe.

Right now, I know I look doe-eyed and deranged, but the list of ways Elliott could get me to surrender to him was stupid.

"Thanks," I say. "I can't believe you remembered."

"I remember more than you think," he hums.

It's not a game, but I want to play anyway.

"Oh, yeah? Like what?"

"Hmm..." he draws out. The tension is electrifying, and I feel it down to my toes. "I think I remember a thirteen-year-old you who really liked Moose Tracks."

He makes the "s" hiss at the end of the sentence. I'm gone.

"Really? That's the best you've got? Anyone could remember that," I swat at his arm and feel the muscle, rigid, beneath my fingers. He pretends to flinch. This banter is treacherous.

"Okay, okay, ouch!" he squeals. "Honestly, Nora, I don't know right now. I remember everything. Your favorite color, the lame guy that gave you the worst first kiss on earth in the dressing rooms at Abercrombie, how your nose wrinkles when you think a movie is funny but not laugh-out-loud funny, the kind of hair gel you used in 2005 when you wanted to try that crunchy hair trend, playing Dance Dance Revolution 'til you almost had a heart attack..." his shoulders meet his earlobes. "I just... I remember *you*."

I'm speechless. Reeling. I'm losing my mind.

When my mind fails to compute and formulate a response, he holds out the package to me. It looks like a book, but it has brown paper wrapped around it and cartoon doodles of people and pets all over it.

"I gave your journal a facelift," he hesitates. "The blue fuzzy stuff is still underneath. But nothing says high school like a paper-bag book cover, right?" A half-grin sneaks across his face.

It's a precipice, and I dive off. I don't know where I'll land, but I'm enjoying the freefall.

Track 19

Still The Longshot

(Elliott's Version)

Being around Nora is like signing my own death certificate with a flourish of calligraphy.

It's a quietly gorgeous demise. Partially because she doesn't ask for attention, and partially because I give it to her anyway. She's been living in the apartment over my garage for seventy-two hours and just knowing she's there gives me goosebumps.

I've been trying to give her the boundaries she deserves. Living this close to someone who feels like a ghost can't be easy. Even when I manage to make her smile, I can see there's something there she isn't ready to share. The joy doesn't quite reach her eyes.

Since we discovered there's no coffee pot in the apartment, and Nora claimed to be an ogre without the first caffeine hit, she's been shuffling into the house every morning to get a fix. I keep my distance, as much as I know how, until she's sipped at least a quarter of the cup. It's a small torment, to be patient while she wakes up and greets the day. But it's worth it, so far, every time.

It feels criminal to witness it. Like I've broken some ancient vow of distance just by noticing the way her hair naturally parts on the side when she always used to part it down the middle. By seeing her silhouetted profile against the kitchen window, as the first light streaks through the trees, and wanting to take a picture. Just to remind myself, she stayed.

Today is the same as the others have been. We dance around each other with no skill. Technique? What's that? With us, it's all style. Timeless and beating. Pulsating through whatever room we inhabit.

The choreography isn't smooth, and we are undoubtedly out of practice. But it doesn't matter, because the music is classic.

She brushes past me to reach the sink, her hand grazing my elbow by accident—or on purpose, and I'll never ask which. I freeze for half a breath. Then pretend to be absorbed in rinsing my spoon.

The closeness and the pale light transport me to the sixth grade Spring Fling. The DJ for the dance hadn't been thoroughly vetted, it was obvious. He had just finished playing *Drop It Like It's Hot* and *Just Lose It*, and I thought I saw the principal's corroded artery burst. It might not have been the most appropriate school dance, but it was entertaining.

As the rap songs were abruptly put out of rotation, our gym teacher was asked to be a stand-in disc jockey and shuffle some songs from his playlist. I wasn't sure I was going to like Mr. McCreedy's taste in music. Then the melody of *Somewhere Only We Know* started to drift over the group and I figured we were in for a solid night of the secret love ballads he cried to when he got home at night. Everyone knew he was going through a divorce and, standing on the sidelines of the dance floor, I felt bad for him.

"C'mon, loser. It's a dance," Nora had said, tugging the sleeve of the sport coat my mom had forced on me. "That means you have to *dance*, El."

El.

She was the only one who ever called me that. To everyone else I was Elliott, or Ashby, or Longshot. The last one had been given to me when no one picked me to be on their team during flag football. One day, Alexander Woodruff chose me, as a joke, so he could blame me when he lost. He always lost.

Turns out I just needed to play in the right position, and quarterback was it.

I was kind of scrawny, and my cleats were busted. But I had a killer spiral. Once the secret was out, that the longshot had proved himself, the nickname stuck. Nora, though, *refused* to use it. She said it reminded her that I was underestimated.

I swear I feel that tug on my sleeve more than I feel the cold water running over my hands at the sink. *C'mon, loser*, she'd said back then. Maybe she'd say it again if she knew how often I replayed it for motivation.

"Hey, uh," she says behind me, "I couldn't find the milk frother. Do you have one?"

"Um… might've thrown it out." I bite my lip. "I never used it."

"Oh. Okay then… I mean, I wasn't going to mention it and I don't want to pry but… what happened to all your stuff? The house is like…empty."

She wasn't wrong. I had gone a little crazy throwing things out. Even more, recently. I didn't feel attached to anything. If it didn't serve a purpose, I didn't need it. The fewer possessions I owned, the less I felt confined. To this house, to this town, inside myself.

I survey the room, like I never noticed how sound ricochets off the walls, or how the dust ghosts the surfaces. It's a mausoleum. An abandoned altar to my parents.

"It's… sparse, I guess. It's very zen, don't ya think?" I say, taking another swig from my mug.

"*Zen?* Elliott Ashby, you've never used that word in your life. It's sterile in here."

Again, not wrong.

"Sterile. Zen. Same thing." I roll my eyes.

"Not the same thing," she replies, running her hand along the credenza. She wipes the dust onto her shirt. It's a handprint from another dimension. Like proof that something human once happened here. "And why is it so dark in here all the time? Don't you ever open the windows?"

A woman's touch.

They say the right woman can transform a home. They say that's what men need when they're bachelors, when they live alone. People say that when you bring that very special woman into your home, they'll rebuild the place right before your eyes. Nora was already doing that.

It wasn't because she was putting up flashy wallpaper or tossing throw pillows onto the couch. All she needed to do was stand there, looking at me like she used to, and the room was transfigured.

Nora didn't need paint swatches and scented candles to resurrect the life that was here once. Her presence rearranged everything. This house. My vital organs.

"I don't know about dark," I reply. "I thought it was kind of a vibe. Tim Burton meets *Saved by the Bell*."

"El…," she deadpans. I'm twelve again. And I'm thirty-three.

Her hands are on her hips and she's looking at me with disapproval and something brewing. Waiting for the real answer maybe. But, staring back, all I see is a pre-teen girl with the world at her feet. Me, on my knees. A girl who broke my heart. And the woman who is unknowingly stitching it back together.

Track 20

Hey, Stranger

(Nora's Version)

Saturday, June 13, 2026

Dear Journal,

Is it okay if I call you Wendy? You're blue like her nightgown. And you keep my secrets like I imagine she would.

I'm delusional. It's fine. Everything's fine.

Anyway, I've been in the garage apartment for almost a week! Another week in Moonridge and, long story short, I'm alive to tell the tale! Not that El hasn't made it as effortless as possible to coexist. Major props to him.

I've been thinking a lot about Elliott and the way things are here. Not romantically... well, that too. But, besides that, I think there's a lot of grief he still carries around. A lot of sadness is locked up inside.

I'm not sure I can be the kind of Rainbow Brite he needs, right now. Could I be the catalyst for something better? Maybe.

An idea has been sliding around in my brain since he started opening up a little more about Mark and Lisa's car accident. A way to pay homage to them. To pave the way for healing.

Healing. I'm one to talk about that… But, Wendy, I'm on my way.

I keep thinking about how grief can rearrange a person's insides. How your stomach gets twisted to make room for the heart that's suddenly enlarged, your lungs collapse, your ribs separate and crack. It's more than a redecoration of the home you carry around with you. It's the gentrification of you as a resident.

Feeling uneven in my own skin sometimes, it was something I could relate to. I'd always mourned the figurative loss of my own parents. The death of wondering if they'd ever care or listen, because I knew they wouldn't. But it barely registered on the Richter scale next to the impact of losing both of his parents, who adored him, at once. The anomaly is that Elliott is still standing, and functioning—mostly.

For a lot of people, grief siphons their vitality and leaves them hollow. But Elliott isn't excavated in that same way. His foundation is cracked; the hinges of his heart hang a bit crooked. But overall, he is enduring. Proving he is built on bedrock, instead of sand.

Every day, I orbit him. Fascinated that he can absorb the tremors of his past and still be looking toward the future. I wonder if I can learn to do that, too.

I got a job, I write. *At the diner in town. It doesn't pay much, but it's not a five-foot cubicle in corporate America either. I think I traded up.*

Tania, the waitress here, is showing me the ropes. I've got to hand it to her, she's quick-witted and smart. She's only eighteen, like I guessed, but she's mature. A lot more so than I was at that age. She's really got her head on straight, ya know. I'm over thirty and I still can't make that claim.

My schedule is rotating, but I'll be here at least four shifts a week. I figured that it's a good enough start for someone who has no degree and is virtually couch surfing. Though I intend to give Elliott every extra penny I get.

It's humbling, honestly. Folding napkins, refilling sugar caddies, memorizing regulars' orders and favorite booths.... But I'll manage it. Somehow.

I glance up and see the clock on the wall says my fifteen-minute break is almost over. I grumble about my feet hurting and the backache that's been persisting since I started spending so much time on them. Though it doesn't make me miss my cushy office chair as much as it makes me respect hard workers like Tania.

I flex my ankles, roll my shoulders, and suck down the last of my pop. The straw slurps, and I feel five again—blowing bubbles in my chocolate milk. I always got scolded for doing it. I got scolded for a lot of things.

Sighing, I regain enough strength to stand and retie my apron. Only an hour and a half left of this shift. It's my first *real* one, where I'm not just shadowing Tania. Going at it alone is nerve-wracking, but I'm doing okay. I think.

I force myself to focus on taking, delivering, and cleaning up after each order for the last part of my shift even though my thoughts keep drifting to what time it is and when Elliott's going to be here. He insisted on picking me up in his truck, even though I can very easily walk back. I'm also craving a shower. I smell like chicken-fried steak and sweat.

The wall clock clicks forward, and I glance at the window. It's a few minutes before seven and I'm starting to wipe down booth nine when he rolls up outside. I expect him to roll down the window and wait, impatiently, for me to finish my tasks so we can get to whatever it is he's anxious about. Or, as obnoxious as it would be, maybe he'll beep the horn to let me know he's arrived.

We still haven't exchanged our new numbers. It feels too intimate.

I press the damp rag in slow circles on the sticky surface, even though it's already clean. Just buying time, maybe. It's a test of sorts. To see if he or I will break first and let the other one in on the fact they're watching. I know I'm visible since the blinds are open and all the lights are still on.

"Hey, stranger." Elliott's voice comes from the diner's doorway. The phrase hits too close to home. But I stay composed because I'm realizing two things—

> — Elliott is going out of his way for me. Something Grayson had always refused to do.

> — We are strangers in loose connotation. But still best friends in the margins.

The rag smells like lemon and is dripping grease all over my trusty Chuck Taylors. I'm ogling and he notices, because what he does next is deplorable.

He peels off the chambray overshirt he's wearing—down to his undershirt—and lays it over a stool at the bar, revealing the tan he's gotten that spreads down his arms. Flipping his snapback backwards and adjusting the fit, he steps into my space.

"Your ride's here," he says gently. Then he takes the rag from my hands and begins wiping down the booth.

I should be annoyed. Instead, I nod, untying the apron with fingers that feel clumsy now, every movement louder than it needs to be.

"Let me grab my bag," I say sliding the apron into a bin beneath the register.

Maybe I should say something about boundaries. About how I could've cleaned the table without his help, thank you very much.

But this is about more than Pine-Sol and Palmolive. It's about everything and nothing.

"I figured we could do something fun tonight, workin' girl," he hollers as I disappear behind the counter.

"Like what? Because, honestly, I just want to stand in hot water until I'm a prune and then crash out," I whine. But he doesn't even give me a hint.

"Get in the truck and find out, Goose," is all he says. And, as much as I want to protest and explain all of the reasons why I can't or won't—all of the reasons why it's a bad idea to get reattached to me—I get in the truck.

Soon, we're on the outskirts of town. Cow pastures and cornfields pass. Cicadas hum and wheat sways. The breeze blows through my hair.

It's a small-town summer Saturday night and Elliott has one hand on the wheel, the other hanging out the window. My bare feet are kicked up on the dash and the smell of fresh-cut hay floods the air around me.

Right now, time doesn't exist. Only the eternity of what was, what is, and what could be.

Track 21

Maimed and Glowing

(Elliott's Version)

It's not grand or dramatic, but it's quiet. A place where I can hear myself think. Thankfully, not many people veer from the beaten path back here, so I've mostly had the place to myself. Though tonight is different.

Soft moss covers the rocks next to the murmuring creek, and there's a fallen log that frogs and turtles perch on. The mushrooms that grow along the edge glow in the hazy evening ambiance. Deer watch us from afar, curious about our visit to the woods.

"The fireflies are showing off for ya," I point out to Nora. "Here," I say, and hand her a mason jar. There are small nail holes in the top and I gesture for her to unscrew the lid. Then I pull out another jar for myself.

"Catching fireflies is your idea of a fun night out?" she asks dryly. But from the amusement in her eyes and the way the corners of her mouth turn upward, I know she's saying it for a reaction. To see if I'll stay in character. What she should know, though, is that this isn't an act.

"I'll give you twenty minutes. Whoever catches the most at the end wins. Deal?" I smirk.

She studies me for a few seconds, heaves a sigh, and jumps down from the tailgate of my truck. "You know I'm gonna smoke you," she threatens.

I wink. "That's my girl," I laugh. The sound rolls through the darkening sky and into the distance.

The twenty minutes go by slowly. It's cinematic—us, rushing around in the meadow grass and through the tall trees with glowing jars in our hands. It's a reprieve from everything we've carried that hasn't been as luminous.

I stop, mid-chase, and watch Nora. She stops, just shy of the creek, mouth ajar with childlike wonder. It's breathtaking. But it's also a scene full of sorrow. Something tells me she hasn't had that many stunningly simple moments since leaving Moonridge.

This is still on my mind as I sneak up behind her. A firefly is hovering over her and she's unaware. Within an instant, I position the jar overhead, scoop up the insect, and clap the lid on top.

"Time's up," I whisper to the top of her head.

Nora whirls around and playfully punches me in the shoulder. "Hey! No fair!" she shrieks.

"Ya snooze, ya lose, Goose," I say nonchalantly.

She throws another punch—this time to my chest, right over the pectoral.

I reach for her jar, which probably holds six or eight fireflies, while mine glows with twice that. Nora tries to hold it out of reach behind her, but my arms are longer—it's easy to overtake her.

Only, I trip over my own foot, lose my balance, and suddenly I'm falling.

We're falling.

Me into her. Her into the creek.

We're both soaked and muddy. The lids to our jars have popped open and the escaped fireflies swirl around us like confetti. Nora's sitting a little deeper in the creek than I am, the water lapping past her thighs while her knobby knees jut up into the air. Her hair is stuck to her forehead and neck, and I'm about to point out the crawdad swimming in her direction when she starts to laugh.

It starts out muffled, her shoulders shaking from the effort of holding it in.

Then it builds—a rumble in her chest, rising until it bursts into a full-fledged belly laugh.

It's not nervous. Not mocking.

It's free. And contagious.

I haven't seen her laugh like this in too long.

It unlocks something inside me—something that convinces me we're fifteen again.

That we're counting down the days until school starts, 'til we can get our licenses, 'til we can get out of this town.

I wonder if we're still those same high school kids underneath it all. If we can recapture the magic we had back then.

Recreate all the shimmering memories that replay inside my head—like a film reel stuck on loop.

Are they flickering in her mind too?

I get on all fours and slink over to where she's sloshing around in the cool ripples of the creek. Propping myself up beside her, I lean against her shoulder and feel that the lighthearted shakes from her hysterics have turned into shivers. I glance at her sideways and see that even though she's got a smile pasted on, tears are streaming down her cheeks.

"Nora," I say gently, placing a tentative hand on her knee. "What's going on?"

I'm confused. Concerned. I hate seeing her sad. If I had any superpower, it would be to heal others. To heal her.

"I didn't come for the funeral," she sobs. "I… I wanted to tell you…" But she doesn't finish. Another wave of convulsions overtakes her.

I wrap my arm around her shoulders and draw her into me. "We've already been over this," I soothe. "It's in the past." But she rocks back and forth, arms wrapped around herself, shaking her head.

"I wanted to, El," she says, desperate. "I wanted to fly out here, but I didn't find out until it was too late. I'm always too late." A tremor wracks her body, but she pushes on. "I was in the hospital. When everything happened with your parents—that's where I was."

Her bottom lip quivers. I take her chin in my hand and press my thumb to it.

Her eyes are a sea of bronze, chocolate, and flecks of fern. They beg me not just to hear her—but to feel her words.

"Your mom and dad never mentioned anything," I say.

Her explanation doesn't quite add up. If she was in the hospital, you'd at least think I'd have heard it through the rumor mill in Moonridge.

"They didn't know," she whispers. "No one did."

"What? Why didn't you say something to someone, Nor?" I'm fighting to understand.

She looks up at me—into my eyes, and through my soul. Her tears have slowed; lips pressed together with determination.

I let my thumb trace a line over one of her dimples and down her face.
"I tried to… to end my life," she says. "Let me just tell you—kitchen knives and Xanax don't mix."

She attempts a chuckle. I, on the other hand, am traumatized.

"W-why? I mean… wait—*when* was this?!" I'm explosive. Raging.

Not because I'm angry at her for feeling that way—but because something, *someone*, made her believe she had to.

"It was probably two weeks before the funerals," she says quietly. "I went to the emergency room because I was having these thoughts… bad, bad thoughts. Everything was out of control."

She closes her eyes. Shutting a window to her mind.

Open them, Nora. Open up. It's me.

"I guess I was there for a couple days, answering questions, doing tests. Eventually, they gave me the option to check myself in. To be evaluated." She grimaces. "Mental health sucks."

"Oh my god… How long did the evaluation take?"

"It was just more questions. Some group therapy. Art therapy—that wasn't so bad." She shrugs. "I ended up staying ten days."

"Don't do that, Nor. Don't shrug like it's nothing. My best friend goes off and tries to hurt herself and I haven't heard about it for *eight years*? That's a huge deal."

I'm borderline screaming. My vision blurs. My fist curls at my side.

"I couldn't tell my parents. They would've judged me—made me feel like there was something wrong with me. I mean, there *is*, but it's no one's fault. Just some stupid chemicals in my brain."

I don't agree. But I don't argue. I put a pin in the topic for later.

"Why didn't you call me?" I ask.

"I… I don't know. Everything was so messed up by then, and I didn't know if you'd even want to hear from me. Plus, by the time I heard from my parents about the accident, it felt like bad timing."

"You can always call me, Goose," I say, nudging her in the ribs. "I've got your back, kid."

"I wish I would've. I wish a lot of things."

"Me too," I nod. "Me too."

I take her wrist, gently searching for scars with my fingertips. Then I pull her to her feet.

Her mascara—what little she wore—has been washed away by tears. The tip of her nose is red from sniffling.

I take one step forward and wrap her in a hug. An embrace so secure, so strong, I hope it chases away every doubt in her mind—that she should be here, should be alive, should be wanted.

I *need* it to. Because if it doesn't, I might lose her again. I might lose her anyway.

"Are we *hugging*?" she asks. It's muffled and her breath is warm through the sleeve of my shirt.

"Don't act like you don't love it," I chuckle.

"It's not that," she says, as she wraps her arms around my waist. "It's that now, I don't know how to stop."

Track 22

Say Less, Be Less

(Nora's Version)

Tuesday, June 16, 2026

Dear Wendy,

Everything inside me is screaming: RUN.

Leave Moonridge. Leave Elliott. Just go.

I'm supposed to be braver than this.

But the truth? I'm just as scared now as I was when I left the first time. Maybe more.
For once in my life, I talked too much. I didn't think that was possible. Elliott's always been the outgoing oversharer—not me. What was I thinking?

cue dramatic background music (preferably Beethoven's Fifth Symphony)

I had the opportunity to be vulnerable—to be real—for the first time since I got back.

And I overshot it.

Elliott probably thinks I'm a freak. Tainted. Sick. Unworthy.

Why wouldn't he? I think those things about myself.

And that line—'I don't think I can stop'—when he hugged me? Puke.

WHO EVEN AM I?

Who even am I?

Nora Elizabeth Lowe.

But that name doesn't mean anything. Not really. I was taught—growing up the daughter of two successful members of Gen X—that identity was earned through achievement. If you asked my dad how he got hired at Buckeye Logistics and worked his way up, he'd make it sound like sheer willpower and work ethic.

In Moonridge Creek, he was admired—president of the country club, regional manager at Buckeye, always shaking hands and giving speeches about grit. People looked at him and saw stability. People saw him as proof that hard work paid off.

Truth? He was a chronic workaholic. Present only as a breadwinner and a strict disciplinarian. Resistant to change. Confrontational.

Thomas Lowe knew how to charm the neighbors, the country club members, and my mother. But his smile was always too tight. And, when he lied—which was often—he blinked too much.

Some of his greatest hits were pretending to advocate for my honesty, then telling me to "suck it up" when I mentioned being depressed. Or belittling me. Telling me I was 'too sensitive'. 'Too much'. 'A troublemaker'.

My mom was no better. She labeled me "dramatic from birth." More concerned with her body image, or the next fad diet, than the impact her example had on my own self-worth.

She taught me how to count calories before I learned how to multiply. How to work out on an elliptical before I was ten. She called it "discipline". I just wanted to disappear.

Being in Moonridge is like looking at my reflection in a broken mirror, I tell Wendy. *Every corner of this town reflects a version of me I tried to outgrow. But the cracks are still there.*

I've been hiding in the garage, sneaking out to my shifts at the diner, ordering DoorDash so I don't have to go into the house. I can't face him.

Elliott's embrace—the calm that settled over me in his arms—was a kind of stillness I've never known.

How can he see my humanity—the ugly, broken, bumpy parts—and still accept me?

I don't have the answer. Not even after pacing the worn floorboards for hours, trying to find it.

To make matters more complicated, last night, when we got back, I unblocked Elliott's number.

I told myself it was just a test—a harmless flick of the thumb.

I may or may not have sent a text to it, hoping it wouldn't go through.

It was just a test. Except it wasn't.

Elliott had wanted to walk me up to the apartment last night. I was drowsy and lightheaded from crying so much, but I still said no. It felt like pity—even if it wasn't—and I didn't want it. I was embarrassed enough.

But, by the time I made it to the landing, just outside the door, I felt a surge of regret.

Thanks…for being there, the text said.

I had rested my head against the wall and exhaled. Closed my eyes and said a prayer, but I'm not sure if it made a difference. Because less than a minute later, my phone chimed. New message alert.

Anytime, Goose. Sleep tight.

Track 23

Tangled / In the Trees

(Elliott's Version)

I pull out my phone and scroll to the text Nora sent me. I'm surprised she has the same phone number. I'm even more surprised she felt comfortable enough to send a message at all—especially after what she shared with me at the creek.

Fifteen years of silence aside, Nora—my Nora—had almost snuffed out her own flame.

The thought makes me sick to my stomach. Dizzy.

I look at the top of my phone screen. 2:22 AM.

Guess it's one of those nights. Sleep's not happening.

I roll onto my side and stare toward the garage. The bay doors diagonally from here and the apartment was built over the one farthest from my bedroom.

I can't see if there are any signs of life. But I hope she's okay.

The Messages app is still open on my phone and Nora's words gaze up at me. In my mind, the letters rearrange themselves into what I think she's really trying to say.

Don't leave me.

I'm restless, and the room is too muggy to sleep. So, I wander down to the kitchen in lounge pants and a Moonridge Rebels Football sweatshirt.

The number of these I own as head coach is, honestly, embarrassing. But chugging milk from the carton isn't exactly a fashion show.

And if nothing else, coaching gets my nose out of the books.

My fridge door is a mess—takeout menus, grocery lists, a coupon that expired in 2019. But one thing's stayed exactly where it was.

One of the only things I kept in its place after my parents' collision with a drunk driver.

A refrigerator magnet they'd gotten on a trip to Mexico.

It was small and cheaply made. I've already superglued it back together a couple of times.

The front of it used to be brighter—sun-washed and vivid. Now it's faded by time. But the words are still there, in bold lettering.

Donde nunca se pone el sol.

Where the sun never sets.

My mom and dad lived by that phrase. Embodied it.

For them, the sun was its most dazzling when it lifted up the people you loved to its light. When the warmth and glow was reflected onto you as a bystander of someone else's success, renewal, joy.

It intrigued me, the way they made it look so easy. Caring for me, and each other.

They kept their disagreements behind closed doors, their gratitude foremost, and their pride dead last.

And above all, they always wanted to see me happy.

Tonight, as I fumble for the handle to grab the 2%, my eyes adjust to the darkness.

After a moment, I see it—the outline of something beneath the magnet, held up by it.

I pluck it from the door and hold it closer, waiting for my vision to clear.

When it does, I prop the fridge open, letting the light spill out—bluish-white, clinical, but enough that I can make out the two faces in the Polaroid now in my hand.

The same one that's floated from pocket to pocket. The one of Nora and me.

How did it get here?

I'm starting to wonder if my house has a mind of its own or if someone's been rummaging through my stuff. Whichever it is, it's creeping me out.

"Time for a midnight snack?" Nora's voice comes from the darkness. Slow and unsure. But it's there. I'd know it anywhere.

"I couldn't sleep," I confess. "You?"

"Same," she replies. "Felt kinda stuffy in the garage."

I don't doubt it. But I know that's not the reason she's here.

She's not awake because the ceiling fan in the apartment stopped working last week and I forgot to fix it.

Nora wouldn't admit it though.

"Sorry. I keep forgetting about fixing the fan," I say. Then pause.

She doesn't respond.

I can't see her face clearly—even in the combined light coming from my appliances and the moon that's come out from behind a cloud. My blinds are open for once, and the whitewashed rock in the sky is the only witness to this awkward exchange.

"You're welcome to crash in here," I croak.

"I don't want to intrude."

She knows, by now, I wouldn't have made the offer if I wasn't sincere.

"Because I have so much going on at the moment?" I say with a grin.

"Obviously." Nora gestures at my attire and the sweating milk carton, as the door to the refrigerator remains ajar. She takes a hesitant step closer. "What's that?"

She means the photo I have clutched in my hand. The one of us—young and dumb. Or possibly the smartest we've ever been. I haven't decided.

"Nothing," I lie. I'm bad at it. Lying to Nora is pointless. So why am I trying?

"Lying isn't your forte, Elliott," she states, like she's reading my mind. "Take it from someone who's been doing it to herself for a *long* time."

"It's not a lie exactly…" I stammer. "I guess I'm not sure what it is."

I close the fridge door. I'm parched, but thirst feels irrelevant now. Because nothing in this room can satisfy me. Except her.

"Oh? So, a photo of us on the boardwalk in Myrtle Beach—eighth grade class trip—is just a memory that *slipped your mind?*"

She waits while I squirm. Usually, it's the other way around. The reversed roles leave me tongue-tied.

I glance at the photo again. Us, arms slung around each other. My goofy grin, her dimples. Like we knew exactly who we were. Like that version of us would last forever.

How did she know I was hanging on to this exact memory? That I was still holding space, for her.

"Relax, El," she giggles. "It fell out of your pocket the other day. I didn't mean to snoop," she says, quieter now. "But I saw it. And I remembered."

I consider asking the question that burns the back of my throat like bile.

Can we stop pretending?

Maybe that's impossible. Maybe the recording of our history is too long to rewind. Maybe we can't edit out the hard parts.

But can we move forward? Push past everything holding us back.

"Ya know what we should do?" I ask, ignoring the persistent berating inside my head. "We should watch a movie. Stay up all night, make popcorn—the whole shebang."

"I think staying up all night is already taken care of. It's almost 2:30."

"Yeah," I wave off the suggestion that we should go back to bed. "Who needs sleep anyway? We can sleep when we're dead."

I head over to the entertainment center, and she follows, watching me as I dig through the collection of DVDs.

"Can't we just put on Netflix or something?" she asks.

I shake my head. "Too fast. Too easy. You know I'm not that kind of guy, Goose."

The innuendo is subtle, but she laughs anyway. It sounds like hope.

Somewhere between the end of *Tommy Boy* and the beginning of *10 Things I Hate About You*, I realize Nora's fallen asleep on the couch.

She snores lightly, eyelids fluttering like she's dreaming of something soft.

It looks so serene. I get out my phone and take a picture.

Maybe, in another life, I'd hang it on the fridge with the Polaroid. Maybe with a magnet that says, *Two Lives, One Love*. Something cheesy like that.

I stare down at the frozen image on my phone screen.

It hurts—how many moments like this I haven't stopped to capture. Before she left. Since she's been back.

I guess I'm afraid to, because, what if it doesn't last?

I fall asleep with that question lingering in my mind and a knot in my neck.

A few hours later, the sun dapples the room—and my face—with specks of light.

Blinking my eyes open, it takes me a minute to get oriented.

I'm in the recliner. The same one my dad used to sit in to watch Cleveland's baseball games.

Sometimes, when I sit in it, I imagine being a kid again—on his lap, his finger tracing the screen as he pointed out the starters.

I miss him. Them. But I rub my eyes and try to adjust to the present, instead of curling into the past.

I remember the movie marathon. The awful IPA I found in the back of the fridge.

Three hours of sleep.

I am *not* sixteen anymore.

Nora stirs and mumbles something in her sleep.

When I offered for her to hang out here last night, I didn't expect to be waking up to her on my couch.

But here she is. Tangled hair. Arm up over her head. And I'm starting to remember what home feels like.

This is dangerous territory.

I haul myself up and grab an Afghan out of the basket next to me. Quietly, I tiptoe over to Nora and spread the blanket over her. Tucking her in gently feels ceremonial.

As I step back and admire her, all unfinished edges and emotional safety pins, I smile.

But despite it, I'm afraid. Because this feels like the beginning of something. Or the echo of something we never finished.

So, I stand there, wondering if you can rewrite a story without erasing the past.

Track 24

Same Ol' Same

(Elliott's Version)

The day was ushered in slowly.

Almost as if dawn itself realized it would be ruining the mood if the sun rose too quickly. Like it would wreck what last night had rebuilt.

The semblance of trust we have is balancing on breaking branches that will come crashing down if the wind blows too strongly. All the feelings Nora divulged will pile up among them. It'll be impossible, then, to separate the splintered truths keeping us going from what's better left for the fire.

This is all so delicate.

Delicate isn't a word I use often. It doesn't apply to much in my life. There's not much I have left that I'm afraid will be easily damaged.

But this reconciliation is something I don't have another way to describe.

I did my best not to think about it all day. Not to be swallowed up by the possibility of things between us reverting to disdain or silence. But the more I ruminated on all the protective instincts coursing through my veins, the stormier my temper became.

It's an intensity I can hardly put into words, having Nora so close and yet so far from me simultaneously. Hearing how she wanted to disappear from the earth made me furious—with life and circumstance and whatever force is out there powerful enough to put Nora into such a dark place.

I'm a zealot for her happiness. An advocate for her cause.

Yet, standing here tonight—in front of my bedroom mirror, rolling up the sleeves on my shirt and straightening my collar—I'm not just passionate about Nora finding her way back to me. I'm angry that she didn't do it sooner.

It's concern, and irritability, and aggression in a way I haven't experienced before. A cocktail of emotions that I don't remember consuming. Though the effect is undeniable.

I'm supposed to meet Marquis at Trudy's in twenty minutes for our typical weekly roundup. Admittedly, I'm not going to be very good company, but it's too late to cancel. Maybe once I down a tumbler of bourbon and get some food into my system, my mood will lighten.

Highly doubtful, but I'll attempt it.

With a tug on the brim of my snapback, the only accessory I usually have on, I step back and take in my reflection.

When did I turn into a man? Is it something physical, or does it just come with the territory of getting older?

I'm older now than my parents were when they had me. Is it too late to want a family for myself? What about in another year? Or five? Will it be too late then?

Marquis and I are the same age, yet he's settled down with his college sweetheart and has two little girls. They're talking about maybe having another baby in a year or two. He's responsible and reliable. The type of guy who was meant to be a husband and father.

I'm not sure what that means except I don't think I qualify.

Maybe that's ironic, considering I spend my days teaching other people's kids how to think, how to write, how to make sense of the world. I know how to listen. I know how to show up. But when I imagine being a father, it feels different.

There's no curriculum for that kind of love.

I'm still considering this as I wind through the streets on the way to the pub. We've been meeting there for ages and I could get there with my eyes closed. It's only ten minutes from my house and I practically sleep through the drive, in this self-assessing haze.

Marquis is already at our regular table near the back when I stroll in, trying to look like I'm not quietly losing my mind. But he knows me well enough by now to catch the strained expression I'm wearing and lack of greeting as I sit down.

"Geez, man. What's eating you?" he asks.

"Long day," I reply.

"Someone pee in your Cheerios again?"

I shake my head glumly. "Nah, it's just… I don't know how I got here."

"Well, if you mean to Moonridge specifically…"

"You know what I mean, Marq. How did we get to be over thirty? How did things get so…serious?"

Marquis sighs. "Can't answer that for you, Elliott. Time moves, we age, things change. The evolution of life."

He says it like he's Gandhi or some other philosophical genius.

I roll my eyes.

The server sets down my usual drink.

"What's really goin' on?" he presses.

It's my turn to sigh. "Nora…"

"Ah. Same ol', same ol'," Marquis chuckles.

"It's not like that," I shoot at him.

"Of course it's *like that*," he mocks. "It has been since we were kids. So don't try to give me some crap about how you've changed or things are different."

"And what makes you think things *can't* be different this time?"

"You've been hung up on Nora for ages. I was here to clean up the pieces, or did you forget that? And did she ever reach out, look for ways to include you in her life? No. And now you're handing her the hammer to smash your heart again."

"You haven't talked to her. She's not the same kid she was back then," I say.

"I don't need to talk to her to see that you're distraught. More than I've seen in the last fifteen years, besides your parents' accident."

"I'm just upset. I guess… I don't get why she didn't come back sooner. She's had her own problems, I know. Big ones. But I've been a steadfast guy. I've waited. And now what?" I admit.

"Now, you hold her accountable," Marquis replies, and takes a swig of his bourbon. "You tell her that your patience has limits. That you're not on standby for her indefinitely. She has to answer for *something*. If you don't do this now, it's going to be a repeat of high school."

I nod, but it's slow. Not agreement—just acknowledgment. The kind that doesn't settle anything.

"C'mon, Ashby. You're not gonna be a doormat again, are you?"

"I'm not a pushover. I just haven't found a way to bring it up," I say truthfully.

"Better figure it out quick before history repeats itself, my friend."

Maybe Marquis is right. Most things don't wait for perfect timing.

Some things arrive unannounced.

They demand to be reckoned with, even if you aren't ready.

I finish my drink, let the burn settle in my chest.

Maybe it's time I stop waiting.

Track 25

Forced Outcomes

(Nora's Version)

Lying in bed and staring at my ceiling isn't an effective way to start my morning, but I'm feeling depleted.

A long day of work yesterday, coupled with the minimal amount of sleep I got on Elliott's couch the night before completely crippled me. Last night, when I got home, I barely registered that his truck wasn't in the driveway and climbed the stairs with only the thought of clean, cool sheets on my mind.

Now, watching the blades of the ceiling fan—collecting dust, stuck at a standstill—I wonder where Elliott was when I stumbled through the fading light and into the apartment.

We aren't at the point where we have each other's agenda memorized, or where we update one another every time we step out for a few minutes. But I'm just nosy enough to wonder who he was with.

It's a self-indulgent thought. Vain, maybe. It creeps in before I can catch it and toss it out.

He's a big boy. He can do whatever he wants.

I scold myself for making his absence about myself.

A gentle knock suddenly comes from the other room. For a moment, I think I'm hearing phantom sounds. There's a long pause and I consider rolling over and trying to snooze a bit more. But then, a bit harder this time, the thumping comes again.

I groan, throw back the blankets, and pad to the door, still half-dreaming, half-dreading. The tile floor feels cool under my feet, but the muggy air of the day surrounds me the moment I answer the persistent knocker.

Elliott. Who else would it have been?

"Hey," he says. "Sorry if I woke you up."

"You didn't," I assure him. "Just enjoying having a morning off."

"Then maybe this isn't the best time…" His voice fades.

"Best time for what?"

"I was just hoping we could talk. I realized last night that I haven't been completely honest with you."

I step back with a puzzled look on my face and Elliott squeezes through the small opening I leave between myself and the door.

He's wearing dark jeans and Nikes, a plain white T-shirt. He doesn't have a snapback on and his hair, which he now keeps cropped short, makes him look mature and serious.

His eyes are wide and sincere.

Wow. It's so easy to pretend in moments like this. Effortless to imagine we're just two people and everything is brand new.

"Look, Nora…" he begins.

"Uh-oh… what did I do?" I chuckle. I'm trying to lighten the tension, but I can tell he's intent on telling me what he set out to say.

"When you told me about your hospital visit, it really helped me to understand a lot about why you weren't around when my parents died. I can imagine that things have been complicated, to say the least, since you left. And I feel awful about what you went through."

I can feel that there is a 'but' coming. So, I decide to get to it before he does.

"But it's not enough," I clip.

"It's not that…exactly," he replies. He looks at his feet. At the wall behind me. Anywhere but in my eyes.

"It is. Just say it, Elliott. You're mad at me."

"I'm not mad, Nor. I'm just hurt. You were gone seven years before my parents' accident. I never got one text, phone call, letter… You never reached out. Why?"

"Are you truly asking me that?" my voice comes out shrill. I'm furious at him for making me feel sad, guilty, and responsible for his feelings. Even if I know I am, at least a little.

"Yeah, I am. You up and disappeared. I was supposed to, what? Feel nothing?" he asks.

"It's not like you chased after me either, ya know," I defend.

"You're right. So many times, I thought about getting on a plane and coming out to Portland, showing up on your doorstep. I never did," he admits. "Even if I had, though, what was I going to say? 'Hey, why'd you run away without so much as a goodbye?' What would your answer have been anyway?"

"Probably that I was better off being alone. I mean, look at you, Elliott. What *could* I have ever said that would've taken the pained look off your face?" I answer.

"I would've tried to understand. I would've done whatever it took, for you."

"I was broken. I didn't know how to say goodbye. It was too hard. You following me wouldn't have made it easier. Closure doesn't always come with proximity," I promise.

"Closure was never what I was looking for. I was looking for *you*," he breathes.

"I was a mess."

"A mess I wanted. My best friend missed fifteen years of my life. I would've waded through the chaos with my hands tied if it meant that time wouldn't have been lost. I didn't even get a say."

The morning light catches his face, and I see the desperation there. Not for repair, but for understanding.

"I made the decision I thought was best for everyone. For both of us," I confess.

In that moment, I realize it's something my parents would've done. Forced the outcome they wanted. The one with the least fuss. The path of least resistance.

Elliott raises his eyebrows, like he can see the thoughts weaving their way through my mind. His eyes glisten with fresh despair. They communicate all the misery he isn't putting to words.

"Oh my gosh…" My hand flies to my mouth. "I'm so selfish."

He wraps his hand around my wrist and moves my hand away from my face. His fingers tap the inside of my arm lightly and he takes a step closer.

I feel pathetic—barefoot, in pajamas, hair in tangles—realizing I'm the reason things fall apart.

"Goose, you were young. We both were. You were trying to preserve yourself for whatever reason. I just need you to know that while you thought removing yourself from your life here would make things better for everyone, they didn't."

I shake my head. "I must've thought the world revolved around me." I squeeze my eyes shut.

"Call it what you want. But what's important now is how you move forward, now that you know," he reasons.

"I'm sorry, ya know?" I say. It's more rhetorical than anything because I know he does. "Running away… I framed it as a fresh start. I was lying to myself."

"I didn't knock on the door just now looking for an apology, Nora. I came looking for truth. Just someone willing to see my side. Someone who realizes I'll never be the first to leave. But I don't want to be the one left behind either."

"Next time I need an escape plan, I'll at least let you be co-mastermind," I offer.

"Deal," he nods. "Now, how about some breakfast?"

My stomach grumbles in response and we both laugh. Any remaining animosity shattered.

I have a feeling that there's not much Elliott's smile and a stack of chocolate-chip pancakes can't fix.

Track 26

Girls Like Us

(Nora's Version)

Friday, June 19, 2026

Dear Wendy,

I think I made an ally. Besides you. Don't be jealous.

I've never had a real girlfriend before, so I'm not sure how this works.

I was working my shift at The Bent Spoon yesterday and met someone new.

I know. Shocking. Considering the only new things in Moonridge Creek are that bookstore where I found you, and the Subway on the way out of town.

A woman stopped in and sat in our booth. Mine and Elliott's.

Her eyes were puffy; her hair was graying and thin. She fidgeted a lot. More than anyone I've ever seen.

Constantly scratching at her arms and wrists. She was sweating and shaking.

I noticed the judgments of my parents surfacing inside me and tried to tamp them down.

I wasn't sure if I should serve her. But I was going to try.

When I got closer, I could see the track marks on her inner arm and the dilation of her pupils. I know the hallmarks of an addict when I see one.

She asked for coffee. Black.

Her voice was raspy, like it had been borrowed from someone older.

She wouldn't make eye contact and, instead, kept trying to see behind me. Stealing glances at the door to the kitchen.

Then, she requested Tania by name.

Imagine my shock when Tania rounded the counter and said hello to her MOTHER.

Her mother, the cocaine addict. Her mother, with trembling hands and pasty skin. Her mother.

Tania didn't flinch. She didn't cry. She just said, "Hi, Mom," like it was any other Thursday.

I left them to talk, but I kept a close eye on Tania from afar. Her body language was stiff, and she looked a little queasy. Like she was bracing for impact.

The visit didn't last long. A few minutes, maybe. But Tania wasn't the same after.

We've never discussed our personal lives, but the air in the diner felt thicker after her mom left. And it seemed like Tania was choking on it. Trying to breathe through smoke.

"Are you okay?" I had asked her on the way out, after closing. I knew she wasn't, but I didn't know how to approach it.

How do you say, *Wanna sit around and discuss our childhood trauma?*

Exactly. You don't.

As badly as I wanted to know how her mom got where she is now, I wasn't going to be the one to bring it up.

She slowed her pace, like she caught my meaning. But she just nodded and said, *I'm fine.*

She wasn't. It was obvious.

Only people that are completely *not* fine try to convince others that they are.

I knew from experience. I had told everyone I was 'fine' since I was old enough to talk. Another circus trick. To keep the illusion from being spoiled.

Smile wide. Voice steady. Hands still. Don't let them see.

I wanted to soothe her somehow. I don't know why. It just felt right.

I grabbed her arm and dragged her down the street to the ice cream parlor and bought her a waffle cone of chocolate-chip cookie dough. That was as close as I could get to, *Alright, spill it.*

At first, she looked at me like she wasn't sure whether I was sane.

Valid.

Then, she took the cone and gave it a tentative lick.

We ended up on the curb outside, counting cars, and squinting into the sun. We pretended that things were normal. That drug users don't show up at diners. That moms aren't substance addicts.

Eventually, she looked at me—really looked. I thought maybe she was ready to talk about what had happened. Instead, she gave me an ornery smile and asked a question I wasn't ready for.

"So is Coach Ashby your boyfriend?"

It should've been easy for me to say no, Wendy. Why wasn't it easy?

Instead, I got tongue-tied and clumsy, and dropped my own cone of raspberry chip into the street.

*"Why do you ask?" was all I could manage. *facepalm**

"I think he likes you," she replied. For her, it was that simple.

"We're just old friends." I wave off the suggestion.

"Really? Because it sure seems like there's more to it," she replies, looking at me like I'm holding something back.

I am. But even I'm not sure what.

Because the truth is, Elliott isn't my boyfriend. I don't even know if we are friends. We might just be two people who knew each other once. Maybe that's all it'll ever feel like.

"You guys are living together," she says with a nod. Like it's fact and not a rumor.

I mean, it *is* technically a rumor. We don't share the same space. I don't see how we ever could.

I wanted to tell her that living together isn't the same as *being together*. That roommates—I shudder—aren't always romantically involved. That sometimes, longing glances and damp hugs in the middle of a creek don't mean anything. But I didn't.

I just shrugged. "It's complicated."

"That's what they all say. Especially when it's not," she laughed.

I laughed too. But I didn't feel the amusement, because my chest was imploding.

I think he likes you. That sentence will remain forever etched into my brain.

The shared moment must make something bloom inside her though. She tells me about her mom, the addiction, rehab—three times—and the dream she has of leaving Moonridge. Being a world-renowned chef and getting awarded a Michelin star.

It's all packaged so pretty, the way she says it. It sounds possible and I don't tell her it's not.

Girls like her—like us—need all the dreams we can collect. And all the courage to chase them.

Courage is something I'm still working on.

But, Wendy, I think Tania might be able to help me with something. Something special. And that excites me.

I haven't been excited about something this big in a long time. I'll be crushed if Elliott thinks it's stupid. After all, it's for him. Because of him.

Everything is for him? Does he know that?

Track 27

I'm Still Here

(Elliott's Version)

"Remember that time we decided to go on an *adventure* and ended up out in the woods in the middle of deer season? We were so oblivious," I chuckle and shake my head. "Our parents had to come looking for us by following the ridge all the way out to old man Kessler's!"

It's late June now. I find it repulsive.

Summer should be endless. Final answer.

"I'm more than happy to remind you," Nora says, "that we got grounded for three weeks after that and had to pick up the dog poop out of Mrs. Wegman's yard while everyone else went to Soak 'n' Splash City."

"Worth it," I say. "I'd do it again."

"You're psychotic," she replies. But it's a tease.

"If you *really* thought that, I doubt you'd be living in my garage." I raise my brows.

Go ahead, try to tell me otherwise.

"For all I know, you could have bodies stuffed in that extra freezer," she quips.

"For all *I* know, *you* could be plotting to usurp me and make off with my millions. Guess we're both taking a risk."

This is comfortable. *This* is what I remember.

The back and forth. The push and pull.

I just don't recall my heart racing quite like this.

It's taken three weeks, but I've finally managed to peel back a couple of the layers she's shrouded in. I know it's hard for her to let go of the veil she's hidden behind since leaving so long ago.

Still—it's nice to see this side of her. Even if I have to work for it.

She lies back on the grass in my backyard and runs her hands and arms over it. It looks like she's trying to make a snow angel. I tilt my head and watch, but I don't know what I'm witnessing. Maybe something sacred.

"Uh, Nora… what are you doing?"

"Imprinting," she says. "Ya know?"

I have no idea what she's talking about, but it's cute—the way her forehead wrinkles in disbelief that I don't.

"Isn't that something baby birds do? Like that one who thought the robot was its mom?" I ask.

"Not like that, dummy! I'm talking about just…leaving a mark," she says.

"You leave your mark everywhere, Goose."

The words leave my lips before I realize that I'm letting out a truth I can't take back.

She sits up halfway, propped on her elbows.

"I'm talking about the kind of mark you leave when you put your hand in wet cement and it's there forever," she explains. She exaggerates her words so she sounds exasperated. But her smirk betrays her.

She's not as tough as she tries to be.

"I *know*," I say, drawing out the words the same way she did. "So am I."

She doesn't answer right away. Just blinks up at me.

I know that look. She's trying to find a hint of insincerity. But there isn't one.

"I don't do that," she finally breathes. "I don't have that kind of personality."

"Is that so? What kind of personality do you have, then?"

"A bad one," she claims. No other explanation.

"Okay." I let her have that thought for herself.

They're her feelings, not mine. I shouldn't try to change them.

But I will tell her my opinion.

"You think you have a bad personality. But I don't. I like it," I begin. "Maybe you're just afraid that someone might see those good parts. Like I do."

"You're a softie."

She laughs, but it wobbles in the middle.

I know she doesn't want reassurance. She wants to stop feeling empty.

No matter how hard I fight though, she has to make up her own mind. To try. To let me in. Anyone in.

"I'm okay with being soft. So are freshly baked chocolate-chip cookies," I grin. "And everybody loves them."

Her eyes roll back in her head, and she feigns annoyance.

"Did I mention that you're also a pain?"

"You love me," I say. But I don't want to hear her deny it, so I turn towards the grill and flick on the propane.

The flame catches with a soft *whoosh*. I stare at it like it's more interesting than it is.

Behind me, I hear Nora getting to her feet and moving closer to where I stand.

She's quiet. She's thinking. It gives me a beat to think too.

"You haven't changed much, ya know." My voice comes out louder than I want.

I grab the tongs and start rearranging nothing. Scrap pieces of aluminum foil and leftover bits of wood from my meat-smoking phase.

"You don't think so?" she answers. "I think we both have. In our own way."

I haven't been able to get much out of Nora since the creek, and this information dump is feeling a little overwhelming.

So why do I keep initiating the questions?

Maybe I want her to say she's the same girl who used to forget to feed my Neopets when I went on vacation, or that I'd still be in her top five on MySpace.

That her MSN Messenger status was a cryptic lyric about her secret crush. Better yet, maybe she'd say that crush was me.

Maybe I want her to say she's not that person at all. That she doesn't love me. That she never did.

I don't know which would be more painful.

It's not until I feel the silence stretching around us that I realize I've said the majority of that out loud.

The nostalgic part. Not the part about being her crush.

"My messenger status was a lyric from that Snow Patrol song—the one you hated," she says.

The melody to *Chasing Cars* immediately begins playing in my head.

"The one from that *One Tree Hill* episode? Ugh. Why are we friends again?"

"I guess… some things just stick," she considers, and bites the inside of her cheek.

"Indeed," is all I can manage. If I let myself say more, I won't forgive myself.

Instead, I pivot to the most injurious topic I can think of. Dating.

"So, anyone special back in Portland? Someone waiting for you to make a grand re-entrance?" I ask.

I pray the answer is no. Please, don't be in love with someone else.

Her cheeks turn red and she looks at the ground. "There was someone," she murmurs. "But it didn't work out."

I nod, pretending it's neutral information. Like the response has no effect on me and my lungs don't feel like collapsing.

"He wasn't the one, then?"

Nora shakes her head. "Definitely not the one," she confirms.

"Not as handsome as me, huh?" I joke. I do it to preserve myself. Not because it's funny.

"He was emotion-phobic? I guess that's what you'd call it."

"So, what you're saying is, he was Jack and you were Rose… In the end, you let him go?"

Titanic reference. Classic.

But she goes silent and hugs herself around the shoulders.

"Oh gosh, Goose. He broke up with you?" I say, but I don't expect a reply. "What a jerk. I shouldn't have asked. I'm sorry."

"It is what it is," she responds. But that's not a real answer.

"Do you want to talk about it?"

"There isn't anything to say, really. He said he wanted space. That we weren't headed in the same direction. That I was two different people."

"Two different people? What does that mean?" I probe.

"I don't know." She puts her hands palm up and shrugs. "I guess I just wasn't what he needed."

That's when something inside me snaps.

"What *he* needed? What about what *you* need?"

I'm trying to keep my composure, but I'm already fired up.

"What about it? I don't even know what I need, El. Probably more psych meds and a straitjacket at this point," she sighs.

"Nora, you really don't give yourself enough credit. You deserve way more than some grown-up version of Sawyer Collins."

"Hey, he was nice!" she squeals.

"Nice? Nor, he had the personality of a dead fish. And whoever this guy is that let you leave Portland— I can guarantee he was worthless too."

"You can't make that call. Not just like that." She's defending him. This dimwit who didn't know what he had with her. How good it could've been.

"I can actually. Just like that," I shout. "I can," I say again, softer. "You know why? Because you're not like everyone else. You never have been. You're not the imitation, Goose. You're the collector's-edition. You don't just throw that away."

Her mouth opens like she's about to argue, but nothing comes out.

The flame on the grill flickers.

"I'm not a collector's-edition," she says finally. But her voice is soft. Uncertain.

"You are," I insist. "Limited run. One of one."

She doesn't answer. Just looks at me like she's trying to memorize the moment. Like maybe, for the first time in a long time, she feels seen.

Track 28

Broken Hearted Girl

(Nora's Version)

Friday, May 21, 2010

Dear Journal,

It's been two weeks since prom and I still can't bring myself to do more than shove my hoodie on and shuffle from class to class like I'm one of the doped-up band kids.

I avoid eye contact with everyone. I escape even the possibility of conversations.

There's still glitter on the hardwood floor of the gym. Girls still reliving every moment in their hallway chatter.

Meanwhile, I'm a ghost of the person I was before that night. A shell of the girl I was before I knew the cruelty of a boy.

I still haven't told my parents what happened.

They probably wouldn't have believed it anyway. So, I've resolved to just get through graduation and move on.

Elliott and I have barely spoken.

The Monday after prom, he left a box of stuff I stashed in his locker on my front porch.

No note. Nothing.

Just a box of us.

Ready to be buried.

I tried to form the questions I wanted answers to…

Why? That was the most pressing one.

But, deep down, I know why. Because I broke him like a promise the moment I let Alexander put his hands on me—at that first dance.

Maybe even before that. When he was charming my parents with false modesty at the country club. When I was letting him borrow my AP Chem notes, trying to be nice.

And then I lost the one real thing I'd ever known. Elliott.

I'm not sure if he even knows what really happened that night. Maybe he doesn't need to.

I don't want him like a best friend, ya know?

I want our secret moments in crowded rooms.

For him call my name, and for everything to just stop.

The first entry I opened to tonight when I absentmindedly flipped through the high school journal Elliott had refashioned for me.

I don't think he made it this far into his reading. Now I hesitate to ever come clean and address what happened. How could we talk about it without displacing the scabs that have grown thick over the injuries?

Sitting on my window seat back then and writing all my feelings down only ever led me to two conclusions.

First, I was damaged goods.

Second, Elliott was the only guy for me.

For years, the incident from that night in 2010 followed me around. Hid behind corners and stepped out of the shadows when I thought I was finally allowed to be happy.

Late in the night, when Portland was asleep, my mind always drifted back to Moonridge. Back to Elliott. But, by then, enough time had passed that I figured he wasn't waiting around for me anymore. If he ever was.

How could I show up and reiterate the feelings I'd only ever told the pages of a journal and expect him to accept them?

My love was frozen in inky words on pages meant for my eyes only.

Even without seeing the journal itself, I could've recited it from memory.

Those memories are what drove me to ask for Xanax to be prescribed to me. So the panic would stop. So the anxiety could end.

But it all took a turn when I started to experience extreme irritability on top of my depression and nervousness. Suicidal thoughts dominated my mind. I was a slave to chewing over every action or inaction that might have led to my overwhelming worthlessness.

It wasn't just that night.

The panic and sadness had been living in me long before prom—before Alexander, before Elliott stopped speaking to me.

That night was just the match.

Everything else—the loneliness, the self-doubt, the ache I couldn't name—had already been soaked in gasoline.

It didn't ignite all at once.

It flickered, flared, and finally caught.

Not a beginning. Just a breaking point.

By the time I landed in the hospital, the fire had already been burning for years. Prom just gave it oxygen.

That's why I missed Mark and Lisa's funerals. But no one knows that it was because of the downward spiral of a high school kid who should've known who not to dance with.

And now that same kid is heartbroken over the same boy all over again.

Track 29

I Wish I Was Normal

(Nora's Version)

My Spotify account is mocking me.

My top three recommended mixes are currently as follows—

— The Playlist I Made Instead of Texting You
— Love Songs That Ruined Me
— Lo-fi That Sounds Like His Smile

I scroll, looking for a playlist that looks a little safer.

There's one called Feel Good Fever Dream.

Sounds good to me.

I press play without looking down, and slide my headphones on.

Soon, the familiar beat of *I Think I'm In Love With You* pounds in my ears. Jessica Simpson's voice is so sugary, I grind my teeth against the sound. Like I'm chewing glassy sugar shards.

I resist the urge to spit.

Right now, the sweetness feels heavy. Cotton candy spun from purl—thin, metallic, and impossible to swallow.

And when she sings about her mind being blown by one look in his eyes, I think I might heave.

I yank the headphones off and toss them onto the bed.

I just got home from work half an hour ago. Early-bird shift. Which means the rest of the day to myself.

But the fan in this apartment still isn't fixed, and we're getting closer to July.

I'm not in the mood for swimming, even though I broke down and bought a swimsuit.

The library doesn't have any books on my wishlist. Not even the sad ones.

Coupled with the love songs that are played on the jukebox at The Bent Spoon for hours on end and the fact that even my music choices when I'm off the clock aren't cooperating, I'm bored.

The kind of boredom that feels like a symptom.

I check my pill bottles. I've only got enough to make it to the end of the week.

My doctor is just a phone call away and I know getting my prescriptions sent to the pharmacy down the street won't be a problem.

It's the act of calling. The hassle of it. The necessity.

I wish I was normal.

Not *better*. Just less… complicated. Less maintenance.

I stare at the bottles again. At how the small white pills in each of them look so similar when, my psychiatrist promises me, they do very different things.

It's not fair. That I'm cursed with a disease no one can see. That I can't explain.

It'd be easier if I just had a broken limb. Those heal. You come back stronger.

When it comes to me, the list of broken parts gets longer all the time.

— Broken personality
— Broken brain
— Broken heart

I could probably list more, if I let myself.

Maybe I'll ask for the list to be included in my eulogy. That way, all of the people who thought I was just a difficult person to be around—too hard to be friends with, a nightmare to live with—might finally understand.

If they even hear it.

I'm sure they'll all be too busy to go out and buy something black last minute to come say goodbye.

Even if they did, they'd demand blood.

Not closure. Not comfort. Just proof.
Proof that I was as mad as they all said. Proof that they had good reason for their judgment. For their preconceived notions.

I told you so, they'd whisper. *I told you so.*

As if my mother heard my intrusive thoughts and wanted to contribute to the conversation, my phone chimed. New message alert.

Lunch tomorrow? If you're not too busy.

If I'm not too busy…

I feel like asking what that is supposed to mean. What she thinks I'm occupying my time with when she wasn't selling me on intermittent fasting. When she isn't telling me to smile more because I'm "so much prettier" when I do.

I don't have the energy for this today.

I'm right across the road.

She brings Elliott meals and patches the holes in his pants. But has she ever bothered to walk into the backyard and see how *I'm* doing? To check if I'm getting along alright, or just to have a mother-daughter chat?

No.

Have she or my father ever asked about my schedule at the diner so that they could come in for lunch and visit me hard at work?

Again, no.

I wasn't raised like Elliott. By people who championed me and wanted me to use my intelligence for the good of humanity—even if the humanity was mine. Parents who hung on my every word and kissed my forehead when I did something good.

Doing something good in my family was always just reason for them to say, *do better.*

I'm not jealous of him. Just living in a constant state of grief.

Getting robbed of your childhood will do that.

On the outside, we looked like the portrait of a family, living the dream. A JCPenney photo of the three of us hung squarely above the mantle at my house. Next to other photos of the so-called happy memories we shared.

Updated year after year.

We looked healthy. Happy. The model family.

But on the inside, it was World War III.

Love is complicated. Love is messy.

But how would I know? I never really had it.

I move swiftly down the stairs and beyond Elliott's truck. Hoofing it down the driveway at record-speed.

Headed nowhere fast. I'm pretty good at that.

"Whoa, Goose! Where's the fire?" Elliott gasps as we collided on the sidewalk.

I huff out an angry sigh.

I don't want him in my way. Looking too tall, too tanned, too perfectly Elliott.

I want to dissolve into a puddle and evaporate into the sky.

He blinks, puts his hands on my shoulders, and leans closer—until we were face to face.

"What's going on?" he tries again.

I start twirling a strand of hair around my finger and look away.

"Just got a lot on my mind," I say.

"Doesn't sound like anything a charming young man like myself can't fix," he smiles. It's dazzling. "I'm just getting in from my run. Let me take a shower and then, I've got an idea."

My eyebrows nearly meet my forehead. I'm skeptical. But diffused.

I eye him warily.

This could either be very good, or very bad.

"Trust me, you'll like it," he says, and sprints toward the house.

I watch him disappear into it, all sunlit limbs and easy promises.

I don't trust easy these days. But this is different. Elliott is different.

So I sit on the stairs of the porch and wait.

I hear the metallic groan of the shower turning on echo through the house, and watch dandelion seed heads scatter across the lawn.

Somewhere inside, over the sound of rushing water, Elliott is singing a Morgan Wallen song.

I always swore country music was the death of culture. But he doesn't sound half bad.

I close my eyes and let the sun warm my face.

Maybe, just this once, I can be the exception to the rule. I can be here, and I can be happy.

Track 30

I Don't Wanna Be Safe

(Elliott's Version)

Seeing Nora sit on my front porch steps is like hearing my favorite song for the first time, and knowing it'll live in my head forever.

My favorite song is *Wonderwall*.

I know—it's cliché.

But right now, in a babydoll dress and Doc Martens, she looks like the kind of girl who *could* save someone. And maybe, if I'm lucky, it's me.

The afternoon is just beginning to bloom and it's one of those rare Ohio days that doesn't feel perpetually overcast. It hasn't rained in a week, and the grass is already starting to turn brown. Funny how quickly things fade here. Grass. Plans. People.

I'll probably perish here. Nora? I'm not so sure.

Nora and I have wanted to get out of Moonridge Creek since we were nine. From the first time we saw the difference between our tiny world and the great big one we hadn't even begun to understand.

And standing here now—in the light of a beautiful Midwestern morning—I feel the shadow of the first time I couldn't protect her.

September 11, 2001, was a turning point. For us. For everyone.

And it was certainly the first time our generation had seen unprecedented times affect us personally—our families, the economy, our sense of safety. The collective trauma settled around us like fallen stars.

I guess those feelings never really left.

We were at school when it happened. Our class was preparing to learn decimals. Though Nora was busy perfecting the folds of her cootie catcher so that later she could tell me my fortune was to marry Jessica Biel.

Her mom was deep in a *7th Heaven* phase.

It was a typical Tuesday. Until it wasn't.

Our teachers tried to stay calm. Tried to keep us from seeing the fear in their eyes, the tremble in their hands. Tried to reassure us that the police showing up at the school was just a routine check.

But, when my parents arrived too, I knew something wasn't right.

My mom's cheeks were tear-stained when I got to the principal's office, and the creases in my dad's forehead were deeper than I'd ever seen.

It wasn't like them to seem so burdened. To be so stoic.

"What about Nora?" I asked when they told me they were taking me home.

Where you'll be safe, they said.

But I didn't want to be safe. I wanted to be with her.

"Can't you just ask if she can come with us?" I pleaded.

"Nora's parents aren't here, son." My dad placed a hand on my shoulder. "She's not our kid. I don't know if there's much we can do."

My parents shared a knowing look and my dad wandered over to the secretary's desk. The two of them started speaking in hushed tones and I got the very distinct feeling the news wasn't going to be good.

"Don't be too upset if Nora can't come with us," my mom soothed. "She's a brave girl. Smart. I know she'll be okay."

It was meant to make me feel better. To give me comfort. Make me trust.

All it really did was confirm to me that Nora was going to be left behind.

I watched as my dad's shoulders sank and he thanked the secretary, still whispering.

Adults always made it seem like whispering kept volatile things contained. Like silence made it easier to pretend.

"Unfortunately, Nora has to stay at school, Elliott. We aren't her guardians. I'm sorry."

I'm sorry. Sorry wasn't enough.

Sorry wasn't going to explain to Nora why I left her in the classroom and never came back.

It wouldn't make her feel less abandoned. Less anxious. More secure.

I'll never forget the guilt I felt—or the way I excused myself from the dinner table that night.

Images of planes, skyscrapers toppling like the LEGO towers their children built, and clouds of black smoke—those were the terrors that plagued adults that day. And for years after.

But I was kept up that night by the horror of leaving Nora behind.

I didn't see her for three days after that.

Three days I spent wondering if she felt like I'd betrayed her.

That Saturday morning, she shuffled over in her pajamas, clutching her sapphire build-a-bear and a worn VHS of *Little Giants*.

The relief in my chest was instant.

I wanted to tell her how sorry I was. How much I had wanted her to leave with me.

How no amount of begging my parents would've made a difference.

I wanted to say, *the school rules are stupid.*

But we never talked about it.

The silence became a pact.

And she doesn't know it but, I still have that VHS tape.

Faded label. Cracked case. It's a relic.

It was planted like a seed inside me, and it had grown—into an entire forest of similar moments.

The kind of invasive species that took root anywhere it pleased.

Some days, I feel more memory than man.

"Why are you looking at me like that?"

Nora's voice cuts through my thoughts.

"Oh, um... I was just thinking about how little summer is left," I say. "Do you think you'll stay? After it's over?"

She tenses and her gaze drifts to the porch swing.

"I-I haven't really thought about it. I should probably be on my way back to Portland by then. I guess I'm just... buying some time right now."

Go ahead. Break my heart again. I'll still be here.

"We'd better get going," I reply.

The keys jingle as I grab them off the hook by the door.

I'm not getting into this right now.

Apparently, neither is she, because the entire drive through town is quiet.

She stares out the window, braiding and re-braiding a section of her hair.

Like she's trying to keep her hands busy. To keep her heart from tumbling out of her mouth.

By the time we pull into the parking lot of Bass & B-Sides, the best record store in the surrounding area, I can't handle the silence anymore.

"Can I ask you a question?"

She turns to me, expression unreadable.

I press on.

"Do you ever just relax?" I ask.

She frowns and narrows her eyes in disapproval.

"You don't know the answer to that already?" she shoots back.

"I mean, the answer is plainly no. But can you just try? For *me*?"

I bat my eyelashes and stick my bottom lip out. Pouting is not beneath me.

She rolls her eyes. She always does. But her mouth twitches.

"You're incorrigible," she says.

"No debate," I confirm. "But I've got better taste in music than you."

"Prove it," she says.

"Oh, I plan to, Goose. Don't you worry."

Walking up to the store, Nora pushes open the door. The smell of vinyl and incense hits us, and I can tell she's feeling nostalgic. She takes a deep breath.

I hope, when she lets it out, she feels like she's gotten her girlhood back.

Track 31

Mad & Lucid

(Nora's Version)

Monday, June 29, 2026

Dear Wendy,

Dare I say, Moonridge is growing on me?

Not like climbing roses or decorative clematis. But like English ivy or Spanish moss.

It's wrapping around my cracked foundation. Draping itself over limbs in the landscape of my mind.

I'd never tell Elliott, though.

I can tell he's getting used to me being here.

He shouldn't.

In fact, I need to start planning my departure.

I would use the word escape, but it doesn't seem to fit anymore.

I don't want my leaving to feel the same this time.
At least not where he's concerned.

I'm not sure if things will ever be the same between us, but, right now, they're better than I ever expected.

Walking back into his life—willingly—wasn't something I thought I'd ever have the chance to do.

But he extended his hand.

I think I'm finally starting to reach back.

To meet him in the middle.

Maybe we don't have to talk about what happened all those years ago.

Maybe we don't have to talk about why I left.

Maybe we can avoid bringing up Alexander Woodruff ever again.

That's the only way I know how to keep things from unraveling.

Yesterday, when we went to Bass and B-Sides—for the first time in ages—I was carried back to senior year.

The good part of it.

The part that didn't hurt to think about.

Elliott still couldn't convince me that he has better taste in music. But hunting through the stacks of vinyl and rows of cassettes was like a treasure hunt.

At any moment, I thought I might look up and see the eighteen-year-old Elliott staring back.

That I'd see the red and black color of his varsity jacket hanging over his shoulder.

His wavy hair falling onto his forehead the way it used to.

That impossible grin on his face.

The memory was clear.

But I was just watching it.

It felt too risky to try and grab it—to have it the way I used to.

After Elliott insisted on paying for my Fleetwood Mac record and the NOW 1997 CD, we went to Piggyback Saloon.

It's weird seeing adult Elliott drink.

Even just beers at his house.

We weren't really party-goers in high school. It was more like him to be playing Grand Theft Auto on the weekends, than to be chugging a keg.

And my parents didn't allow me to go to any high school parties where there weren't parents as chaperones.

Everyone knew that.

Eventually, I just stopped getting invited altogether.

I feel like I wouldn't have been able to relax at one of those parties anyway. Just like I can't relax now.

Elliott called me out about that yesterday.

It was casually affronting. But it seared my pride.

I don't do passive-aggressive.

It's one or the other.

At least it was with my parents.

I pause writing and glance at the time.

Speaking of parents, my day's final entry says.

My mom is probably already waiting for me to join her at lunch.

Lend me some pixie dust.

I'll need it.

I stare in the mirror at myself, tapping in the concealer dotted on my under eyes with my fingertips.

In my head, I can already hear my mother.

Telling me how tired I look.

How uncivilized it is for me to work at a diner.

To befriend the daughter of an addict.

She'll bring up my living arrangements again, no doubt.

She might even break out some Prosecco when I tell her I'm heading back to Portland soon.

But not yet.

I have a few things to finish first.

It's been a long time since the last time we had lunch together—just the two of us.

Since we've done *anything* together, alone, actually.

On the way to the restaurant—Cornelia's Garden—my palms are sweating.

It's the fanciest place to eat in a forty-mile radius.

White tablecloths. Linen napkins.

Dishes like beet salad with goat cheese and pistachios.

We'd come here to celebrate every special occasion growing up.

As if, when we were in public, we were the typical American family.

My mom probably viewed it as a rebellion that I worked at The Bent Spoon. Serving tater tots and onion rings to off-duty truck drivers with ketchup stains on my apron.

The thought that she might feel insulted by my work ethic being applied to plating fried foods and ice cream sundaes made me giggle—quietly, to myself.

As I'm escorted to the main dining room and approach the table, she rises but doesn't move to embrace me.

Once was enough.

That was over a month ago.

I'm just her daughter.

No big deal.

I notice Prosecco, already chilling in the ice bucket next to her.

What a coincidence.

"Sit, Nora."

She says it like I'm a dog.

An animal, trained to obey.

No objection. No resistance.

I sit.

"Would you like some Prosecco?" she offers.

It's too polite.

"Uh, sure," I reply. "What are we celebrating?"

"Celebrating?" she muses. As if the beverage choice isn't calculated.

As if this overly orchestrated lunch isn't an elaborate scheme.

"Yeah. It's not every day we come to Cornelia's Garden and have lunch, Mom," I say. "Is there something special going on?"

"Something *special* has to be going on for me to want to have a nice meal with my daughter?"

We blink at each other.

She's taunting me.

"What can I get you ladies?" a voice asks.

The server doesn't detect the emotional undercurrent.

The overwhelming effort my mother is putting forth.

"We'll have two bowls of French-onion soup with side salads," my mother answers.

"What type of dressing?"

"Vinaigrette."

She didn't even let me order my own food?

"Soup, Mom? It's ninety degrees out," I say.

"Also, I'll have ranch dressing, please," I tell the server.

"Very good," he nods, and disappears behind the heavy curtain that separates the two dining areas.

"Nora, do you realize what the fat content of ranch dressing is?" my mother sighs.

She clucks like a disapproving hen, shaking her head at her straying chick.

"Honestly, Mom, I don't care." I catch myself mid-eye-roll.

"Don't use that tone with me, Nora."

"Can you just tell me what this lunch is all about?"

She sighs again.

I'm losing patience. Fast.

"Your father and I want to help you," she begins. "You're living in a garage apartment, working ungodly hours at that diner… you're obviously not taking care of yourself."

"What does *that* mean? I'm doing just fine," I refute.

"Have you seen the shadows under your eyes, honey? You look so tired."

Called it.

I don't respond.

"What I'm saying is, we want to give you a chance to start over. We found some nice apartments in Portland online, and you're all set to meet with the rental manager next week."

"What? I didn't even say when I was planning to leave yet!" I exclaim.

"Nora…" her voice softens. "It's time."

"Time for what exactly?"

She shifts slightly and retrieves a crisp white envelope from her purse.

She pushes it across the table toward me.

"What is it?" I ask, suspicious.

"It's the opportunity for something new. Open it," she urges.

Hesitantly, I take the envelope.

It's unsealed.

I'm reluctant, but I take a look inside anyway.

Staring back at me is a check for five thousand dollars.

And a plane ticket.

CLE > PDX

Tomorrow afternoon.

"You're… buying me off?"

It's a relocation package.

A severance.

A rebranding of my life.

My stomach drops.

Not because I'm surprised.

I'm not.

Nothing surprises me anymore.

"Don't act like you don't need it," she says as our salads arrive.

I watch as she fluffs the lettuce with her fork and mixes the dressing like it's a ritual.

She puts the homemade garlic bread that comes with it to the side.

Of course. Too many carbs.

"I'm *not* taking this," I say firmly.

"Don't be ridiculous. Of course you are."

I recoil at the suggestion that my integrity has a price.

That I can be paid to slip away silently.

"Why do you want me to leave so badly?" I demand.

"We don't *want* you to leave, sweetheart. But things are…complicated for you here."

"Or is my being here complicated for *you*?" I shoot back.

"Nora, don't do this. You're an adult. Now it's time to act like one," she says, setting down the fork. "Living in Elliott's backyard? Really? Haven't you considered how that makes him look? As a respected member of the community? A teacher? The football coach?"

"I've considered that people need to keep their mouth shut," I charge forward. "In fact, I'm thinking that the only people really concerned with how things *look* here, are you and dad," I reply, through gritted teeth.

"We're concerned about you. Everyone is."

"Who is everyone?"

"Hon', people see you walking around town. And with that addict's daughter? You really need to consider your image. Our image," she responds.

"Image?" I scoff. "You *do* realize that by saying it's an image you are admitting that our whole lives—what we've portrayed to everyone, all our friends, for years—isn't real, right?"

"Personal appearances are *very* real."

"And, apparently, so is bribing your own daughter."

I stand from the table and set the envelope down in front of her.

There are no words for how I feel right now.

"This is appalling," I state, steady and clear. "I'll be staying. Indefinitely."

With that, I storm out of the restaurant—leaving her with her mouth gaping, her salad uneaten, and her payoff returned.

But my integrity?

It's at an all-time high.

Track 32

Showgirl Energy

(Elliott's Version)

July is for lovers.

At least that's what the banner across Main Street says.

It has every summer since I can remember.

Fireworks, picnics, lake dates, outdoor concerts.

All made for you to spend with the person you can't live without.

Moonridge Creek even dedicated an entire festival to the idea.

It was colorful and loud, and it reeked of funnel cakes and corn dogs.

I went once.

With a woman named Cassie. Cassandra.

She had curly red hair that refused to be tamed.

Pale skin that burned the moment she stepped outside.

A bashful smile. A nervous laugh.

We dated for four months.

I won her a stuffed monkey at one of the carnival games.

She wouldn't touch it because she was a self-declared germophobe.

Apparently, the monkey with Velcro hands was a breeding ground for bacteria.

And, she claimed, it shed microplastics.

She didn't want to inhale them.

That's when I knew. We weren't soulmates.

The evening ended on a park bench.

Me, trying to explain our obvious differences.

Her, sobbing her way through a bucket of caramel corn.

The more I talked, the redder her eyes got.

I started counting the pauses between her sniffles, like they were seconds ticking toward the end.

A side effect of noticing too much.

This year, I was gearing up for a special event I was much more excited about.

July 30th is International Friendship Day.

Nora and I used to use it as our unofficial anniversary.

Every year, without fail.

We even exchanged gifts.

One time she bought me a *Jaws* T-shirt and made me watch every Richard Dreyfuss movie she could find.

Another year—the last one—I gave her a collage.

Ticket stubs, doodles, scraps of us I'd saved without meaning to.

I hoped she'd hang it in her dorm.

So she wouldn't forget about me when we were on opposite coasts.

Nora was supposed to go to USC and study screenwriting. Become the next great writer and follow in the footsteps of her namesake.

But I heard she withdrew her tuition a week before classes started.

Suddenly, I realize that I've been staring at the same page in my book for the last twenty minutes.

And I'm holding it upside down.

Of course I am.

"Afternoon, Elliott," comes a voice from the lawn.

Tommy, Nora's dad, is making his way to the porch. I haven't seen him in a few weeks.

My visits to their house have thinned out since I realized he wasn't just strict. He was a dictator.

"You got time for a quick one-on-one?" he asks.

"What's on your mind, sir?" I ask.

I've never called Tommy *sir* in my life. I do it now, not out of respect for him—out of respect for Nora. It's a delicate balance.

There's distance between them now. And I'm trying to honor both without igniting the flame.

Growing up, Tommy was just another picture-perfect—yet rigid—dad in the neighborhood. He was stern and had a long list of rules he expected his daughter to follow. But he never came across as cruel.

Now, I wasn't so sure.

Back then, I thought his structure was love.

Curfews meant he cared. Chores meant he believed in responsibility.

Even the way he monitored Nora's outfits—I chalked up to fatherly concern.

But lately, it feels as if it was less like guidance and more like surveillance.

Even now, it seems he's still trying to parent a version of her that doesn't exist anymore.

Then again, maybe I'm trying to hang on to that same version.

"I was hoping we could talk about something we both care about," he says next. "Nora."

"I'm not sure I want to discuss anything about Nora without her being here too, if I'm honest," I reply.

"Oh, Elliott. Don't think I don't know what's going on here," he continues. "I know how much you love

Nora. So does Cindy. How you'd do just about anything for her—am I right?"

"I don't think Nora needs me to do much. She's pretty set on being independent."

"Independence is overrated for a girl like her," he states.

"I'm not sure I get your meaning, sir."

"She needs you to do something for her that she'd never ask you to do herself, son," he explains. "She needs you to let her go."

My brows furrow. My mouth goes dry.

I stand and walk to the edge of the steps so he can't get past me even if he does climb them.

"Let her go?"

I stammer, but he doesn't flinch.

"We both want what's best for her, Elliott. For heaven's sake, I know you've been pining for her and hoping she'd notice since you were kids," he shakes his head. "But I think we both know that you were too impulsive for her back then. And you have such a good thing going on in Moonridge now. What about that principal—Miss Sorrell? I thought you were giving that a chance."

"Jessica and I only work together," I say dryly.

"Could really be something though. I wouldn't give up on it."

"I haven't," I assure him. "Because I never saw it as an option in the first place."

"Don't sell yourself short. Besides, I don't think Nora's gonna be around much longer. From what I understand Cindy went to meet her for lunch and talk about her plans for heading back to Portland," he tells me.

The words hit me like a bag of bricks.

"Nora's…leaving?"

"Mmhmm…probably sooner than you think," is all he gets out before Nora comes striding up the sidewalk.

She kicks the neighbor's trash can and hits my mailbox flag with a stick. She looks frenzied and miserable.

Then she sees her dad. And it's just anger.

Tommy turns to walk away. Back to the house, I'm sure. Off to hide behind his ego and whatever instigation he thinks passes for parenting.

Nora seethes. "Here to gloat?"

"I was just telling Elliott that some parting words may be in order," Tommy says to her.

"Parting words? Because you tried to incentivize my leaving, you mean?" she says, glaring.

"Don't be dramatic, Nora. Getting all bent out of shape isn't going to change the facts. It's just time to close the curtain on this little hiatus from real life."

"Hiatus from real life? You think I'm just taking a break? That I've got my feet up, eating bonbons all day?" she replies.

I can see the effort it takes for her to physically restrain herself. She probably wants to run right now.

Nora is very anti-confrontation. I haven't seen her stand up to anyone since kindergarten—when a kid stole the burnt sienna crayon she needed to finish a picture. She shoved him and he ended up with a broken nose after face-planting into a desk.

"What exactly is going on?" I ask into the void between them.

I'm thoroughly confused at this point, but equally worried that Nora might break her dad's nose too.

The look on her face says, *Try me*.

"Do you want to explain?" she nods to her dad. "Oh wait—you'd probably just lie to preserve yourself. So,

I'll do it. I'll explain, for the entire neighborhood to hear, how you bought me a plane ticket and signed a check because you thought erasing me would be *that* easy," she bellows.

Her voice echoes down the block. Ricocheting off porch lights and picket fences.

"You didn't…" I whisper behind Tommy.

I come down the porch steps and stand behind Nora, close but careful.

I place a hand on her back—steady and supportive.

She doesn't falter.

"You thought if you handed me an envelope—a way out without having to earn it—I'd disappear."

Her voice is like a scalpel.

Precise. Surgical. Unforgiving.

"I'd quit embarrassing you, and mom, and you'd have something else to hold over my head," she goes on.

"We just want you to start living responsibly. Is that so much to ask?" Tommy replies.

The look in his eyes says more than his words.

They are cold. Calculating.

Oozing Machiavellian pragmatism.

"You're not *asking* anything," she points out. "You're *forcing* your way, as usual." She pauses, just long enough for the weight to settle. "And I'm done."

I'm proud of her.

This Nora.

The Nora taking control of her circumstances.

The one deciding what's best for her, instead of being told what that looks like.

Maybe she'll finally wear the black nail polish she was never allowed to.

Maybe she'll get that cartilage piercing like she's always wanted.

Maybe she'll start living like she belongs to herself.

Tommy doesn't respond. He just turns and walks back toward the house, shoulders stiff, hands in his pockets.

Nora doesn't watch him go.

She turns.

And I follow.

Track 33

Not A Phase / Don't Forget

(Nora's Version)

Indefinitely.

How many years is that?

I'm standing in a tattoo parlor with Tania, staring at an incredibly detailed *Terms of Agreement* form.

Getting my cartilage pierced at thirty-three is scarier than I anticipated.

Elliott insisted I do something for myself since I called out my dad last week. Following a similar situation with my mother. Who knew that wanting to erase me from Moonridge would draw two people so close together?

I feel looser since it happened.

Like I can finally stretch my achy joints and sore muscles, without being told I'm doing it wrong.

Originally, I came back to Moonridge hoping my time here would patch the hole in my armor that Grayson put there when he gave up on me like a bad habit. But it turns out, they haven't changed. They probably never will.

That realization—and the obvious toxicity they've fostered into my life—left me with no choice but to be extreme. No choice but to say I'd be staying for the foreseeable future. No choice but to choose me.

When I told Tania what happened the next day when we met up at the mall, she looked at me with wide eyes and crossed arms for the first five minutes. The rest of the time she appeared to be plotting how to commit arson without it tying back to her. If my parents' house burns down in the middle of the night one of these days, I'll know exactly who to ask.

"I think you should get the bumblebee one," Tania says beside me.

"Why?" I wrinkle my nose. I still haven't signed the form.

Procrastination is a skill.

"Because…you sting like a bee. Like Muhammad Ali." She grins and puts up her fists like a boxer.

I laugh and it sounds jubilant.

Triumphant.

Like I'm more myself now than I have ever been.

"Maybe I'll just do the butterfly," I say. "It's…cute."

"It's *safe*," Tania whines. "How about the skull and crossbones?"

"Or something that doesn't advertise that I'm dead inside," I joke.

I can tell the inside isn't as hollow as it used to be. There might even be a little bit of hope blooming in there.

"Which one do you think Coach would like more?" Tania asks.

"Does it matter?"

"Isn't he the one who said you should do this?" She tilts her head. "You should've asked him to come."

I glance at her, surprised. "He's probably busy."

"I bet he's fun. More fun than he seems when he's yelling on the football field."

"Ha. I guess he has you fooled then," I huff.

"Have you told him yet?"

"Told me what?"

Elliott's voice comes from the doorway, like Tania summoned him herself. Only I remember that *I'm* the one that texted him where I would be.

It's disrupting. Grounding. Maybe even slightly comforting.

But he's already seen me in a state of flux—always in motion—during this entire trip. I'm not sure I can stay still enough for him to see me for what I am now.

It's like my identity is finally crystallizing and I'm afraid of being stuck in whatever his perception is.

Come to think of it, I don't even know what it is.

"Oh, nothing," I panic. "We were just talking about what piercing to get."

"Hmm…" He rubs his chin. "I'd be a forward helix man myself. But it looks like you came with the real expert." He nods at Tania and flashes her a smile—more friend than former educator.

I watch her visibly melt.

Tania has an entire row of small silver hoops cascading down her right ear and a constellation of other piercings on the left. This tattoo parlor, she said, is the only one she trusts to not give me an infection.

I nodded when she told me. Like that settled it.

Now, I'm not sure I should be here.

"When you said you were actually going through with it, I figured I'd swing by," he shrugs, stepping up beside me like it's no big deal. "Make sure you didn't pass out or something."

I scribble my name on the signature line before the doubt can creep in.

Handing the clipboard back to the receptionist and reaching for my wallet to pay for the hole about to be punctured in my upper ear, I glance down and see it. The perfect earring. A design that encompasses everything I am transforming into.

After my choice is confirmed, I'm led through the salon to a narrow space in the back. It's not so much an actual room as a makeshift station—needles of varying sizes, cotton swabs, and Q-tips. In the center is a client chair with an adjustable headrest and footrests.

Let's get this over with.

Once the curtain is drawn and I'm lying back in the chair, the body piercer begins surveying the terrain of my ear.

There's no roof to this space. No door either.

I can hear everything.

The buzz of the tattoo machines, the snore of a client who's getting his fiftieth tattoo, and Tania chattering to Elliott about the latest recipe she came up with.

She's prattling on about how she wants to attend the culinary arts program at Stark State this fall. But every dime she's made has gone to keeping the lights on at home. Her mom is in the middle of a relapse. Her little brother is only eleven. When she's working at the diner, he stays with the neighbor—eating snack cakes and watching cable TV.

I admire Tania for not being ashamed of her life. For accepting things as they come. For letting go when it's time.

She's learning those lessons young. It'll serve her well when she gets where she's going.

She's meant for bigger things than Moonridge.

"How long have you and Nora been friends?" I hear her ask.

"Oh, thirty years, give or take, I guess," he estimates.

"You *guess*? You don't know?" she presses.

"We kinda…lost touch for a while," he explains.

"I'll bet you're glad she's back now. And that she's staying."

"I think it's more about whether Nora is glad about it."

"True. But it seems like you guys make a good team," she says.

"Ya think?" he chuckles. "I do too. We always have. In fact, she's the reason I'm a teacher. And coach too, really."

I gasp. More because of what he says than the pressure on my ear.

"Did she encourage you to chase your passion?"

"Well, yeah. But it was more than that," he starts. "When we were kids, Nora would stand in my backyard and run fake drills with me, watch all my favorite sports movies and games. She cheered when I cheered, yelled when I yelled…and when the team lost, she would throw a fit like me too."

Tania laughs at this.

The image of Elliott throwing a fit over a particularly painful loss resurfaces.

"But when I got into college on a football scholarship, I was terrified," he adds.

"Why? Didn't you think you were good enough?"

"It's not that I didn't have talent. But I knew talent wouldn't last forever. I had to have something to fall back on."

"So, what did you do?"

I can tell Tania is hanging on his every word.

"As you can imagine, I was really stressed out about it. But then I remembered something Nora had told me when we started high school," he paused.

I could hear the emotion in his words. This wasn't just a story he was telling for the sake of it.

It was a core memory. An undeniable truth.

"She had been afraid to go to ninth grade. All the high schoolers seemed so cool and intimidating. But, of course, we went and everything was fine. And after that first day, she turned to me on the walk home, and said, 'El, you're the kind of person who makes other people feel like they matter. You do that for me. I know you do it for other people too, even if they don't say it out loud.'"

"Wow," Tania breathes.

"I know," Elliott chuckles. "Nora has always had her fingerprint on my life. But that day, she made me believe I could leave mine on other people. And I've tried to live up to that every day since."

"All done," the piercer announces.

"Done?"

"Yep. You were so calm and still, it's like nothing ever happened."

I get up from the chair without glancing in the mirror and exit into the main area.

I see Tania and Elliott side-by-side on the wooden, pew-style bench in the entry, laughing together.

And I have a bronze snake winding its way up my ear.

Track 34

Small Town First String

(10 Minute Version)

(Elliott's Version)

Leaning against the wall in this arcade, checking out the girl working the *Mortal Kombat* joystick is very 2010-coded of me.

Just so happens, I'm over thirty and the girl at the gaming cabinet is Nora.

But that's the way it should've been all along.

I've built my life around constancy.

Nora was always a constant.

We didn't need a common denominator.

We were just Elliott and Nora.

A part of me—the part broken by her skipping town after graduation—had always wondered if maybe our two-person club had lasted longer than it should have. If maybe coming back here after college and swallowing the ache was the only way to mourn the loss of the loyalty we once had to each other.

But now—after this summer, after watching her recalibrate herself in real time—I see it.

She's spent years curating herself. To be chosen. To be agreeable. To absorb blame.

The more I revisit what happened at senior prom, the more I understand.

Nora was crying for help.

And I wasn't there to hear her.

And the more that realization takes shape, the more I hope we never have to bring it up.

What we've got now is too fragile. I can't risk shattering it.

I think about the innocence that's colored this summer. How Nora's softened, slowly, like ice cream left out too long—melting into something truer.

How we've stayed up late listening to the *Delilah* radio show like we used to when we were young. Laughing at the first-time callers and mimicking the voices of distraught advice seekers. We've even called in to request cheesy love songs—dedicating them to our exes, like it's all just a joke. But sometimes, I wonder if Nora's listening for something more.

The ice cream truck still makes stops on our street too. On especially hot days, when Nora's off work and I'm bored of working on lesson plans, we chase it down and order our favorites. A strawberry shortcake ice cream bar for Nora, and a firecracker popsicle for me.

I think the only thing we haven't gotten to yet is a hula hooping competition.

I'm convinced these hips still have it.

Nora's unconvinced.

Today is International Friendship Day.

Nora's gift is supposedly arriving later this afternoon.

Mine's still tucked away—I'm too nervous to hand it over just yet.

So, the arcade, with its neon glow and pixelated screens, was my first suggestion to stall.

I'm in it for the coin drops and chaos, and maybe the way she scrunches her nose when she loses. Definitely *not* to see how attractive it is when she scrunches up her face and sticks out her tongue when she's concentrating on a game she already knows she'll lose. And *not* to memorize exactly how gorgeous she looks when she doesn't try.

Because the Nora that's not performing for anyone? That's the one I like best.

I'm honestly surprised I was able to get her to agree to celebrating this year. Especially since I was sure she'd probably forgotten the tradition.

I didn't ask what had become of the collage I made her. Instead, I reframed the day as a celebration—proof that our friendship still held.

Friendship, I'd said. Like I'd never wanted more.

As if what could've been—and what might still be—wasn't quietly devouring every thought.

As if it's not the only thing I'm thinking about right now.

I'm aware I'm hopeless, but when you've only dated a handful of women in over a decade because no one can compare to the one that got away, there's no other way to live.

It's not like I've been marking calendars with red X's for fifteen years.

Still, the number hits harder than I expected.

"You think you're ready to try something other than a katana blade yet?" I ask Nora, breaking free from my musings. "I think Donkey Kong might be more your speed, Goose."

"Shut up," she scowls. Her hand balls into a fist and she aims directly for my right bicep, but I catch her hand in mine mid-swing.

"Okay, okay. Let's not resort to violence," I croon.

"Video games hate me," she says.

"Maybe," I reply, still holding her fist in my hand.

Her fingers are cold. I'm suddenly burning—head to toe, heart to bone.

This is not the first time Nora and I have had physical contact.

My mom even labeled a photo in my baby book as "First Kiss"—me grabbing Nora's face and planting one on her cheek.

I don't remember it. But it's there. A still frame of affection, long before I knew what it meant.

There had been piggyback rides and school dances over the years too. But nothing ever felt like this. Nothing ever made my heart beat so loud it echoed in my ears.

"I'd also like to formally request that you stop trying to beat me up," I say.

She blushes.

"Sorry," she says, pulling her hand back. "I guess we're not kids anymore. Feels more like assault than affection."

My eyes widen.

"Affection, huh?" I say, tilting my head. "Is that what it's been all along?"

But I've struck a nerve and we both know it.

Nora avoids eye contact.

"You know what I mean," she mumbles.

"I do. I just thought maybe you'd finally say it out loud," I smirk.

"Seeking validation, huh? I'm fluent in that language," she says, half-smiling.

"Goose, your parents…they don't *see* you. But I do."

It's only then that she looks me in the eyes.

Hers are flecked with green, warm gold, and stormy brown—a precise brew of memory and the burden of knowing too much.

They change in the glow of the neon lights around us.

They stay unreadable.

She's still deciding if it's safe to be seen.

"Ya know, I'm man enough to admit I haven't always been the most observant, Nor. Haven't always said the right thing. Or done it. Especially when it came to you. To us," I continue.

"El—" she interrupts. But I press on.

I've got to get this out.

"I think I was so focused on being a good son. On football. On sacrificing for the greater good. I never stopped to think what my best friend might be going through without me. I didn't realize you needed me. Not like that."

Not like that.

Even as the words left my mouth, I wasn't sure what they meant.

Or maybe I did. And that scared me.

Just then, her purse begins blaring with the chorus to *Beautiful Things*.

I think about how lucky Benson Boone is—to say it out loud. To tell the girl he loves that the man who stands to lose her is the most terrified man alive.

Nora looks at me with puppy dog, sad eyes.

Like she hates that the moment's slipping away.

Like it's not a relief her phone rang.

"Sorry, El. I've gotta get this."

She's putting me on hold.

Nora puts the phone to her ear and disappears around the corner.

I hear urgent whispering—brief, breathless.

The call lasts seconds.

But it costs me everything.

When she returns, she has a huge smile on her face.

Like I wasn't just about to announce that I wanted to be her endgame.

That I wanted everything we ever had and so much more.

Sixty seconds ago, I had the courage. Now, it's gone.

"We have to go," she announces. "That was Tania. Your present is finally ready!"

She does a victory dance and tugs me toward the parking lot.

She's already halfway to the truck, practically vibrating with excitement.

I trail behind, slower now.

She dives under the passenger seat like it's a treasure chest.

"What are you doing?" I ask. My voice sounds flat.

Maybe it's my squashed ego.

My wallowing barely has time to breathe. Nora's back—grinning, glowing, holding a box out to me.

A plain shoebox. No brand, no story. Topped with a white plastic bow, the kind that crinkles when you touch it.

Dollar Tree chic. Childhood nostalgia. Emotional roulette.

This is all screaming Christmas in July.

"Open it," she says. "I'm dying to see your reaction."

Wordlessly, I take the lid off and place it on the hood of my truck.

At first, I'm not sure what I'm looking at.

The entire box is filled with tissue paper. But it's heavy.

I look up at Nora with confusion.

"You have to dig." She makes exaggerated unwrapping motions. "Don't just stare at it."

I do as she says, though my heart feels heavy.

But, once I get past the paper, it feels like it might explode.

Inside the box are three things:

1. A vintage Polaroid camera
2. Several Polaroids of the two of us I've never seen
3. A framed photo of my parents laughing on our porch swing

I stare at the contents like they might vanish if I blink. The camera is old, but beautiful—cream-colored with a faded leather strap. The Polaroids are tucked in a bundle, tied with twine. I flip through them slowly.

Us at the lake. Us in the back of her dad's Camry. Us laughing at something I don't remember.

Moments I didn't know she'd kept. Moments I didn't know *mattered* enough to keep.

And then the photo. My parents on the porch swing, mid-laugh. My mom's head thrown back. My dad's hand on her knee. I don't remember this day. But seeing the candid capture fortifies me.

I look up. She's watching me. Not smiling now. Just waiting.

I'm speechless.

"Nora...I..." I stumble. "I don't know what to say."

"Don't say anything, silly," she grins.

"I don't know how I'm ever going to thank you for this. Especially... my mom and dad..." my voice trails off.

"You know how you can thank me?" she asks. But she doesn't wait for an answer. "You can keep remembering, El. You notice *everything* and I don't want you to stop."

"Photography?"

"Maybe not in the traditional sense. But that Polaroid of us in Myrtle Beach got me thinking," she says. "About how you watch things. All the things you've collected in that brain of yours. How you remember stuff the rest of us forget. I just thought... maybe it's time you had a way to keep them."

Taking pictures as a pastime. I'd never considered it.

For other people maybe. Never myself.

The way Nora said it, it felt like a truth I'd missed. Like the wanting had always been there—just waiting to be named.

"I've always kinda seen my watching and noticing to be a weird thing. A quirk I couldn't shake," I admit.

"Nah. It's a superpower."

And she says it like it's obvious. Like it's always been true.

I can tell she means it.

I believe her.

"Now, before you start crying," she continues, "in the spirit of preserving things… part two of your surprise awaits!"

"Part two?"

"Just get in the truck, Coach."

"Yes, ma'am," I tease, tipping the brim of my snapback in her direction.

She rolls her eyes, but I catch the smile she's trying to hide.

I get behind the wheel, heart thudding like it's knocking on the door to my better judgment.

Right now, though, I'm pretty sure no one's home.

By the time we get to the house, she hops out of the truck and I see Tania standing on the front steps with a pair of giant scissors.

Like, comically large.

There is also a very large red ribbon hanging across the entryway.

What is going on here?

I blink. Tania waves the scissors like she's hosting a game show. Nora's already halfway to the porch, grinning like she's won something. I haven't even stepped out of the truck, and somehow, I feel like I'm crossing a line I won't come back from.

"Welcome home, Coach Ashby," Tania hollers as I round the truck bed and, hesitantly, make my way toward the house.

"Am I supposed to know what's happening?"

"Nope," Nora laughs. "That's the best part of *surprises*, El."

I shrug. Apparently, I have no options here.

I glance at Nora. She's not looking at the house—she's looking at me. Like *I'm* the thing being unveiled.

She clears her throat and starts speaking in her most theatrical voice.

"Elliott—Coach Ashby for all intents and purposes—I have taken the liberty of putting together a proposal that will knock your socks off. And, provided you agree to it, you will never be lonely again."

"I beg your pardon? Lonely?"

"Yep," she says, taking a few steps closer to me. "Lonely."

"And the theatrics are going to fix that?"

"Not all of it. But it's a start," she replies. "I am proposing that because your house is empty and tomb-like, we turn it into something you're proud of."

"And what's that?" I ask. I'm skeptical.

"A bed and breakfast."

"You want strangers to sleep in my house?"

"Not strangers. Guests," she explains. "Your mom and dad were always so hospitable. They loved entertaining and making people feel special. They taught you how to do that too. But, no offense, you don't show that side of yourself to very many people anymore. At least from what I've seen. And it's tragic."

I blink again.

Not because I'm confused—because Nora's not wrong.

My mom used to set out extra plates, even when no one was coming. My dad used to leave the porch light on like it meant something.

Now I barely turn it on at all.

"You think a bed and breakfast is going to fix me?" I ask.

"No," she says softly. She places her hand on my arm and drags me a few inches closer. "I think it might remind you how to let the world in."

"Pfft. I don't shut people out," I refute.

"Maybe not on purpose. But is there a chance you've suppressed the part of you that resents being in this town? Maybe you started keeping people at arm's length without knowing it because you've been grieving?"

My eyes are welling up with tears now.

"I thought I was the therapist in this relationship." I chuckle through the tightness in my throat.

Nora doesn't laugh. She just squeezes my arm.

"You're allowed to grieve, El. You're allowed to be angry. But you're also allowed to want more."

I swallow hard.

"I want more than you can imagine," I confess.

"That might be a bigger conversation," she murmurs. "For now, what do you think of this idea?"

"It's…it's great, Goose. It's also a massive undertaking."

"Well, if it helps, you have two long-term boarders practically breaking down the front door, if you'll have them. And one of them cooks really well. I'm sure she'd help out with the kitchen logistics," she nods at Tania.

"My brother and I would love to rent a room. If it's something you want to think about, I get it," Tania says. "But my mom is heading to a rehabilitation facility next week and I'd really like to provide a better environment for him."

"Tania, that's amazing. You're the kind of sister everyone needs," I reply. "But I don't even know how to get started with all this."

"I've done all the permit and zoning research. There are even grants you can apply for. But I didn't go any farther, in case you decided not to go through with it," Nora chimes in.

I look at the porch. At the ribbon. At the house that's held so much silence.

"You really did all that?" I ask.

Nora nods. "I even made a Pinterest board. Don't judge me."

I laugh. I wish my parents could hear it. Hear her plans.

"Okay," I say. "Let's start small. One room."

Then, I do something that surprises even me.

I grab the giant scissors, cut the ribbon, and walk through.

"Guess we're doing this," I smile.

I think Nora Lowe has just saved me from the man I've become.

Track 35

What I've Been Waiting For

(Nora's Version)

I was taught, growing up, that anything new or different was something to fear. Or worse—something to shame.

In all my years of therapy—all the money that was spent—I was never changed in the same way that Moonridge has changed me.

Turns out, making a little room for compassion and empathy makes all the difference.

Especially when it's for yourself.

For the things you've survived.

For the people around you who carry more than they show.

For the truth that emotions come in waves. Trauma doesn't define you. And love—real love—is out there.

I'm still wondering if I can work up the courage to claim it.

But at least now, I believe it exists.

I wonder if my parents are inside on the couch.

If they can see me here on Elliott's porch swing.

If they can sense my thoughts and know that I'm healing—in my own way.

I don't have the perfect words or circumstances.

But I have quiet mornings in my apartment.

Mismatched mugs.

And the kind of silence I'm not afraid to sit with my own thoughts in.

To people who benefited from your silence, boundaries feel like rebellion.

To those who expected you to stay insecure, confidence looks like arrogance.

To the ones who romanticize loving you *their* way, the bare minimum is the golden standard.

Instead, I have Elliott. Again.

Astonishing, but true.

And maybe, the ache between us has softened—just enough to let something new in.

I think he might've been trying to tell me something about that earlier today. But the moment passed.

Though it transitioned into the best surprise I've ever been able to pull off.

Elliott's face when he opened the box of Polaroids and the camera undid my mental faculties. I never imagined his reaction would be so enthusiastic. But I hoped it would.

The photo of his parents was buried deep in my own family's archive.

My dad's office was mostly full of odds and ends. Old research materials. Outdated textbooks.

But I found a Tupperware container tucked inside my dad's filing cabinet—after I watched them pull out of the driveway one morning and let myself in.

Some of my school pictures were scattered among the belongings.

Grades three, seven, and eight.

Always the same handwriting on the back—my name, the year. No notes. No affection. Just documentation.

And then—vacation photos. My mother in a bathing suit and matching swimming cap. Posed. Smiling. Taken before I existed.

Toward the bottom of the stack was the photo of Mark and Lisa.

Young. Alive. Candid.

It was exactly how I remembered them. Like they were encapsulated in time that way.

I'd always thought Lisa was glamorous, Mark was handsome. Together, they were the power couple of Moonridge. My parents' best friends. The surrogate mom and dad I wish could've adopted me for real.

They had always been ready and willing to listen to anything, everything I said and felt. Lisa complimented me on how smart I was and made sure to tell me that it was more important than being pretty.

Even though you're drop-dead gorgeous, too, she'd said and winked.

Elliott winked at me like she had. And he had his dad's easy, trustworthy smile.

A smile that says, *I see you. You're safe with me.*

Their family gave me permission to matter. It wasn't only that Elliott and I were inseparable. It was the nurturing atmosphere—warm and intentional. A home that had space for emotion, softness, and growth.

And now, as we rebrand it into a bed and breakfast, I want to restore that feeling.

Not just for Elliott. For anyone who's ever needed a place to land.

It was my safe place all those years ago. It's been my safe place since I've been back.

It probably always will be.

"My mom and dad would be proud of you, Goose. I know I am," Elliott states as he comes out of the house with two cold glasses of lemonade and a mini bottle of vodka for us to split.

"Me? I didn't really do anything," I reply.

My cheeks are hot but I'm not sure why.

Maybe it's the way he says he's proud of me. Or the memory of us sitting here a thousand times as kids. Dreaming up what our world would be like when we grew up. How we'd leave this town and never look back.

I guess that didn't really work out for either of us.

"You did more than you think," he says. "This is officially the friendship day to beat."

"It *has* been pretty great. Although the year you gave me the collage is still my favorite."

"Yeah? I didn't even think you'd remember that," he confesses. "Thought maybe it was too painful, or weird, looking back."

"I mean, it's hard to go through the archives of the past," I say. "When you come across the bad, you want to throw it out. Forget it ever happened. But you giving me that collage? It's stored up here forever." I tap my temple.

"Too bad you don't still have it. That would be the ultimate trip down memory lane."

"Who said I didn't have it?"

"Do you?"

I nod.

"It's packed up and sitting in an air-conditioned storage unit in Portland right now. But I never once thought about getting rid of it."

"I guess I assumed that, when you left, you'd get rid of every trace of me. Or try to," he replies.

He pours half the bottle of Tito's into his cup, eyes fixed on the liquid.

Doesn't look at me. Just stirs.

The ice pings against the glass—sharp and rhythmic.

"El, I never wanted to forget you. In fact, that's impossible." I tilt my head and place a hand on his knee. "I think I was just running from my own feelings. The confusion of everything that was happening back then."

He raises his eyes to mine. Trying to decide if I'm lying.

But those azure irises are like truth serum.

And Elliott's trust is too precious to lose.

Right now, it's not about romance. It's about honesty.

His breathing slows.

Mine doesn't.

My pulse picks up—like my body knows the risk of truth.

"I was hoping you'd say that," he chuckles.

The sound is effortless and melodic.

"Otherwise," he continues, "it'd be pretty awkward to give you this."

He retrieves a sachet from his pocket, tied up with string.

My name is scribbled on the front with what looks like a tagline.
If memory were a melody, it would sound like this.

Carefully, I untangle the string and unwrap a hard plastic rectangle.

My brows furrow as I realize it's a cassette tape. But not just any tape.

A custom mixtape, entitled:

Goose's Mix—The One and Only

"You made me a mixtape?!" I squeal. My excitement cannot be contained.

"Mmhmm…might just be the last great mixtape of our lives. All inspired by you."

"This is *the* most thoughtful gift anyone has ever given me," I sigh. "But I don't have anything to listen to it on."

Before I finish the sentence, though, Elliott is holding a Walkman and headphones out in front of me.

"Don't say I never did anything for you," he smirks. "eBay has everything."

I take them and open the cassette case.

He put a lot of effort into this. I can tell because there is even a folded track list that accompanies the tape. As I unfold it, I recognize some of my old favorite songs and some I don't know offhand.

"There are sixteen tracks. One for every year we spent apart. Before Portland hijacked my best friend. And, one for this summer," he explains.

I'm breathless, but I search for words anyway.

"Are the songs symbolic? For the years?" I ask.

"Some of them are. Some of them are just songs I heard that whispered to me, 'Nora would like this one.' So, I tucked it away for when I might need it again."

My chest aches and I feel woozy.

"It's amazing," I whisper. "I can't believe you did this for me."

"I'd do anything for you, Goose."

He reaches out and presses the spot where my left dimple hides.

Like magic, it appears.

I laugh.

"Like…listen to this entire tape right now? Backyard karaoke performance of 3 Doors Down? For old times' sake?"

"How can I listen? There is only one set of headphones," he points out.

"Well just… get closer. We'll share."

So—huddled close, buzzing on spiked lemonade, inhaling the santal and citronella candle burning on the porch—I slip the headphones over both of our ears and press play.

A few seconds later, the opening notes to *Wonderwall* begin to play.

Track 36

Rewrite That Night

(Elliott's Version)

August is bittersweet.

Back-to-school activities are in full swing.

I'm not ready to go back.

I feel like it's a Sunday night and I'm bartering with the universe to delay tomorrow as long as possible.

Between last-minute curriculum prep, football tryouts, and the promise I made to Nora about the B&B permits, I'm swamped.

Adulting doesn't pull punches.

And the days? They feel different with Nora back.

Sometimes I flash back to that day in June—outside the American Airlines terminal—when I asked her to stay.

I'm not a guy who takes risks. I've built my life on being dependable.

I've lost myself in trying to be a role model.

Made my heartbreaks almost invisible.

I've endured. Forgiven. Loved.

And for a long time, I thought it was all in vain. Like I was chasing a life I couldn't reach.

But Moonridge? I'm realizing it's not the trap.

It's the imperfect, aching solution.

Nora showed me that.

She came back here to recalibrate.

Despite her parents.

Despite the past.

Despite Alexander Woodruff.

That alone tells me everything.

And the way she looked at that blue, fuzzy journal when I showed up on her porch?

It probably holds more than one secret about him.

I'm positive she wouldn't have done it if she knew he was still around.

It's amazing we haven't run into him in town.

Nora would lose her mind. And I can't say I'd blame her.

Even I have steered clear of Alex since prom. He's bad news. Always was.

I should've known he was a total creep from the time he harassed Nora about her body at our pool party one year.

She almost puked in the bushes. I almost wrung Alex's neck.

But Alex was being Alex.

The same way he'd been our whole lives up to that point and would be for the foreseeable future.

He was a certifiable sleaze. And he preyed on anything with boobs.

Calling him out didn't make him stop. Neither did the complaints lodged by dozens of female students.

I eventually learned to ignore him. But ignoring his victims? That was harder.

Especially when one of them was my best friend.

And the girl I secretly had a crush on.

I tried to pretend everything was fine when we went to football practice.

Pretend I didn't see him groping the cheerleaders.

Pretend I didn't see him smoking pot behind the bleachers.

It was easier that way. For me.

I never knew how hard it would be for Nora.

Because the problem was, I was pretending around her, too.

I thought I was protecting her. From getting involved with me and ruining our friendship.

From making things awkward for our parents if we got together, then broke up.

What about people at school? What kind of ridicule would I get for pining for my closest friend?

What if our first kiss was like kissing my cousin?

Being *friends* with Nora was easy.

Being Nora's *boyfriend* would've been complicated.

Complicated wasn't in my vocabulary back then.

I chose easy. I chose silence.

In hindsight, it's easy to see why she'd stop choosing me.

Also, Alex wasn't just a dumb jock.

He was highly intelligent and manipulative.

Nora wasn't just a casualty. She was targeted by him.

And I didn't just miss it.

It was my fault.

I saw the signs. I just didn't want them to mean what they meant. Because if they did, I'd have to do something. And I didn't.

Alex was already inside the walls. Charming her parents. Winning over teachers. Making me look like the jealous best friend.

Worse yet? He knew I had feelings for her.

"When are you gonna stop being a putz and show her who's boss?" he'd say.

It's not like that. I care about her too much, I'd think to myself.

But, if I had cared *enough*, things would've been different.

I thought love meant staying quiet. Letting her choose. Letting her figure it out. But love should've meant showing up. Even when it wasn't easy. Especially then.

Love definitely wasn't letting some sycophant take advantage of her emotions.

I made plans with Nora to go to senior prom together.

May 7, 2011.

A night we had waited four long years for. A night that would signify our freedom.

A night we would remember as a turning point.

We were heading to different colleges that fall, and everything was changing so fast.

It was one of our last chances to let loose and forget the stress of it all. Of becoming new adults.

I didn't know it then, but that night wouldn't be a beginning.

Instead, it was the start of the unraveling.

I remember stepping away from Nora for a split second to step outside for some air. The gymnasium was loud and humid.

The next thing I knew, when I came back, she was in Alex's arms on the dance floor.

One hand was on the small of her back. The other was sliding up her neck. She was laughing and blushing.

I froze at the edge of the crowd, half-hidden behind a curtain of metallic streamers.

The music was something upbeat—too cheerful for what I was watching. I don't remember the lyrics, just the thrum of bass against my ribs and the way Nora tilted her head toward him like it was muscle memory. Like I'd never been there at all.

But, really, I hadn't. Not the way he was.

Not in a blatantly obvious, *I want to be with you*, kind of way.

She was looking at him in a dreamy, cinematic haze.

Seeing her like that stuck to me like glitter. Impossible to hold but already clinging to everything.

But it was when Alex caught my eye and winked that I knew nothing would ever be the same.

She was lost to me, and he was twisting the knife in. Slow and painful.

He *wanted* me to know that he had the one thing I truly wanted.

My girl. Mine.

Only she wasn't.

I'd spent years memorizing her—every freckle, every favorite song, every way she said "shut up" when her joy spilled out sideways. I thought that meant something. I thought knowing her meant I had a claim. But love isn't a ledger.

What haunts me about that night is that I still don't know the full story of what happened after that dance.

How things escalated or didn't.

Nora never told me.

We were too busy fighting. Shutting each other out.

Then, she packed a suitcase and a couple of boxes.

No note. No phone call. No goodbye.

She just vanished. Like everything good does when it's over.

For weeks, I kept expecting a knock at the door. A text. A scrap of... anything. Something to make it feel less ghostly. But all I got was silence. And the silence said everything.

I screwed up. And I couldn't take it back.

Now, I'm determined not to repeat that mistake.

I can't rewrite that night. But I can make sure all the ones I'm here for end differently.

Track 37

Ripped Up Prom Dress
(Live From Moonridge)
(Nora's Version)

Thursday, August 7, 2026

Dear Wendy,

Time is running out.

To tell him how I feel. To apologize for that night.

In my head, I go back to it all the time.

All the things I should've said.

The most important of those being no.

Sometimes I'm almost able to remember it without all the details.

Sometimes I'm just a girl in a purple dress.

Spinning under gymnasium lights.

Laughing too loud.

Careless. Weightless.

Fearless.

And then I remember.

That girl danced with the devil.

Now, that girl is scared of ghosts.

I regret it all the time.

And Elliott has spent however long wondering if I'd tell him what happened.

Once upon a time, I told him everything.

Once upon a time isn't enough.

Elliott grew up with the girl in the purple dress.

The one who plastered on a smile and didn't know how to ask for help.

The version of myself I'm shedding.

This summer has been an outstanding game of make-believe.

But he goes back to his real life in just a few days.

I think, sometimes, he's trying to tell me something.

Maybe that he doesn't need an explanation. Wouldn't that be nice?

And I've almost given him one anyway—more than once.

We've always been fluent in almosts.

The last few months feel like the longest-running sentence...

Neither of us knows how to end it.

I look down at the last sentence I wrote and sigh.

The problem with all this is that I love him.

And I'm in love with him.

The difference used to matter.

Now, it's all tangled. Love, longing, fear.

If I don't confess soon—light a candle, say a prayer—it'll all end in flames.

If I do tell the truth, it still might.

What do I do, Wendy?
What would you do?

Early morning silence seeps in around me as I look out the apartment window, down into the yard, and across the wooded tree line.

If someone walked in on me right now, they might think I was studious. Organized and academic.

I'm sitting in a rickety armchair. My feet propped up on the windowsill. Journal in my lap and coffee steaming on the table next to me.

Yes, on the outside, I'd look very put together.

My vital organs are in all the right places on the inside, too.

Even my heart.

The problem is that the stitches keeping it together are coming loose.

I keep pressing my fingers to my chest like I'll feel the fraying.

Like anguish might have a pulse.

But all I get is the steady thud of a heart trying its best.

Trying to hold shape.

To hold space.

I'm supposed to meet Elliott after football tryouts.

I'm nervous.

It's the first time I'll have visited the high school since graduation. Even that was painful.

All dressed up in a cap and gown.

I was supposed to be proud of myself. But all I felt was guilt and isolation.

What ought to have been happy tears were tears of worthlessness.

Saline evidence that I was falling apart.

But no one knew.

Not even Elliott.

Especially not Elliott.

I take a sip of my coffee and wrap my hands around the warm mug.

I wonder if he's thinking about me, right now.

Standing on the fifty-yard line—thermos in hand, whistle around his neck, barking plays to the quarterback.

I wonder if he can tell there's something I'm holding back.

My phone vibrates and I startle, almost spilling the entirety of my cup.

Elliott's name lights up my screen. New message alert.

Wrapping up here. See you soon, Goose.

I send back a thumbs-up emoji—something I never would have done to Grayson—and toss my journal on the counter.

Throwing my hair into a ponytail that trails down my back and slipping into my favorite pair of jeans, I take stock of what needs to be done before I leave. What part of my face needs to be prodded. Painted. Made presentable enough to pass.

It's rare that I go without makeup these days.

What I wear lets my freckles show—just enough to look natural. Even if I'm still hiding behind foundation, the illusion is that I'm not.

That I'm comfortable. That I'm confident. That I'm okay.

Instead of saying *this is me trying*, it says *I woke up like this*.

But today, I do something radical.

Today, I shrug off the insecurities.

I go without makeup—because I can. Because I want to.

No amount of skin care, primers, and blush will make what needs to happen any easier.

No swipe of mascara can make something ugly look like anything other than what it is.

I'm not trying to make a point. Just giving myself grace.

I let the moment spool out.

Twenty minutes later, I'm walking through the end zone.

A group of teenage boys push blocking dummies at the thirty-yard line.

I keep walking until I spot Elliott looking very *in his element*.

He sees me too. His smile beams down the sidelines.

Like it's meant for everyone but still finds me.

A whistle blows.

"Alright, boys, listen up! I want to thank all of you for waking up early to come for tryouts today. I know getting back into the routine isn't easy. But each of you showed a lot of heart out there—dedication and love of the game. That goes a long way with me," Elliott bellows.

He tells the boys—some rookies and some former teammates—that the final roster will be posted online on Monday morning. That, for now, they should enjoy what's left of summer.

I wait for them to disperse before I approach Elliott.

I don't want anyone thinking we're something we're not.

We're just friends.

"Hey, Coach," I say with an easy grin. "Team was lookin' great out there."

"Yeah, the potential team, anyway. Gonna be tough to cut some of those kids," he shrugs. "Sometimes I wish our third string roster could fit everybody."

"Has anyone ever told you that you're the most empathetic head coach ever?"

"Not in those words," he jokes. "Truthfully, there are a lot of people out there that think I need to be tougher on the boys. More of an authority figure than someone they can come to and talk."

"Coming from someone who didn't have that growing up, they're fortunate to have you. Having someone come down on you all the time—someone tough and unreadable—is exhausting." I slump down onto the bleachers. "You're doing something right. They trust you."

"Do *you*? Trust me?"

"Yeah, why?"

"Because you shouldn't," he laughs.

The next thing I know, an entire cooler of Gatorade is poured over my head.

I'm soaked. I'm sticky.

My shoelaces are blue.

I blink. "You're a menace."

He's doubled over laughing.

I wipe Gatorade from my eyes.

"Isn't this what you're supposed to do to *coaches* when they *win*?" I manage. "Not to innocent bystanders."

"Eh," Elliott grunts. "I've already won. Trophies, a scholarship, another summer with you."

He says it like I'm the real prize.

Like it's obvious. Like it has been all along.

Elliott sits down next to me on the metal bench, and we stare at the other side of the field.

At the bleachers for the rival teams' supporters.

We stay like that for a while.

"You ever miss playing?" I ask eventually.

He shakes his head. "Not the game. Just the feeling of being part of something bigger than myself. But you gave me some of that back with the bed and breakfast idea."

There's a long pause as I ponder what he's implying.

"You've given me back a lot of things, Goose," he adds.

"El," I breathe. "I'm flattered, but I think you're overestimating me."

"I'm not sure that's your call," he replies. It's playful, but direct.

I let the silence stretch, unsure whether to argue or absorb it.

There's a flicker in his expression—something like amusement, something like ache.

"You always do that," he says finally. "Downplay the good."

"I don't always," I say. "It's just… things aren't always as simple as you try to make them."

"I believe things are only as complicated as you let them be. It's easiest to start small and add more later."

"But, sometimes you can't," my voice breaks. "Sometimes you can't because you've already made it complicated in your head, and starting small feels like lying."

"Something tells me we aren't talking about this summer anymore," he says.

"We are. And we're not." I shake my head. "It's about everything. It's about this place. And you. And prom."

He blinks at me without speaking. But his eyes are expectant and accepting.

I could drown in them if I tried hard enough.

I could deflect and pretend this conversation isn't happening.

"I have to be honest with you, El. About that night. Alex and I… it wasn't what you thought."

"You don't know what I thought, Nor. We didn't talk about it."

"We didn't need to. I saw the disappointment on your face. I walked home alone that night. That was all I needed to know," I say.

"You think I was disappointed in *you*?" he asks. "I was disappointed in myself. For not asking. For letting you walk away thinking I didn't care. If I'd have spoken up you would've been *dancing* all the way home."

"Well, I wasn't. I was crying in a ripped-up prom dress. Trying to figure out how I would explain to my mom that I was coerced into a situation that never should've happened. That I had been abused by the same manipulative person I swore I'd never get involved with."

He doesn't speak at first. Just blinks, like he's trying to unsee the version of that night he's carried for years. "Nora…" he says, voice breaking. "I didn't know. I swear I didn't know."

I swallow. Wipe my eyes. Clear my throat.

"I kept replaying it. Your face. The silence. I thought maybe I deserved it. Maybe I ruined everything. Maybe it was all my fault," I reply.

"Geez, Nora! No! You were alone, because I let you be. With him, of all people. And I don't mean just then," Elliott explains. "It was ignorant of me to assume that Alex wasn't planning something all along. Looking back, there were signs. I should've paid closer attention."

"Maybe you're not the only one. Maybe I was just stupid, or weak—or both."

"No," he whispers. "You're not any of those things. You're strong. Witty. You didn't deserve for some slimeball to victimize you."

I'm full-on sobbing now.

Elliott pulls me into his arms like he's trying to hold together everything I've just let fall apart.

I let him. And I don't apologize.

"What did your parents say?" he asks when my convulsions subside. "Did they ever report anything to the school? Anyone?"

I shake my head. "I never told them. I just wanted to keep my head down. Make it through graduation. But I knew I'd never make it at USC. I was trapped inside myself. Clawing my way out took a long time."

"You were going through all that, and I was just... living my life. Thinking you'd ghosted me. Thinking that you chose him. I feel like I failed you," he sighs. "I wish I'd known."

"I wish I'd let you," I reply. "But I didn't know how to be known back then."

"And what about now?"

"Depends on the day," I say, rubbing my tear-stained cheeks. "Today? I'm somewhere between the girl who hid and the woman who wants to be seen. Not where I want to be yet. But closer."

Then, I look at him. Really look and wonder if being known means being held together by someone who doesn't flinch when you fall apart.

Track 38

Ex-Almost-Somethings

(Elliott's Version)

Maybe she needed to lose me to love herself.

That's what I keep batting around inside my head.

I turned over the facts a hundred times. All the truths that she laid out for me at the football field.

Just two kids sitting on the bleachers.

Dew-soaked sneakers.

The earthy smell of turf.

She was soaked in Gatorade. Shoelaces stained blue.

Nora had shown up to Moonridge High in a pair of light-wash jeans, a Rebels tank top I swear I'd seen her wear in junior year, and the most girl-next-door looking ponytail I've ever seen.

Leopard sneakers with glittery stars.

She was the kind of pretty that walked straight out of a yearbook photo.

She belonged leaning up against a locker door.

At a high school pep rally.

One look from her, and I was #11 again.

Searching for her in the stands.

Scoring the winning drive against our archrivals.

Trying to impress the girl who never needed impressing.

Nora finally telling me what happened between her and Alex—reframing the optics of the situation—gave me the clarity to finally let go of some of the condemnation that's been piling up.

Realizing that was a five-step process.

1. Complete and utter devastation
2. Spend months building a case against her/them
3. Brood about feeling guilty for being a coward
4. Pine for the next fifteen years, to the point of self-sabatoge

5. Fall back in love with the girl I thought I'd lost forever

Somewhere between steps three and four, I was convinced she'd forgotten about me.

Moved on and found fulfillment in her new life. Maybe even in *someone* new.

If I was in her story at all, by that point, I was sure I had been reduced to a footnote.

But, when Marquis called and told me he'd seen her at a red light, I knew I was the same boy who was sitting on his front porch steps, wearing a wrinkled tuxedo, head in his hands.

He's called to check in at least once a week since step one. Sometimes to talk me down. That was particularly helpful when I was at UNC and felt insanely isolated.

Since Nora has been back, we've kept up our biweekly trip to Trudy's for bourbon and brats.

At first, I think he was afraid I might lose myself in the idea of who she'd been when I knew her last. That my heart might get broken all over again. That I'd trip over the past and land on a cactus.

But I didn't. Not exactly.

At first, I fumbled over myself.

That playful punch in the shoulder at the creek? Almost did me in.

The dimples that were buried until she was genuinely happy about something? I surrender.

I didn't say anything, of course.

Just smiled like it didn't matter. Didn't mean anything.

Like I hadn't spent all that time apart wondering if I'd ever have the pleasure of making her laugh again.

I made excuses. That it was just nostalgia.

I was in love with a ghost.

It was a reflex.

But the truth is, that was a lie.

I had a big-time crush on her. One that was only made worse when she answered the door in a threadbare t-shirt and shorts, in the middle of a rainstorm, and her body language told me to buzz off.

I stood there like an idiot. Rain dripping off my baseball cap, heart doing that thing it hadn't done since senior year. Begging her to open up, when she had no reason to.

She didn't smile. Didn't invite me in. And I knew I was in trouble.

"You alright, Coach Ashby?"

Tania's voice comes from the couch.

I'm supposed to be working on the roster that gets posted in the morning, but my mind keeps drifting.

"I'm fine," I say, offering a tight smile. "And, Tania, you and Bash can call me Elliott, ya know. Coach Ashby isn't necessary."

She shakes her head. "Okay," she nods. "Well then, *Elliott*, you are a horrible liar."

"I'm sorry. I thought I heard you say I was a liar."

"Yeah," she replies. She rounds the corner and strides over to the table, covered in my playbooks and player profiles. "Nora said you were really bad at it. She was right."

"Nora is mistaken. I happened to be a master liar," I laugh.

"Did you forget that I live with an eleven-year-old boy?" she asks.

"Fair point."

"All I'm saying is, it's *obvious* you are into her. I don't know why you don't just go for it."

"Tania, do you have a boyfriend?" I ask.

"No," she replies.

"Why not?"

"Because. Boys are stupid," she states. "No offense."

"None taken. We are a pretty special brand of idiot sometimes," I confess. "But, if you realize that, then you see my problem."

Tania narrows her eyes. "So, you're saying you're too dumb to tell her how you feel?"

"Precisely."

"Please tell me this isn't one of those times when you're going to use the excuse of not wanting to ruin your friendship…blah, blah, blah."

"I happen to think that's a valid reason."

Tania rolls her eyes. "You're not friends. You're ex-almost-somethings."

I blink. "Ex-almost-somethings?"

"Yeah. You know. She loved you. You loved her. Neither of you ever confessed and then there was some mystery event that tore you apart. She ran away. You didn't go after her and spent your whole life regretting it. And now, she's miraculously back in your life. It's pretty much a Hallmark movie."

I stare at her.

"You've been watching too much TV."

"Or maybe you've been living in a rerun," she says.

"You're terrifying," I reply.

"Don't forget it." Tania gives me the *I'm watching you* signal and struts out of the room.

I stare at the roster sheet, but the names blur.

Nora's name isn't on it. But she's the biggest player in my life.

I pick up a pen and write her name in the corner.

I stare at it. Underline it. Her name, small and crooked in the margin.

I think about adding a position next to it.

But what do you call someone who is the only definition you have left of home?

I don't add a position.

Just leave her name there.

Because if home has a name, it's hers.

Track 39

Every Little Thing

(Elliott's Version)

I stand to stretch—arms overhead, yawning—and shake my head with exhaustion, trying to break free from the fog that crept in while I was chained to the kitchen table.

Everyone seems to think that coaching is ninety percent on the field. But a fair bit is actually grueling hours spent poring over paperwork and game plans. My aching back and groaning joints can attest to the bad posture that comes from such duties. I'd much rather have my feet planted on the turf.

A game without strategy, though, is motion without meaning. Effort without aim.

So much of life off the field is the same way.

Just as I'm stacking my printouts and closing the thick three-ring binder I just committed to memory for the last four hours, Nora sprints through the screen door and into the kitchen.

Her hair, once tied up in a neat bun on the top of her head, is beginning to unravel. Stringy pieces hang down into her face and the knot bobbles as she walks with determination in the direction of the coffee pot.

The Docs she chose to wear to work today must be killing her feet by now. She's wincing with every step.

Unmistakably, the smell of grilled onions and industrial soap wafts toward me with her movements. I know she is probably counting the moments until she can scrub off the grime of her shift and be alone. Though I can't help but relish the sight of her, disheveled and fatigued, groping for the carafe.

"I'm guessing your day was…difficult?" I ask.

"Try impossible," she answers, rifling through the fridge for her special creamer. "Benny Apgar sent his order back three times because he said the scramble on the eggs 'wasn't quite right.'"

She makes air quotes when she says this, further emphasizing how ridiculous the request to recook them more than once was.

"That was just during the first hour," she sighs. "The entire day went on like that. Hence…coffee," she continues, displaying the brown liquid in the carafe like she's displaying a prize on *The Price Is Right*.

"Sure you don't want decaf? It's pretty late," I reply.

"I'd rather choke than drink that dirt water," she scoffs.

I grin. "Okay, just a thought."

Glancing around the room and into the living room, I notice stray items of Tania's and random articles of Bash's lying around.

A lip gloss tube is on the coffee table next to earbuds. Multiple chargers hang out of the wall, tangled like vines. A half-drunk iced coffee is on the counter.

Bash's abandoned socks are next to the couch and crumpled sheets of what look like homework are tossed into the corner. At least he hung his backpack on the hook by the door.

"Kids," I say aloud to no one in particular.

Nora spins around and takes in the state of the house. A little messy, a lot lived in.

Tania and Bash have only lived here for a couple of weeks, but they have a surprising amount of stuff between the two of them. Watching them carry box after box into the house on move-in day was slightly jarring, considering the emptiness I've grown accustomed to.

"Looks like this house is turning back into a home," Nora states with a wink in my direction. She wears a sheepish smile as she looks down into her mug and stirs.

I scratch the back of my neck. Take off my hat and toss it on top of the binder. Cross my arms.

"Uh-oh. I've seen that look before," she says.

"What? It's nothing," I brush off. "I'm just getting used to the changes."

"Yeah, and...? With changes come feelings. You've lived in a tomb for a long time, El. Fess up."

"I'm processing," I reply, truthfully. "Since my parents passed, it's been hard to hold on to almost anything. I tell myself that things don't hold memories. That's why I tossed out or donated most of their stuff. But I think I really did it because physical memories are harder to ignore."

"Ah, and if all you have is the ones inside, you can keep yourself busy enough not to dwell on them?"

"Something like that," I admit. "Filling the house back up with people—their bits and pieces—it reminds me how little time I took to grieve my parents' absence. I emptied the house, slapped a Band-Aid on my broken parts, and kept going. That's the truth."

"I'm not sure you'll ever finish grieving them, no matter how long you tell yourself it should take. They were titans. Irreplaceable. You love them. Even now, you love them," Nora says softly.

"I guess life's not a very straight line," I mumble, pinching the bridge of my nose. I can feel tears stinging my eyes, but I'm not prepared to let them fall.

"Joy and sorrow. Unfortunately, those are two emotions that can coexist. And sometimes that sucks."

"I've never been very good with the sorrow part," I say. My eyes blink open and I realize Nora has moved to stand behind a seat opposite me, and I can see her freckles dancing under the yellow kitchen light.

"You don't have to be," she whispers. The reply is simple but it's real.

"It's been a long time since I let myself fall apart," I confess.

"Then I'd say you've earned another breakdown," she remarks. "Maybe not one that swallows you. But one that lets you find the space between aching and melancholy and nostalgia. Somewhere you can visit when you miss them."

"I miss them all the time."

"Then find something worth holding onto in the middle of it all. An anchor so you don't lose yourself."

I already know what it is.

It's her.

It's them. Tania and Bash.

It's the rebuilding.

"An anchor, huh? I like that," is all I manage.

"Good," she smiles. "I'll be supervising to make sure you don't let go of it."

She takes a sip of her coffee.

She doesn't know I've already wrapped both hands around it. And every little thing she does makes me hold tighter.

Track 40

Love Story Season

(Nora's Version)

Wednesday, September 9th, 2026

Dear Wendy,

Fall is almost here.

It shows in the way the leaves sound—crunching under my feet.

It's almost time for candles and cardigans. Soft blankets and warm apple pie.

The smell of cardamom and honey. Vanilla and bourbon.

Pumpkin everything. Obviously.

A Gilmore Girls rewatch.

But not A Year In The Life. Just the OG episodes.

"It makes me want to buy school supplies." — Name that movie!

I'll give you a hint: Meg Ryan and Tom Hanks are the ultimate rom-com duo.

Autumn makes me think of my mom's cinnamon muffins—the only thing she knows how to bake.

Hot chocolate and homecoming games.

Homecoming is only two and a half weeks away.

And for Moonridge Rebels, that means facing their biggest rival.

Elliott has been in full-on panic mode about it.

He doesn't think I notice. But it's the same way he used to get before playing.

Coaching hasn't changed that side of him. In fact, it might even be more intense.

The adorable thing about it is that he tries to push those kids to do their best. Not so they can win championships—so they can feel good about their effort. And have it transfer into every other aspect of their life.

I'm a little jealous of him being so motivational. I feel like my only skill is asking, "Do you want fries with that?"

I used to be so much more creative. More generous with the color in my world. Now everything seems beige.

Is it too late to tap back into that part of myself?

I don't know when I stopped.

Maybe it was gradual. Like the way summer fades into fall—quietly, without asking permission.

I want that part of me back. The one who saw potential in the most abstract ideas.

Is it selfish to miss her?

I don't know how to return to her.

I keep hoping she'll show up in a dream, or a song, or a sentence.

It doesn't need to be anything large or fancy. Just something that wakes up the imagination I've let sleep too long.

Speaking of sleep, I'm craving a nap.

The diner's been my second home lately—especially with Tania studying nonstop.

Tania reads without letup. Not novels and magazines though. Cookbooks and autobiographies of famous chefs. She has such a knack for flavors and unique ingredients.

She's hoping to get into the culinary program in person for the second semester. Right now, she's working her way through the prerequisite courses online.

College is something she never thought would be attainable. But now that she and her brother are boarding at Elliott's and don't have exorbitant bills to pay, it's within reach.

I don't mind the extra hours if it means she can pursue her dreams. The coffee burns my tongue and my feet ache by the end of the night, but it's worth it.

And at home, Bash quizzes Tania on French sauces like it's his job.

It warms my heart.

Elliott pretends to be absorbed in his playbooks or grading papers, but I've caught him scribbling down recipe names in his notebook.

It's funny.

For a house that used to feel like a waiting room, it's starting to smell like possibility.

Or is that the fumes from Elliott's muffler?

I stick my head out the window just in time to see a cloud of black smoke puff up from the back of his truck and collide with his face.

He looks like a chimney sweep.

It's ridiculous. And weirdly endearing.

"Should I fetch Mary Poppins?" I giggle from my roost.

"Ha. Ha," Elliott mocks.

"Sorry," I holler. "It's probably just the fuel injector."

"What are you, an auto mechanic now?"

Elliott looks thoroughly confused.

I hold a finger out the window to signify *hold on*, and rush down the stairs and out the door.

"What do you know about fuel injectors?" Elliott asks as I catch my breath.

I flash a grin that says wouldn't-you-like-to-know, but it's all a bluff. I've never been good at playing coy.

"I know absolutely nothing about fuel injectors," I declare proudly. "But I made you think I did."

Elliott cocks his head.

"I just repeated what some guy at the garage told me once. When I had black stuff pouring out of my car. Like that," I say, gesturing to his dirty face.

"I'm impressed," he says with a chuckle.

"As you should be," I say, dropping into a dramatic curtsey.

"Well, as a reward for your suspiciously confident, entirely fraudulent advice… I have something for you."

He opens the rear passenger door to the truck and pulls out what looks like, a bouquet wrapped in kraft paper. Only I can't see any flowers. In fact, I smell wood shavings.

"I wasn't sure if you like Ticonderoga or Mead. So, I went a little crazy and used both," he says.

Elliott hands me the bundle.

It's the same size as what I image a dozen roses would be—though no one's ever gotten me flowers. But this is definitely not roses. It's too heavy.

"It feels prickly," I reply, shifting the weight of it awkwardly.

"Unwrap it," is his explanation.

I hesitate for a second before peeling back the edge of the paper and then see rows of long yellow stems. Rigid and—do I see hot glue?

The scent that wafts up at me is reminiscent of craft supplies. Sketch pads and eraser burns.

I eagerly finish tearing the paper away and my eyes begin to well up.

Why do I cry so much around him?

I'm holding a lavish bouquet of freshly sharpened pencils, tied with a bright green ribbon and a gift tag.

I flip it over.

About time for a You've Got Mail movie night?

Right on cue, Elliott pulls out a daisy-embroidered handkerchief—Kathleen Kelly's signature—and dabs the tears from my cheeks. I laugh through the wetness.

Of course he remembered.

Elliott is the most attentive, confidently masculine, and emotionally intelligent man I've ever known. This seals it.

This combination has never existed in one person. Not in my world. Not in anyone else.

Only now, with cedar, varnish, and graphite in the air, do I feel that thought taking root. By the gentle ways he's caring for me.

My mind flashes back to him telling Tania the story about why he's a teacher and coach. How it's because of me. Because once I told him he made people feel like they mattered.

The fact is, he's always been taking care of me.

"What's with the waterworks, Goose?" Elliott asks.

"I was just thinking," I reply, "I've never had anyone give me a bouquet. Of anything."

I didn't realize how much I'd wanted that. Until now.

"I know it's not New York in the fall. But it's the best I could do on short notice," he grins.

"Oh, no," I say, shaking my head. "Don't sell yourself short. NY152 would one hundred percent approve."

"Well then, let's go get our Nora Ephron on," he teases.

My face is trying to smile. But my whole body feels brighter. More relaxed.

Elliott knows I was named after Nora Ephron.

It started in 1989, with When Harry Met Sally. My mom became obsessed.

In 1992, when This Is My Life was released, it was confirmed. I was going to be named after the most amazing screenwriter of the twentieth century.

Thank goodness I didn't end up being a boy. My name probably would've been Dan Aykroyd.

And somehow, Elliott knows all of this. I don't know what's more astounding—that he knows it, or that he remembers it all.

Either way, the sun isn't as high in the sky now. The air is turning crisp; the leaves are rustling.

I want to cling to his neck. To tell him this moment matters. That I'll carry it with me. Always.

But I don't. I stop *just* short.

Because choosing this now means risking what comes after. And I'm not sure I'm ready.

Track 41

Friendly Flame

(Elliott's Version)

Her love languages?

Gifts.

Acts of service.

What's mine? Her. Just her.

I didn't make Nora a mixtape or a pencil bouquet for the heck of it.

I made them because Nora is the kind of person that makes you want to try.

Not for the recognition or thanks.

Not because I think she's broken and needs fixing.

But because she makes you want to fuss over her. Makes you want to choose her over yourself. Every time.

I'd take a literal bullet for Nora. And I know she'd do the same for me.

The last few months have taken us from cut ties to unexpected circumstances. Unrequited feelings have been a recurrent theme. But lately, we've been inching toward something else. Something mutual.

So, what does mutual understanding mean, exactly? Because I'm starting to worry it's code for the friend zone.

Sitting here now, watching Joe Fox slog through *Pride and Prejudice* to impress a woman he met in a chat room, I'm struck by how ridiculous love can be.

And how willing I am to be ridiculous for Nora.

It's not all grand gestures and clever quotes. Sometimes it's just trying. Fumbling. Loving.

With the right person. Forever.

I've been fumbling for a long time.

Kicking myself for not stepping between her and Alex. Wishing I'd followed her to Portland. Hoping she'd come back.

All of this without action.

Without knowing what play to call.

That all changed the day that a Florida license plate was staring at me from the Lowe's driveway.

The strategy was clear—

Be back in Nora's life. Somehow.

Whatever way she'd let me.

And if she never chose me back? I'd live with it.

That reasoning still stands.

Because loving Nora has never been about being chosen. It's about choosing her. And her choosing herself.

It's a privilege for me to witness her becoming.

It's an honor for me to see her in motion.

Love is action. Not outcome.

I watch her, snuggled into a throw blanket. Hair tossed up into a messy bun. Eyes wide like she doesn't know exactly what's going to happen in this film next.

If I get to sit beside her, like this, while she finds her way?

That's enough.

That's everything.

Affection isn't imposing. It's not something she should ever be made to feel she has to earn.

It's subtle, crinkled at the edges, and hushed.

She deserves it because she exists. Not because she proved anything to me.

Not because she's strong, or clever, or resilient—though she is all of those things. But because she's Nora.

It reminds me of what's happening just beyond this room.

I can hear Tania and Bash laughing. They're a perfect reflection of choosing each other when all else is crumbling. When the world has asked too much of you.

Survival has a lot of different sounds. Laughter is my favorite.

It resembles joy but not just that. It seems like humor, but it's not only that either.

If there were an audio definition next to the word healing, in the dictionary, it'd be the sound of laughter.

Not the kind that slips out when you're watching stand-up comedy.

The kind that finds its way into the silence when your heart is touched.

It's unassuming.

Sensitive.

It's the sound of something fragile choosing to live. And I get to be here for it.

That's the gift.

"What are you thinking about? Your jaw is doing that clenchy thing," Nora says, breaking me free from my thoughts.

I blink, realizing I've been staring at the paused screen for who knows how long. Joe Fox is mid-sentence, frozen in rom-com purgatory.

"I was thinking about laughter," I say.

She raises an eyebrow. "Laughter?"

"Yeah. Yours. Bash's. Tania's. It's been a while since this house was full of that. I'm glad it's back."

Nora shifts closer, her shoulder brushing mine.

I want to do something radical.

But I don't want to scare her.

I don't want to rewind the progress we've made.

So I stay still.

I don't wrap my arm around her, the way every impulse is urging me to.

I don't tell her that the way her eyes change in the light or with whatever color shirt she's wearing is mesmerizing.

I don't say that her presence feels like the first inhale after holding your breath too long.

Because this isn't about me.

It's about being unrushed.

It's about agency.

Giving her agency.

Letting her decide what this moment becomes.

"I've missed this," I say finally. "Just, being here. The two of us."

"Isn't that what we've been doing all summer?" she asks.

"I don't mean like that." I shake my head. "I mean, being present. Taking it all in."

She nods and rests her head on my shoulder.

It's the smallest gesture.

My breath hitches, but I try not to let her see.

I'm afraid to grip this moment too tight.

I don't want it to crack in my hands.

"Yeah," she breathes. It's friendly fire against the skin of my neck.

"I get that. Like, I can finally just rest and *really* be here," she concludes.

It's not a promise. It's just an observation.

I don't respond right away. I just let myself feel it— her weight against my shoulder, the softness in her voice, the quiet miracle of *here*.

Track 42

Into The Dark

(Nora's Version)

"How are you feeling about homecoming?" Elliott asks me, sitting at the kitchen table with an opponent analysis spread before him.

I'm caught off guard because I had never considered how I was feeling about it. Until now.

I want to go. Be supportive of Elliott and the difference he's making in the lives of the young men on the team. But stepping foot into the stands with the rest of Moonridge? That's something else entirely.

"Undecided, I guess." I shrug. "I'm not sure I want to face everyone in town all at once. It's been nice only going to two places—the diner and the library—and then right back upstairs."

"Still hiding out?"

"I wouldn't say that. Just avoiding drama. I haven't found a way to play nice with people who push me too far yet," I admit.

"I push you all the time," Elliott teases.

"That's not the same," I whine.

"I know. All I'm saying is…" he pauses.

"Is what?"

"I'm just saying, you should come. With me. We'll go together, like we used to. It'll be fun," he promises.

I remember the last time I was there. The cool metal of the bleachers through my jeans. The gasps and cheers from everyone around me. The sparkly pom-poms and marching band uniforms.

What if I can't do this yet?

"Do you think people will talk? About us? Me?" I ask.

"If they do, so what? I say, let's give 'em something to talk about," he says. "I'll even let you wear my hoodie. That should do it."

Hoodies and sweatshirts were something Elliott leant me a lot of growing up. I rarely, if ever, gave them back.

I'd stuff them in the bottom drawer of my dresser or in the back of my closet so my mom wouldn't find them when she did my laundry. She would've thought it was wildly inappropriate for me to wear a piece of clothing from a boy. Probably would've taken it as an improper proposition.

But they made me feel like a turtle. Carrying my home around with me. Tucking into the neck hole when I didn't want to talk or think too much.

Elliott understood that.

It became an unspoken gesture of security between us.

For him to extend it now, I knew, was more than just a habit. It was him saying, just like he did then, *I won't let anything happen to you.*

Elliott reaches behind him, takes the hoodie from the back of the chair, and tosses it onto the table. "It's clean," he says. "Mostly."

I pick it up, press the sleeve to my face. It smells like him.

Forest and brine.

We sit there for a minute, not saying anything. The hum of the fridge fills the space between us. I trace the edge of the hoodie with my thumb.

"Alright." I sigh into the silence. "I'll go. With you."

Elliott must not have expected me to make up my mind so quickly because his eyes widen with surprise. I think I even see his cheeks flush as he turns his *Carhartt* cap around backwards and presses it back down on his head.

In the quiet way he usually accepts things, he doesn't speak right away. Just nods.

That's that.

He seems afraid words might break the moment.

And maybe they would.

So, I nod back, hug the hoodie to my chest, and head out to the back porch.

I stare up at the sky. It watches me back.

Trillions of sparkling eyes in an ocean of darkness.

I wonder if any of them have seen this moment before.

Two people deciding something but not saying it aloud.

Without fireworks. Without fanfare.

Just a nod. Just a breath.

Just the smell of forest and brine clinging to cotton.

Behind me, the screen door creaks open. Elliott steps out but doesn't come close. He leans against the railing, arms folded, gaze tilted upward.

Him, standing there that way—patient and calm—unlocks new pathways in my brain.

Makes me want to buy pretty date night dresses.

Makes me want to belt out love songs in the car with the windows down.

Or believe that dopamine levels might actually cure me.

He's already a ten.

But he doesn't mind that I'm crazy, so for me, he's not even on the chart.

I want to ask him what's on his mind. Something is. I can tell from the way the porchlight hits his jaw and it looks like it's made of stone.

Maybe he's thinking, *kiss her, you fool.*

I know I am.

I shift my weight, suddenly aware of the way my bare feet press into the wood slats.

I think: *this is how people fall in love.*

"I think I'm gonna head upstairs," I say. "Do you want your hoodie back?"

"Nah," Elliott replies. "It looks better on you anyway. All of them have."

I smile, but it's small. The kind you feel more in your chest than on your lips.

I'm suddenly shy.

I wonder if he knows what that line did to me.

All of them have.

It's not sensual or forced.

Just like Elliott, it was casual and cool. Loaded but thoughtful.

I wonder how long he spent noticing. How long he's been waiting.

I take a step toward the stairs, then pause. The porchlight buzzes faintly overhead, casting long shadows across the driveway.

"I'll walk with you," he huffs out. "It's really dark. Don't want you to get lost."

He clears his throat, and I wonder if he's chivalrous because he was taught to be. Or if it's just in his genes. After all, the apartment is just across the yard.

Does he ever wish he'd bitten his tongue and *not* offered to be the kindest human on the planet?

His hands slide into his pockets, shoulders relaxed, but I can tell he's watching me. Though not in a way that demands anything.

After a few strides, he's already ahead of me. Joining the long shadows of the tree line.

I giggle to myself because I know, in a couple seconds, he'll look back and say, *C'mon, Goose. We don't have all night.* Knowing full well that we actually do.

The air smells like backyard bonfires and distant rain, and I swear the stars are brighter tonight.

Northeast Ohio in autumn is pretty magical.

Maybe it's the company or the hoodie I'm hugging tighter.

Either way, I follow him into the dark. Trusting the way he walks. Even when he's a few steps ahead.

Track 43

White Noise And Side-Eyes

(Elliott's Version)

When I told Nora I had to be at the game ninety minutes before it started, I assumed she'd prefer to meet me at the school. But she was in the truck, blowing the horn and hollering for me to hurry up before I even had all my gear in the back.

I could tell her enthusiasm was increasing when she and Tania stood in front of the bathroom mirror putting temporary football tattoos on their cheeks. Smudging glitter into their hairlines. Putting on red lipstick and black eyeliner to match team colors.

And, by the time we all pile into the cab, I'm high on the feeling that it's going to be the best Friday night I've had in a long time.

The only things I miss are my mom and dad.

Coming back to Moonridge and living in the garage apartment—the one Nora sleeps in now—was never part of the plan.

Was it reasonable? Absolutely.

Was it what I was hoping for as a freshly graduated English major with an itch to get back on the football field? Absolutely not.

I was cockier then.

I wanted recognition for my accomplishments.

Praise for my abilities.

Moonridge didn't really offer either.

What the superintendent *did* have going for him though was a large grant from the State and the need for a new head coach. The previous one had just retired, and the super was as desperate to get a replacement as I was to make a name for myself.

I was familiar with how it all worked in Moonridge, too. The hierarchy. The bureaucracy.

And even though the Carolina blue skies were the opposite of somber gray of Ohio, I had to admit, I missed the way it felt to sit on the sidelines of my old athletic field. Crisp breeze blowing past my face mask. Odd-man rush. Trying to avoid being blitzed by the other guys.

So, with a little urging from my parents, I made the drive back up I-77 and replanted myself. Just praying something would bloom.

Unfortunately, in the years since then, I've always wondered *what if.*

What if I had decided to teach somewhere more prestigious?

What if I could've made more money in a bigger city?

If I stayed away, could I have healed more emotionally?

Now, with Nora in the passenger seat, humming along to a country song—I never thought I'd see the day—my hoodie tied around her waist, those questions fade.

They're replaced with the memories of our parents sitting in the stands at my games. Wrapped in blankets and sipping thermoses of cider. My dad, yelling at the refs like a yellow flag was a personal offense.

I wonder what he'd think of me now—whistle in hand, clipboard tucked under my arm, trying to teach boys how to lose with dignity. How to not give up when things get tough—on the field, and off.

I used to think coaching was about strategy. Now I know it's about showing up. Even when you're tired. Even when you're scared. Especially then.

That life skill translates. It's a fact.

The other thing I'm beginning to believe in again is fourth-quarter miracles.

When the tension in the air is so thick it clouds your vision. The crowd is holding its breath. Everything's moving in slow motion.

And then, you take that last chance. You play the last down. You throw the Hail Mary touchdown pass. The seconds wind down. And, just when you think there's no way… You win.

That's what it's been like this summer. That's what it's like right now.

Nora's my Heisman. My Lombardi Trophy. My Super Bowl ring.

The woman who has been the prize the entire time.

I used to chase wins. Now I know. I've already won.

As we pull into the lot, it's already crowded. Players' parents are tailgating. Friends are gathered around propane grills. Party punch is passed around. Alumni and community members mingle with burgers stacked on their plates. The smell of popcorn fills the air.

"You ready?" I ask Nora.

Tania and Bash have already scrambled out of the truck and gone to find their friends. And, alone with Nora, I can see her excitement is now mixed with nerves.

I want to tell her it's okay. That she's got the guts to face the vipers of Moonridge with a smile.

"We'll walk in together?" I prod instead.

Nora nods and hops down onto the blacktop. She rounds the front of the truck and comes around to face me.

"I'm living for the moment tonight," she says, unconvincingly.

"You should," I agree. "We both should."

And without thinking, I take her hand and thread her fingers through mine.
She looks down at them. Then back at me. A grin tugs on the corner of her lips, but she fights it.

"What's this?" she asks.

"Let's call it a confidence boost," I suggest.

She squeezes once. *Let's go.*

We step out from beside the row of cars, and I'm met with a lot of claps on the back, handshakes, and "Hey, Coach" calls. But the greeting Nora's receiving is a little less stellar.

Some folks nod solemnly in our direction. Others keep their eyes trained on our hands, linked as we walk toward the entrance of the field.
Mouths get covered with hands as whispers are exchanged.

It's not about what our relationship *is*. They gossip because of what the potential of our relationship means to *them*.

Nora doesn't flinch, but I know she notices. Her jaw tightens.

But she doesn't ask me to shield her. She doesn't beg me to keep walking.

She keeps her eyes forward, grip tight, and puts one foot in front of the other.

Even though I know she doesn't need my protection, I still want to say something to them.

But I follow her lead. I move further into the crowd, tugging her with me, until we get to the entrance gate.

In my periphery, I see Nora's parents, talking to the fire chief. They glance in our direction and I stiffen.

"What's up?" Nora whispers.

"Nothing. Just your parents."

She peers around me, and I can sense the moment she locks eyes with her mom because she squeezes my fingers and her breath quickens.

I'm not sure if I should let go—like a teenager caught trying to make a move on his girlfriend's couch—but I don't.

"Do you think we should…" she starts.

"Go talk to them?" I finish her sentence. "Nora, you and me walking in here and showing everyone we don't care is louder than anything we could say with words."

"You're probably right," she replies.

"I *know* I'm right. Remember—living for the moment."

She raises her chin a fraction and I push open the gate.

The hinges groan and the grass rustles under our feet.

A few more heads turn. But I hope that the shock value is enough to keep anyone from saying anything stupid out loud.

"Sometimes I wish I could just burn this whole place down," Nora whispers.

"If worse comes to worst, I'll floor it through the fences," I whisper back.

She smiles and I know I've said the right thing.

I might not be a knight in shining armor. But I'll always have a white horse on standby.

"These people are just judgmental. They talk, but you don't have to listen, Goose. It's just white noise," I add.

"You're right," she replies. "It's my choice. I'm not gonna let it ruin the night."

"It's just white noise," I echo, searching her eyes for a sign she believes it.

"I don't even know what I did to them," she confesses.

"You didn't *do* anything, Nor. You left. You found yourself. You came back. Be proud of that." I look around and then nod at the entrance to the player tunnel. "I have to go to the locker room now. But just know, they don't hate you. They hate what they can't explain."

I'm tempted to kiss her forehead before I disappear down the tunnel.

I'm tempted to kiss her in general.

But I hike the heavy bag I'm carrying up on my shoulder a little higher.

In the distance I hear the roll of thunder.

The stadium lights flicker on.

And, suddenly, I'm surrounded by young men who expect me to either lead them to victory or, at the very least, to the endzone.

Track 44

White Noise And Side-Eyes

(Reprise)

(Nora's Version)

I watch Elliott disappear into the tunnel that leads to the locker room.

Whooping and applause echo from the dark concrete hallway and I can only assume Elliott's fan club of players have engulfed him in some sort of pregame ritual.

Suddenly the air feels chillier than it did when we left the house, even though it's not completely dark yet.

There is a low rumble of thunder and clouds have rolled in. Gray and thick, they press low—sealing in the scene below like a lid.

The stadium lights wash out the faces of everyone filling the stands. The green of the grass looks duller. The color noise stretches across the sky and distorts the picture I try to take with my phone camera, of the first Friday night lights I've seen in a decade.

I went on a few date in 2023 with a guy who was obsessed with the Seattle Seahawks. He spoke almost solely in sports jargon, Geno Smith statistics, and repeatedly told me he could bench press three hundred twenty-five pounds. Of course, he never failed to mention that only men who were *elite* in that weight class could accomplish such a feat.

By the end of date number three I told him I was allergic to monologues and excused myself to the ladies' room. When I came back, he asked me if a monologue allergy was something he could catch from me. I broke up with him on the spot and made sure to avoid the street I knew his preferred gym was on for at least six months after.

I lower the phone. The picture's blurry anyway.

Maybe some moments aren't meant to be captured.

The thunder rolls again. Not loud. Not threatening. But rain is still a risk. If it doesn't clear up soon, it'll delay the game.

I hope, for Elliott's sake, that it doesn't.

And for mine.

I already feel lonely enough since he let go of my hand and left me standing here. Even Tania and Bash didn't want to hang out with me. They scampered off with their friends as soon as we pulled into the parking lot. Typical.

I remember being anxious to get here when I was young, too.

Back then, I still hadn't had a lot of girlfriends. But Elliott always made me feel at home with the clique that followed him around the halls. His popularity never rubbed off on me, but I could at least show up to school events knowing people I could carry on a conversation with. People that would invite me to get a snack at the concession stand, or would stand outside the Port-a-John to make sure my purse didn't get stolen.

I scroll through my phone, pretending I'm waiting on a text.

I'm not. But it's easier than looking around and realizing no one's looking for me.

At this point, I don't know if I can force myself to sit among the Moonridge Rebels-enthused crowd starting to fill the stands, and act like I didn't wish Elliott was beside me.

He'll be right below the bleachers. Marking things on his clipboard—x's and o's and arrows. Arguing with the referee. Turning his hat backwards and forwards a dozen times.

He looked like one of those NFL coaches you'd see on *Sunday Night Football*. Stoic one minute and overly animated the next. All he was missing was a fancy headset and a billion-dollar sponsorship.

If I take my place, alone in the throng of fans, maybe I can pretend I'm so enthralled by the game that it doesn't bother me how people were talking about me under their breath when we came around the truck hand-in-hand. Not to mention the near-miss with my parents at the front gate.

Elliott is better at compartmentalizing than I am, so he's probably already forgotten about the handholding.

But I keep replaying it. The way his thumb brushed mine. How he didn't let go, and just kept walking steadily beside me.

He wasn't embarrassed or trying to hide that we'd come together.

I won't lie. In that moment, I felt like a celebrity arriving at a professional game. People murmuring about me around every corner but not caring because I'm there to support my football boyfriend. Not caring because he's a human exclamation point and would literally go headfirst into a mob of paparazzi for me.

My football boyfriend who's charismatic and respects my boundaries and views love as mutual support and not possession would be able to make me believe that the most sanctimonious middle-class moms who carry around wine glasses like their own personal sippy cups were the scum of the earth.

And my parents? All they ever tried to do, my entire life, was contain the scandal that surrounded our entire existence. My knight in Air Jordan cleats would go to great lengths to keep my name out of their mouths too.

Of course, I'm not famous.

And Elliott's not in the NFL.

He's not even my boyfriend.

But for a second, it felt like we were something worth talking about.

Not because we were scandalous.

But because we were real.

The possibility of being the talk of the town when I moved into Elliott's garage was never the problem for me. It was the way we showed up here tonight and got looked at like a headline instead of as people.

But even if my name is the headlines, I guess it's not my business.

Maybe the story isn't mine to fix.

Maybe it's not even mine to read.

I make my way up the stairs to find a seat. It looks like all of Moonridge has come out to support the Rebels tonight. But I find a place in the third row of the center section and pull Elliott's hoodie over my head.

It's way too big and the drawstrings hang down past my knees as I tap my feet on the metal floor.

The teams are entering the field, and the announcer has started to inform the fans about the current standing of each. The band starts playing *Sweet Caroline*, the cheerleaders are doing back handsprings and cartwheels.

Someone's laughter cuts through the hum around me. Just loud enough to carry.

"Did you see that girl with Elliott? Didn't she date Alexander Woodruff in high school?"

A pause.

"Right, that guy who…" The rest gets swallowed by a plastic cup filled with beer. Then the subject changes.

I turn my head just enough to see Kacey, my previous classmate and a former cheerleader, sitting with another woman I don't recognize.

I don't say anything. Just pull the hood tighter and let the drawstrings sway.

The metal bleacher vibrates beneath me as the crowd claps along to the band.

So good, so good, so good.

I could turn back around. Correct Kacey. Remind her that Alexander Woodruff was pure chaos. That he sabotaged my life. That what happened wasn't gossip—it was survival.

But I don't.

Instead, I watch Elliott and the assistant coach, Andy Brewer, take their places next to the Gatorade table.

My shoelaces are still stained.

What they're saying is barely audible above the noise. Something about coverage and the coin toss. There is a lot of gesturing and Elliott points to the clipboard like it holds the secrets of the universe.

Kacey laughs again, and this time I don't flinch. I just reach into the pocket of Elliott's hoodie and wrap my fingers around the crumpled receipt he left in there. It's from the gas station on Route 45.

The wind shifts. I glance up.

I see them before they see me. Dad in his Cabela's jacket, Mom with a gaudy Michael Kors bag. They're climbing the bleachers like they've done it a hundred times. Because they have.

Mom spots me first. Her mouth tightens. She nudges Dad.

He looks at me and then back at the crowd, like he's trying to find *anyone* else to talk to.

They don't wave. They just sit. Two rows behind me, and to the left.

Mom clears her throat. Loud enough to be heard. Not loud enough to be addressed.

Dad leans forward, elbows on knees, like he's watching for the start of the game. But I know that posture. It's the same one he used when I was sixteen and he told me he was done "dealing with me" because I asked for something he didn't want to give.

I couldn't tell you what it was. Only that it was too much for him.

"Didn't expect to see you here," Mom says finally, leaning up behind me. Her voice is flat.

"I live here," I say, still facing forward.

Another pause.

Mom exhales like my response is a personal attack.

"You don't need to respond to your mother that way," my dad says.

I ignore him.

Elliott looks up and scans the stands until he finds me.

He also finds my parents.

"OK?" he mouths.

I nod and he smiles back. It makes me sit taller.

The anthem plays.

I don't think about it.

The crowd cheers as the teams appear to be lining up for kickoff.

I shift in my seat. The whistle blows. Kickoff.

I lean forward, elbows on knees, just like my dad. But I'm not watching the game. I'm watching Elliott.

His dark polo and khakis. Dark red snapback. Signature Nikes.

Then, down the sideline, I catch sight of a fluorescent *Whitetails* hoodie with a large camouflage deer decal on the front and stripes down the sleeves. The man wearing it has his own black trucker hat tugged down low on his brow so I can't make out much of his face, except he has a thick brown beard.

His arm is wrapped around the shoulders of a woman standing next to him in extremely short cut-offs and a gray Ohio State University sweatshirt. Though his body language says that things between them aren't romantic. They both laugh at an anecdote someone in their group of friends shares.

The man's hearty chortle echoes through the crowd and rings in my ears. It sounds eerily familiar.

Where have I heard that laugh before?

He tosses his head back and his coal-colored eyes glint in the brightness of the floodlights. Suddenly, my heart stops.

I know that face. That man. Fifteen years younger.

Alexander Woodruff.

I forget to breathe.

The blood drains from my face. From my extremities.

I'm lifeless. Limp.

I blink and refocus.

Alexander is accepting a Styrofoam cup from the man next to him and shaking hands with another a moment later. He nods and smiles. The energy of the crowd flowing through him.

A cold sweat breaks out on my forehead.

I think of all the nightmares I've fought off throughout the years. All the scenarios I made up about seeing him again that I hoped would never come true. The therapy sessions I spent wishing I didn't have to say his name with bitterness for the millionth time.

Those sessions should've been accompanied by a complimentary wine bar.

But here, now, I have a choice.

I can let that bitterness and the memories of helplessness overtake me, control me, and turn me into the teenager I was when he decided to take advantage of me. Or I can forget he exists and live in eternal indifference.

I can refuse the poison that's been placed in front of me.

I can let him fade into the background noise. A face in the crowd. Nothing more.

I'm the heroine.

He doesn't get to own me. Not past me. Not present me.

I try to focus on the way Elliott's palm pressed against mine on the way in tonight. The way he checked on me when he realized my parents were over my shoulder. And the way we looks so in charge and capable under the darkening sky, right now.

My line of sight follows the kicker practicing his best field goal technique and I inhale after what seems like years of idle lungs.

Maybe it has been.

Now I'm waking up, just in time.

Track 45

Back Then, Right Now

(Elliott's Version)

I'm all worked up on the sidelines by the time the third quarter is almost through.

Sweat is dripping down my forehead, under the brim of my hat. I've rubbed my jaw raw. The team is tired and we're down by a touchdown on the scoreboard.

Andy, my assistant coach, who is frowning under his bushy mustache, has his hands on his hips, pacing back and forth, wearing a hole in the ground. I worry he'll make one big enough to fall through.

Diesel, our team captain, has gritted his teeth around his mouth guard and thrown pass after pass. But the receivers are being double-teamed, the fullback is running too deep, and I'm sure the referee has been paid to penalize the Rebels on every play. Not to mention our running game really needs some work. The Gatorade I'm throwing back tastes like a salt bath.

I can hear Nora, behind me in the stands, cheering louder than anyone else.

Or maybe I just choose to hear her over them.

Her parents are sitting right behind her, and I despise them for it. For making her feel pressured and pinpointed when tonight is supposed to be fun. Supposed to be a Moonridge celebration of community and family, a team coming together, autumn's beginning.

She's isolated in plain sight.

And seeing her fight through the verdict that many people already made when we walked through the parking lot together makes my heart leap into my throat.

It's endearing the way she throws her hands into the air and waves them around, wearing the Rebels friendship bracelets she made with Tania. The shiny plastic beads glisten in the stadium lights and her tousled locks swing back and forth under the hood of my sweatshirt. It's wild and it works.

It's brazen for her not to give a rip what anyone thinks. And might I add, downright sexy?

"That's right! Show 'em who's boss, Miller!"

Nora's voice cuts through like the whistle around my neck during practice.

Sharp. Clear. Pitch-perfect.

I smile to myself and turn to catch her eye, like I'd done every Friday home game we had in high school. Like, the heat of the moment—the time crunch we were under, the pressure I was feeling to win—would all dissipate if I could just see her.

I remember the first time she yelled my name from the stands.

I missed the snap.

Got chewed out by Coach.

Didn't care.

Even now, if I could I'd pull her into the middle of the huddle. Let her call the next play.

Because Nora makes me want to forget all the rules of the game and make up my own.

I could always count on her being the most invested fan. The most intense supporter.

Not because I expected it, but because she genuinely cared. About me and what I thought was important. She wanted to hear about my sense of responsibility in the pocket. It was refreshing. And validating.

Most people asked about touchdowns.

She asked about timing.

About what it felt like to wait, to trust, to throw before you were sure.

She didn't cheer for the score then. And she doesn't now.

Maybe I'm delusional, but I feel like she's cheering just for me.

I plant my feet.

Read the field.

Diesel's lining up again. Our offensive line looks worn out, but there isn't much I can do. The other team is running us ragged.

I call a timeout.

Everyone groans.

I shove the clipboard to Andy's chest and pat him on the shoulder. Nod at him.

"You're in charge, buddy. Be right back," I say.

He's opening his mouth to object, but I'm already walking away. Climbing stairs. Mumbling excuse-mes and thank-yous.

I feel raindrops on my back. On my bare arms.

The humidity tonight has been unbearable and it's finally deciding to forfeit to the clouds that have cluttered the sky since game time.

I love a good rainstorm. We haven't had many of them since that first day on Nora's porch in June. It's been a luminous summer. But this rain feels like honesty. Like both me and the sky can't hold back anymore.

I'm making my way to Nora. Slowly but determined.

I'm not sure what I'll say when I get there but—whatever this is—it's been a long time coming.

My pulse beats out her name in tempo. Like a song.

Her eyes are already on me by the time I'm a row away from her seat. Her forehead is wrinkled and she's already crawling over people to get to the landing.

By the time we meet in the middle, we're breathless.

"What's going on? Why are you up here?" she asks, concerned.

"Because it's where you are," I pant.

"Yeah. But, the game. It's third and short, Coach. You should be out there."

"Only if you come down and call the plays with me."

"I can't do that!" she shrieks.

"Why not? If you're the play caller, there's no rule against it. You've already seen the playbook," I say.

"Yeah, but I didn't memorize it."

"C'mon, Goose. I need you."

It's my only explanation and maybe not a good enough one, but there's nothing truer.

She stares at me like I've lost my mind.

Maybe I have.

But she's still holding my gaze.

Still standing in the rain. And now it's a full-on shower.

I grab the pocket of my hoodie, sagging on her small frame, and drag her closer.

"Please."

It's not clever or brave. It's messy and desperate.

It's me asking permission. To need her.

I press my forehead to hers.

"What are we waiting for?"

She gives in—with a smile that swallows her face in dimples. With eagerness, and it makes me feel like I could fly.

I don't answer. We just run.

Down the steps, past the stunned faces, through the whirlwind of noise.

She's beside me.

It's like I've stepped back in time and flashed forward to the future all at once.

Track 46

Bless My Soul

(Nora's Version)

I never imagined being someone whom others relied on to make the right call in *any* situation. Let alone a football game.

Sure, I know a lot about the rules and special situations that could come up. Elliott taught me. Still, it was rare—okay, never—that a group of *men* asked my opinion about anything. Especially an all-American sport that—it's assumed—most women have little knowledge of.

Now—thanks to a moment of pure trust and spontaneity—I was made the play caller and thrust into a huddle of teenagers. Tired, dirty, moody teenagers.

My head is still spinning from the fact that Elliott had dropped everything and come to find me, just so I could be beside him. Because he *needed* me.

In an instant, I stopped seeing him as Elliott, my best friend. And I saw him as Elliott, the man. Who he'd become when I wasn't looking. In all the years I hadn't been paying attention.

Not just the way his lips quirked when his gaze lingered on my dimples. Or the way his arms tightened around me for a tight squeeze before he stopped hugging me.

I've been officially converted to a hugger.

But it was more than something that had physically changed between us. Even though that way he tugged me close and said *please* had left me swallowing a golf-ball-sized lump in my throat.

It was seeing Elliott as a confident leader. Asserting himself when he wanted something. Making me feel like the main event instead of the freak show.

Elliott isn't steeped in toxic masculinity. He doesn't dominate, intimidate, or control. Instead, he's grown into something tender. Constructive. Authentically himself. He leads in the classroom and on the field with the same care he used when he led me down those stadium steps—like I was something worth protecting, not performing for.

The fact that maybe he wants my dreary days and complications—the whole mess of me—in a way I never thought possible, lets the butterflies in my stomach out of their cage.

After all the times I pretended not to stalk him online, or the nights I painted the town blue just to drown out the thought of him, I can't believe we're here. Standing in Moonridge on a Friday night. Choosing each other. Maybe the stolen glances between us are saying what we haven't yet.

You're the one I want.

I'm sure half the town thinks I'm having a marvelous time ruining everything. Especially Elliott's chances of ending up with someone who isn't just a fragment of who her parents tried to raise her to be.

Well-bred. Polite. Never argumentative. Always sunny.

That girl isn't me. She was my understudy.

I let her take the stage for years.

But now, I'm done rehearsing.

Tonight, there's no script. No spotlight. Just me.

Not even my parents—teaming up to degrade me—could cancel that.

I'm not keeping my head down, tail between my legs, and leaving town with grace.

I'd dig up the grave a hundred more times if I had to.

If it meant Elliott's hip stayed pressed against mine on the sidelines, whispering instructions in my ear. If it meant Tania kept inspiring me to be the role model I've always wanted to be. If Bash's Imagine Dragons obsession kept echoing through the house like a heartbeat.

I'm done changing everything about myself just to fit in.

It's fourth and eight at the twenty. Rain's coming down in sheets. Ten seconds left on the play clock.

We're still down by four.

I'm soaked to the bone. The hoodie's long gone—stripped off, discarded.

Raindrops trail down my arms, collect on the tip of my nose.

Andy's pulling his hair out. Literally.

Two starters are benched with minor injuries.

A field goal's off the table.

An elaborate play? Not happening.

"What's the decision?" Andy asks Elliott, voice tight.

Elliott turns to me.

"It's risk versus reward now, isn't it?" I say.

And then he smiles—stunning, disarming. It makes the whole place shine.

I nearly forget we're in public. Nearly.

"So, what's the play?" Andy presses.

I draw in a breath. Let it out slow. I know my silence is torture for him.

"Okay," I say finally, tracing a path on the clipboard with my fingers. "I think our three best receivers need to run this way. Their safety might be tied up. Number eighteen's tall enough—if we let him break out at six or eight yards, and Diesel can throw high enough to reach him—not so deep it sails past him—we might be in good shape."

"You want to target the tight end?" Andy asks, skeptical.

He doesn't trust me.

"He's tall and athletic enough," Elliott says, stepping in. "We haven't practiced it. But it's a good play."

Andy sighs.

I chew the inside of my cheek.

"It'll have to be perfect on the first try," Andy says, disapproving.

"Yep. And one try is all it takes, Brewer," Elliott replies, calm and certain.

We need to get the ball in motion before the delay-of-game flag flies.

No time for second-guessing. No time for doubt.

The stadium lights pulse overhead. The white eighteen on the tight end's jersey glows against the blackest black of his uniform. Andy looks like he's praying, palms pressed together under his chin.

Diesel calls the snap.

The line shifts.

Eighteen breaks.

Six yards. Eight.

He turns.

The ball leaves Diesel's hand like it knows where it's going.

High. Not deep.

I hold my breath.

Everyone in the stands holds their breath.

Eighteen leaps.

Fingertips.

Contact.

Catch.

He lands hard.

One defender misses. Another grabs air.

Eighteen's running.

The glow of the white eighteen burns brighter as he crosses the line.

Touchdown.

Andy exhales like he's been underwater.

The crowd roars.

I'm stunned. And Elliott's hands are on my waist.

He's screaming, "We won! You did it, Goose!"

Andy hugs me and jostles me back and forth.

The team is hoisting Diesel and Henderson, the tight end, into the air.

Fist bumping. Butt slaps. Helmet taps.

Chaos.

I blink.

Elliott's still holding me.

Like I'm an award he wishes he could pin on.

Or a medal he could hang around his neck.

One try. That's all it takes.

I find his eyes and shrug. *No biggie.*

But it is.

Rain pounds down.

Parents and kids scatter—toward the field, the parking lot, under the bleachers.

The opposing team claps backs and shakes hands.

Andy's grinning like he's won the lottery.

But Elliott doesn't let go.

Instead, his indigo eyes darken. His lips find mine and he grasps me tighter.

I'm locked in his orbit.

My heartbeat skips ahead, dragging my brain behind it.

It's like I'm seventeen and, even if I tried to explain this feeling, no one would understand.

It's too big. Too loud. Too *everything*.

I'm not sure if the rain is still falling or if it's just us. Just this.

Just the kind of kiss that rewrites the rules.

The kind that makes you forget you ever played by them.

Track 47

A Reckless Girl &

A Rooftop

(Elliott's Version)

I've waited my whole life to kiss Nora Lowe.

I don't mean the photo my mom snapped of my grubby little hands on her shoulders, and my chubby face pressed against her cheek.

I mean an earth-shattering, soul-shaking kiss.

And, tonight, I finally went for it.

It was everything I hoped. And somehow, impossibly, more.

With that kiss, it's like a record scratched and the whole world stopped.

I wasn't man or matter or memory.

In that moment, I was celestial. Incandescent.

I can't tell you what song the band was playing at the end of the game, or how long I stood there—arms around her, lips on hers.

Smiling in the middle of it all.

I even forgot the feel of the rain until we broke apart.

And that was the moment I knew that I'd be chasing the feeling of that kiss for the rest of my life.

That home wasn't a place. It was her, right there.

I've spent so long keeping the hand I was dealt close to my chest. Plenty of times, I wanted to fold. Walk away from the table. Though I felt I had nothing left to lose.

Tonight is different. Tonight is electric. Tonight I'm all in.

When Nora's eyes fluttered open and found mine, she gave me a shy smile.

"Was that bad?" I asked, worried that maybe I had been too eager. Too selfish.

She grinned. "Most fun I've ever had. Living for the moment and all."

But the moment was cut short when Tania stomped up, dragging Bash behind her by his shirt sleeve.

She was mid-rant. "Next time you want to tell an embarrassing story about me to all your dumb friends, I swear I'll tie you to a chair and duct tape your mouth shut."

Our magical mess was rain-soaked and stubborn, but softer now than before.

But softness doesn't last long in Nora's world.

Not when her parents are waiting in the parking lot, arms crossed, eyes sharp.

They didn't yell. That would've been too easy.

Her mom just glared. "You made a scene," she'd said.

Her dad added, "We don't need the whole town watching you throw yourself at someone."

"Aren't you embarrassed? And Elliott, I would've expected better from you," her mom scolded.

It hits me that they don't realize Nora is Nora. Their grown-up daughter, who can make her own decisions. Or who might happen to be adored by me.

No. They can only see what might've served as a derailment to their plans for who she should be.

They felt like everything should be whispered. But Nora and I were becoming a declaration. At least, I hoped. Maybe that's what scared them most.

Nora didn't apologize.

She just said, "If you're embarrassed, that's your problem."

She didn't wait for their response. Just turned and got into the truck, revoking any further access to herself.

Now, with the house quiet—everyone dry and warm—I'm looking for Nora. Not just to find her, but to make sure she's not unraveling after that strange confrontation with her parents. But I've checked the garage, the usual spots she disappears to. Even peeked in the dripping wet hammock hanging in the backyard. Empty.

I sigh and trudge up the stairs.

What if she thinks what happened at the game was a mistake?

I probably just ruined everything.

As I walk down the hallway, resigning myself to the belief that going to sleep will help, I notice my old bedroom door open with a light on inside. Only, I haven't been in that room for ages. It was the one I was going to let Nora stay in if she moved into the house. But when she insisted on staying in the apartment, I knew better than attempting to force anything.

I stick my head inside the door, but it looks untouched. Not like a shrine. Just preserved.

Though the window is open and curtains move side to side with the breeze.

I remember climbing out that window a million times to sit on the roof and think. When we were very young Nora and I tried to make a tin can telephone and stretch a rope all the way across the street and through our houses. We thought it would be the coolest thing to have our own secret way to communicate.

Nora's secret communication, though, was always what she didn't say. It was me looking at her and knowing what she was trying to get across.

When our moms saw the tangled gobs of string all over the house, they both put a stop to the telephone idea. Not that it wasn't imaginative. But Nora's mom claimed we didn't need "constant contact". That we already did everything together so why did we need to talk from her bedroom to mine at all hours. It was "too accessible" she'd said.

That day wasn't just about a string being cut. It was about the craving for connection being called inappropriate. Having our childhood intimacy limited wasn't something Nora or I had ever considered.

I always gave her the bigger half of a candy bar. She gave me a lick of her ice cream cone. There was no question about what we would or wouldn't do for each other.

Moments like that should've helped me to realize that behind closed doors, Nora's parents were more uncompromising and sterner than I'd imagined.

I stick my head out the window, fingers resting on the sill, about to close it, when I see the shadow of Nora sitting on the roof.

She looks like a gargoyle, keeping watch with a stony presence.

I climb out and slide across the shingles to sit beside her.

The roof creaks under us as I fold to match her posture. Knees pulled up, arms wrapped tight.

I wait for her to speak.

"Tonight doesn't feel real," she begins. "Feels like I'm living someone else's life."

"What do you mean?" I ask, though I can guess.

"It seems like this whole thing is a giant movie. The tension with my parents, the chaos of homecoming…you kissing me." She looks at me.

I don't look away.

"The thing about movies is that those are paid actors," I say. "I don't need millions of dollars to know that kissing you was long overdue."

"I know. That makes it worse."

I chuckle, uneasy. "I used to think I'd know the moment everything changed," I say. "Now I know it's not just one moment. It's a collection of them. There's no sign or soundtrack. Just rain, a roof, and you."

I reach for her hand, and she leans her shoulder into mine.

"Remember the first time we realized we could get up here from your window?" Nora asks.

"Yeah. Everyone acted like we were kittens caught in a tree," I reply. "Ridiculous."

She laughs softly. "My mom said we were reckless. Said roofs weren't made for proper young girls either."

I glance at her. "And what did you say?"

She shrugs. "That I'd rather fall than keep my feet on the ground."

"And now?"

"Falling feels like flying."

Track 48

Still, Somehow

(Nora's Version)

Friday, September 25, 2026

Dear Wendy,

I couldn't go to sleep tonight without documenting some substantial developments—

> — Alexander Woodruff no longer has a hold on my life. He doesn't get to write my ending. This story belongs to me.
> — I was made the play caller for the Rebels at homecoming
> — We won the game!
> — Elliott kissed me

Maybe the biggest win of all? I didn't run.

Not when I saw Alexander on the sidelines.

Not when the memories clawed their way back.

I stayed. I didn't cause a scene. I didn't let him steal the night.

I'm proud of that. Because I didn't let fear decide for me.

I should be in bed, lying back on my pillow, dreaming about the happily ever after feeling that flooded me when the emotions of the night were at their highest. After Elliott held me in his arms for what felt like a small infinity.

That bubble was quickly popped by my parents who showed up outside the athletic field, standing next to Elliott's truck, complaining that I caused a scene. Accusing me of throwing myself at him. Of showing the whole town a side of myself that was embarrassing.
I know I should still be riding high from both the Rebels' victory and mine, but sometimes parents know just what to say to make you feel like a lesser version of yourself. No matter how old you are or what other support you've found for yourself.

And the support I've got now is pretty great.

Tania is the little sister I always wanted. Seeing her blossom into someone poised and resilient makes me feel maternal in a way I never expected. I always thought I'd be lousy at being an influence on someone. But I think I had the idea of what it meant all mixed up.

Bash is teaching me patience. But, more than that, I'm learning that living life bracing for bad news isn't living at all. He's only eleven but he's the most good-natured, well-adjusted kid. His mom's addiction hasn't made life easy for him, yet his heart is full of nothing but love—for her, and everyone.

When I first got back to Moonridge, I lived like everything was temporary. Everything felt fleeting.

Now, with Elliott's hoodie draped over the chair, the window cracked open, and the sound of an owl hooting outside, I realize that things have shifted.

I'm less guarded. Less armor, more skin.

I pause and reflect.

When I first got here, I lined my shoes up neatly by the door—ready to leave at a moment's notice. Now they're in a pile in the closet. Like I'm no longer poised to run. More relaxed and spontaneous. Not overly concerned with meaningless details.

Elliott's casual reliability—his steady presence—has made me feel like I can breathe deeper. Like I can stop scanning the horizon for what's chasing me.

He doesn't ask me to be brave. He just makes it easier to be.

And our kiss? It wasn't fireworks.

It was gravity.

Something I've been circling forever finally pulling me in.

Claiming me while the whole town watched.

While my parents sat in the stands and saw me stop performing restraint.

Saw me finally give in to the inevitability of Elliott.

And then that loaded stand-off at the truck.

They didn't want me to be reckless.

They wanted me to be quiet.

But every time I try to whisper it comes out like a confession.

I guess I only know how to be loud—even when the moment's wrong.

I'm the laugh at a funeral.

Elliott's the guy who laughs along with me.

For years I've tried to stifle my own chances at joy. I've looked for validation. I know now that I don't need it.

For an entire summer, I've lived out of a suitcase, worked at a diner, and made friends into an entirely new family. I've made something out of myself, albeit small, from nothing. And I've never had to pretend I was something I'm not. To make gains or get ahead.

That's why I didn't let the argument with my parents linger. I didn't in the parking lot, and I won't anywhere else. Because I know I'm lovable. From the inside out. And I don't need to earn it because it's been there all along.

It's strange how clarity sneaks up on you. One minute you're buying Tampax at a corner store and crying alone. The next you're on a roof, feeling the relief of being recognized.

We talked for a long time tonight before I came up to the apartment.

It came in bursts and waves. Sporadic thoughts. Confirmations of what's been left unsaid. What ifs and maybes.

The air was chilly. The street quiet. And Elliott didn't ask me to explain anything.

After a long silence somewhere between the topic of our dream travel destinations and the most-read book on his nightstand, Elliott turned to me in the dark and stared at my profile. I stared at the clouds, eerie in sparse moonlight.

"Did you love him?" he asked. "The guy in Portland?"

It sounded more curious than jealous.

"Grayson? Honestly…" I paused. "I thought I did. I thought I could make him happy. But once we broke up and I came back here, I started to realize that making other people happy doesn't always result in your own happiness."

Elliott nodded like he'd already suspected that answer.

Like he'd been waiting for me to say it out loud.

The clouds shifted, and for a second, the moon lit up his face.

He looked younger. All jawline and swagger. Boyish mischief and charm.

A face that he could use to talk his way into or out of anything.

My hand found his, and I curled my fingers into his palm.

"You're right," he said into the night. "If you're not happy, the relationship won't be either. And I have to say thank you. Thank you for telling me that, in high school, you kept yourself just out of reach."

"I wanted to be found, El. There were so many times when I thought maybe, if things could be different, I could be honest. With myself. With you," I replied.

He didn't let go.

Just held my hand like it was something he'd been waiting to carry.

Not to fix me. Just to know me.

Now, I think back to the me that arrived back in May.

The one who had her defenses up. Who would've refused to fall in love.

If you'd told that girl she would be lying on a roof with Elliott Ashby holding her hand after the most maniacal night, she'd have told you you're crazy.

But I'm not that girl anymore.

I'm the one who leans in when there's an opportunity to be close.

Who kisses boys in the rain.

And it's not about closing a chapter. It's about continuing it.

Even messy and unedited, it's beautiful.

Track 49

Earned Hope

(B-side)

(Elliott's Version)

After last night's rain, the rust-colored leaves are in full glory today.
The smell of wet pavement and decaying wood is in the air.

I can hear the first few notes of a mockingbird's song.

And I'm on the porch, chilled to the bone. But I'm too stubborn to go inside.

I want to soak up every minute that's left of September.

I even snuck a little of the pumpkin spice coffee creamer Nora left in the fridge.

To think that at the start of the summer, I would've been wary of doing something like that. She was still baring her teeth and growling at me then.

It's been four months of me repeating *I don't want you to go* in different words and actions.

When I took over cleaning a booth for her at the diner…

When I straightened her shoes by the door next to mine…

I said it then.

I meant it.

When I tucked her in on the couch.

Making the pencil bouquet and rewatching her favorite movie over and over.

Maybe, in the end, that's how you get the girl.

The leaves are still dripping.

My coffee's getting cold.

I hear Nora padding around the kitchen, making her own cup of coffee.

I still haven't gotten her a coffee machine for the apartment.

Maybe because I forgot.

But it's probably because I like having her close in the mornings.

I like seeing her messy hair hanging down her back and her freckles without a mask of makeup.

Even the way she moves to the silverware drawer and withdraws a spoon captivates me.

She's so real. So beautiful.

She doesn't say anything when she sits next to me on the porch—just sets her mug down beside mine. Our fingers brush.

She doesn't pull away.

We broke each other's hearts once. And remarkably, we're putting them back together.

"Are you insane?" she says. "It's frigid out here."

But she snuggles into me on the porch swing anyway. Her baggy sweatpants and bulky sweater enveloping her until she looks like a heap of material.

I wrap my arm around her and pull her nearer.

With Nora, close will never be close enough.

The mockingbird sings again.

A squirrel races up the oak tree in the front yard.

And September holds on, just a little longer.

"You know it's gonna snow before too long, right?" I grin.

"Ugh. Don't remind me," she mumbles before taking a swig of coffee.

"C'mon, Goose. You can take the girl out of Ohio, but you can't take Ohio out of the girl."

"Well, considering this is Tania's sweater, this Ohio girl needs to restock on some proper winter clothes. One suitcase isn't cutting it anymore," she replies.

Winter.

Nora will be here for winter.

The thought makes me giddy.

It's a promise. Not just for time, but for soup on the stove and her boots by the door. Of the kind of quiet that only exists when someone else is breathing beside you.

For better or worse, that's all I want. And I'd wait forever to have it. Only with her.

She rests against me, the weight of her trust settling in.

Beneath us, the porch swing murmurs—a slow, familiar ache. And September exhales.

I think I do too.

The porch still smells faintly of varnish from the last round of touch-ups Bash and I did. Tania's got her herb garden thriving in mismatched pots along the interior windowsill—mint, rosemary, something she swears is lavender. They've hung curtains in the front windows.

Not the kind you'd find in a showroom. The kind that say, *we live here now.*

The bed and breakfast plans are still taped to the fridge, corners curling, next to the Polaroid of Nora and me. But no one's rushing.

Turns out, the house didn't need a launch date to become a home. It just needed people who chose each other and stuck it out.

Sometimes I think about showing her the other photos. The ones I've taken since she handed me that hand-me-down Polaroid. Not all of them are good, but they're mine—quiet moments but alive. Ones I might've missed if she hadn't named the wanting in me.

I still don't call it photography. But I've started keeping things.

Some things don't announce themselves. They just begin. Like the day Nora and I met.

Three years old. Born into a world of grainy photos, grunge, and the beginning of the internet.

And, over the years, as much as media and school shootings, and Y2K shaped us—we shaped each other.

We were the kind of kids who built forts out of couch cushions and made-up secret handshakes we forgot by morning.

She used to boss me around with a plastic tiara perched on her head, peanut butter on her chin.

I let her.

I have craved that kind of simplicity for years. Wondering if it was crazy to think two people could find their way back to each other.

Turns out, they could.

Turns out, they already did.

Track 50

Earned Perspective:

The Porch Swing Sessions

(Nora's Version)

There's going to be a Harvest Moon tonight.

It's my favorite of the year.

It's especially appropriate now.

It will be September for a few more days.

The transition to autumn is in full swing.

So is my personal metamorphosis.

I'm still figuring out what things to shed in order to take my most beautiful form.

It's complicated, but I think I've earned the right to be.

I've done more living in the last four months than in the last decade.

It's due to more than just being around Elliott.

I thought that my life in Moonridge was a bygone era, faded to gray.

Now, it's all vibrancy and saturation.

A full spectrum of color.

No filters. No fear.

Sitting with Elliott on the porch swing with his arm around me and a warm mug in my hands, I feel immune to the ache. For the first time in years.

Like I'm in a sanctuary that can't be shattered.

I didn't ask to sit beside him when I came outside. Just took my place there, like I'd always belonged.

Maybe I always have.

The way he rocks us gently back and forth—pushing against the renewed planks of the porch with his heels—makes me almost want to admit that I'm becoming too soft for normal life. That this—slow mornings and pumpkin spice, and him—is what could feed my soul for eternity.

He doesn't know it yet, but I started writing a screenplay based on the story of our lives.

They always say you should write what you know. I know me and Elliott.

A love letter to the life I'd thought I'd lost.

I haven't decided how I want it to end yet.

How do you craft dialogue that exposes the people whose expectations led you, until you realize they were what was causing you the most trauma?

How do you write the moment someone else's complications now feel like peace?

How do you script that you were waiting for someone to chase you when you were too afraid to stay? And now, you're glad they never did.

I want a happy ending. But an honest one too.

One where the girl doesn't get rescued. She finds herself.

Where the guy doesn't lead her on. Just proves his loyalty.

Where the porch swing creaks beneath two people who've grown tired of the miscommunication trope. I want the audience to feel the ache of almosts and the relief of choosing sacred new beginnings.

I want them to see that softness isn't weakness. That sometimes, the bravest thing you can do is sit still and let someone love you.

Sometimes the most fearless thing is to love yourself.

The screenplay is just sitting in a folder on my laptop labeled *Untitled* right now.

Eventually I'll find a name that encompasses Moonridge.

Not the town. The feeling. The gnawing. The rebirth.

I've been thinking about legacy lately.

Not the kind you inherit. The kind you choose.

I used to think mine would be escape.

Now, I think it might be presence.

And presence, I'm learning, is built in moments like Tania experimenting with soup recipes.

Sometimes she lets Bash help.

Last week she made a roasted red pepper one. Bash put too much cayenne, but we all tried to pretend it was intentional.

We laughed until my eyes watered and Elliott kissed my temple.

I felt like I was watching my own life play out from overhead.

And I thought, *this is it. I want to write this miracle.*

It's going to be one of those nights when we'll pile blankets on an inflatable mattress in the backyard, begging Elliott to set up an old sheet and projector.

I'm not sure what tomorrow holds.

But I know this: I'm not afraid of winter anymore. I'm not afraid of softness. I'm not afraid of being seen.

Growing up with Elliott, I knew, deep down, he was the right guy. The best friend I'd fall in love with. Sunset setting, sitting side by side, laughing. Credits rolling and an all-encompassing song playing.

But, I guess, I got all that anyway. Without the cameras and scripted conversations, it's better.

Elliott's laugh echoing down the hallway.

The way Tania hums when she's chopping herbs.

Bash's terrible jokes that somehow still make me smile.

We're not perfect. We're not polished. But we're here.

Tonight, when the moon rises, I want to sit in the backyard and let it wash over me. I want to feel the weight of the blankets and the lightness of being loved. I want to remember every detail—how the cider tastes, how the projector flickers, how Elliott's thumb brushes my knuckles beneath the layers. I want to write it all down. Just for me. To remember how it felt.

Inside, someone's laughing at Saturday morning cartoons. Probably Bash.

The air tastes like apples and possibility.

There's a moth circling the porch light that's still on.

I don't know what happens next.

Not for the characters in my screenplay. Not for me.

Elliott shifts beside me. Doesn't say anything. Doesn't need to.

The coffee's almost gone.

I nestle deeper into Elliott's side and the sweater I borrowed from Tania's closet.

And I let them hold me.

Epilogue I

(Elliott's Version)

[Out Of The Attic]

Saturday, April 3, 2027

Dear Nora,

I've never kept a journal. I've never written a song.

Maybe a poem or two for our high school English class?

As an English teacher myself, I guess that's pretty sad.

Anyway, the point is I never realized how important it would be for me to put these words into writing.

In indelible ink. So you can read them over and over again.

At this point, you've spent months writing everyone else's version of you in the screenplay you think is a secret. And *maybe I'm too late. Maybe this will never make it into the final draft. But I'll regret it forever if I don't give you my version.*

The one where you're not a labyrinth. You're layered.

Where you're not hard to love.

Instead, you're worth loving well.

Where my heart is indefinitely reserved for you.

I've watched you shed the persona that was chosen for you when you were born.

I've seen you embrace the version of yourself that made other people uncomfortable.

Lord knows, I've tried to be the kind of man—though I'm imperfect—who doesn't ask you to perform.

To be anything other than yourself.

I just want to be the one who stays. I just want to be the one.

So I'm making it permanent.

This letter might not make the final cut. But I hope I do. Because I'm here for more than just a season, Goose. I bought a luxury box because I want the best view for the rest of them.

I want you to know, you don't have to run sprints. Not with me. My love for you is an endurance race.

You can be messy. You can be magnificent. You can be the girl who rewrites the ending. And I'll still be here.

I'll be here when you're ready to write the next scene. Or tear it up. Or start from scratch.

Because loving you isn't an act. It's not a game.

It's the privilege of my life.

And I'll be the loudest, most obnoxious man there ever was if it means I'm doing it for you.

Not because I need a role. But because I believe in the story.

Yours. Ours.

El

She didn't change a single word.

Not even the part where I called her Goose.

She said it's the only scene that never needed a rewrite.

Said that my version of her is the one she wants to live up to.

Unapologetic. Smitten. Creative.

The one that will one day make people sit in silence.

The one that will make them wonder if it was real.

She told me that if she ever forgot who she was—or who she could be—she'd reread that scene, that letter.

And I swear, when that amazing woman looks at me and tells me she loves me, I hold my head up higher.

When she looks me in the eyes, I know we're unbreakable.

And it's then—when she's head over heels in the moment—that I believe her.

Because in that moment, it's not a production. She's not protecting.

She's just hers.

And somehow—mine.

It's her, in real time.

Choosing this.

Epilogue II

(Nora's Version)

[Unreleased]

Monday, June 7, 2027

Dear Wendy,

It's been a year. I counted twice, just to be sure.

A year since I stepped on a plane and didn't look back.

A year since I stood on my parents' porch and wondered if I'd made a mistake.

A year since I—unknowingly—started letting love back into my life.

Yes, I'm counting proximity to Elliott. Because feeling his presence from across the street was enough.

Today, Bash asked if I remembered the name of the dog from Marquis's barbecue last fall. I didn't. But I remembered the smell of the grill and the way Elliott kept smiling at me from across the lawn.

Marquis's wife, Natasha, is kind and thoughtful—the perfect host. She's got her hands full with their two girls. But we became fast friends.

I still get butterflies when the girls call me Auntie Nora.

Maybe I'm just hormonal, but *cue the waterworks*

Somehow, Tania is still managing shifts at The Bent Spoon and working doubly as hard in her culinary program this year. I can tell she's ready to soak up the summer though.

We all thrive around here when our lives are less hectic.

I ended up quitting the diner. Not because I didn't like it.

I have so many memories there, new and old, that it will always be a special place for me. But I got a job teaching a creative writing class to teens online and I think it might be exactly what I've been looking for. Although I don't know who is learning more. Me or them.

I still haven't finished the screenplay. But I renamed the folder again. It's called "The Birthright."

Not the legal kind. The emotional kind. The kind you carry in your posture when you stop giving apologies.

My relationship with my parents is strained, but it exists.

Sometimes I think about Elliott and me running away from all this. Bolting for more freedom.

Not because we need to avoid anything or slip away into exile. But because we want to experience something more. Things we used to talk about as kids.

Maybe it'll happen one day...

Sometimes I think we're just older versions of the kids who once dreamed of escape.

But now, instead of running, we build.

We plant herbs in the mismatched pots Tania brings home.

We argue about which movies deserve a backyard screening.

We let Bash pick the popcorn seasoning, even when it's chaos.

Elliott still respects my boundaries. The garage apartment. Prom night.

But he still won't take any rent money.

He says I pay him enough in kisses and early-morning coffee dates on the porch.

I don't know what the next year will bring. The next five years.

I used to be like Peter, Wendy.

I never used to want to grow up because I was afraid of what that might mean. What it might look like.

I was afraid to find myself.

But now that I have, I'm not letting her get away.

Dear readers,

Thank you for choosing to spend time with Nora, Elliott, and the town of Moonridge Creek. I hope it meets you where you are—and maybe even helps you stay a little longer.

This story was born from the ache of memory, the quiet resilience of survival, and the belief that healing rarely follows a straight line. The themes in The Last Great Almost—grief, trauma, belonging, and the beauty of imperfect love—are ones I've carried in my subconscious and in conversations with others over the years.

Writing this book was a way to hold space for those emotions and maybe offer a little light to anyone who's felt unseen in their own story.

If this book moved you, I'd be honored if you would share it with anyone you feel might need it. Sometimes the right story finds us when we're ready to feel less alone.

With Gratitude,

Quintana McConnell

Discussion Questions:

The title The Last Great Almost *suggests longing and near-misses. What do you think Nora almost lost—and what did she reclaim?*

Elliott often chooses restraint over reaction. How does his emotional discipline shape Nora's journey?

What role does chosen family play in Nora's healing? How do Bash and Tania shift her understanding of love?

How does Elliott's quiet loyalty contrast with Nora's emotional volatility? What makes their dynamic feel earned?

What does Nora's relationship with her parents reveal about emotional inheritance?

How does the setting of Moonridge function as more than just a backdrop?

What does softness mean in the context of this story? How is it portrayed as strength?

At one point, Elliott reflects on aging, responsibility, and missed chances. How does his internal monologue complicate the idea of masculinity and emotional vulnerability?

In Track 24, Nora realizes she's reenacting her parents' emotional logic. How does this moment shift her character arc?

Reflection Prompts:

Who in your life has helped you feel safe enough to soften?

Have you ever loved someone like Elliott—quietly, without asking for anything back?

Think about a time when you longed for closure—with a person, a place, or a version of yourself. Did physical closeness help resolve it, or did it complicate things further?

Nora says, "Closure doesn't always come with proximity." What does that mean to you? How do you define closure—and can it exist without confrontation, apology, or reunion?

When Nora sees Alexander again, she says: "I'm the heroine. He doesn't get to own me." How does this moment reframe her past?

What does it mean to be chosen, not just loved?

Optional Add-On:

Character Pairing Activity

Match each character with a theme: softness, loyalty, escape, legacy, performance, healing.

Discuss how these themes evolve across the story—and how they intersect.

Final Echo:

The Last Great Almost Playlists

These are the songs that held the ache, the warmth, the almosts.

From The Catalog of Taylor Swift

The Archive of Emotional Ruin

Quintana McConnell writes emotionally resonant fiction. Her stories are rooted in slow-burn intimacy and layered character journeys, often told with restraint and poetic clarity. She invites readers into spaces where emotional truth takes center stage.

A self-proclaimed mood reader and avid traveler, she draws inspiration from life's journeys—whether on a scenic hiking trail or enjoying new foods. Quintana values building genuine connections with her readers, often sharing her personal insights and inspirations along her writing journey via social media @quintanamcconnellauthor.

www.ingramcontent.com/pod-product-compliance
Lightning Source LLC
LaVergne TN
LVHW091656070526
838199LV00050B/2181